ACTING BADLY

ACTING BADLY

Santa Fe, New Mexico, March 2003,
the week before American forces invade Iraq

A Novel
by

MICHAEL SCOFIELD

SUNSTONE
PRESS
SANTA FE

THIS BOOK IS A WORK OF FICTION.
Names, characters, places, and incidents are either the product of the author's
imagination or are used fictitiously.

Cover and author photographs by Noreen Scofield

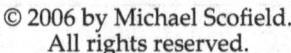

Sunstone books may be purchased for educational, business, or sales promotional
use. For information please write: Special Markets Department, Sunstone Press,
P.O. Box 2321, Santa Fe, New Mexico 87504-2321.

Library of Congress Cataloging-in-Publication Data:

Scofield, Michael.
  Acting badly : Santa Fe, New Mexico, March 2003, the week before American forces
invade Iraq : a novel / by Michael Scofield.
    p. cm.
  ISBN 0-86534-484-1 (Hardcover: alk. paper)
ISBN 978-0-86534-537-9 (Softcover: alk. paper)
  1. Iraq War, 2003---Fiction. 2. Santa Fe (N.M)--Fiction. I. Title.

PS3619.C63A65 2006
811'.54--dc22

                                        2006015623

WWW.SUNSTONEPRESS.COM
SUNSTONE PRESS / POST OFFICE BOX 2321 / SANTA FE, NM 87504-2321 /USA
(505) 988-4418 / ORDERS ONLY (800) 243-5644 / FAX (505) 988-1025

ACKNOWLEDGMENTS

THIS STORY WOULD NOT HAVE SEEN PUBLICATION without the help of my wife, Noreen. For two and a half years she kept our home quiet in the mornings and showed me ways to tighten the story. She also conceived and took the cover photograph.

Thanks to Woody Galloway for participating in the photograph and to my stepson, Brendan Ward, for painting the two large slogans that appear on the vehicles.

I am also grateful to my Vermont College MFA professors, who shared their know-how for maximizing the impact that words can wield, and to the following individuals, who served as fact checkers: Tommy Archuleta, Mary Blisset, Dave Caldwell, Jane Clarke, Laura Cooley, Mary Joy Ford, Wendy Havlir, Juliana Henderson, Chip Lilienthal, Phil Loggains, Clint Marshall, Jan Nelson, Frank Ratliff, Rob Rikoon, John-Paul Ruch, Jeff Sand, Drew Scott, Daphne Sidor, Jennifer Sprague, Susan Tixier, Rick Tashi, and Rick Von Kaenel.

Added thanks to Sunstone's publisher, Jim Smith, for his enthusiasm about the manuscript; to Jim's assistant, Carl Condit, for easing the trials of reaching publication; to Richard Lehnert for copyediting; to Ben Glass for proofreading; to Russel Stolins for formatting; and to Vicki Ahl for book design.

CHARACTERS IN ORDER OF APPEARANCE ___

Ronald (Big Shit) Kirkpatrick—mortgage broker

Lila (Lile) Kirkpatrick—Ronald's wife

Manning (Manny) Barnes—marketing writer

Maxine (Max) Morgan—real estate broker

Joyce (Boodie) Hunt—Manny Barnes's girlfriend

Charles (Chuck) Ridley—CPA

Helen Ridley—Chuck Ridley's wife

Alexis (Allie) Dahl—assists Chuck Ridley

Bret Wilkes—CEO, encryption-software company

Victor Valdez—handyman for Maxine Morgan

Stu Fisher—handyman for Manny and Joyce

Dirk Pellington—retired foreign correspondent

Giordy Morgan—Maxine Morgan's husband

"LILE, BABE, WE GONNA INDULGE IN A LITTLE HANKY-panky?"

"If you'll do me like I like it."

Ron and Lila Kirkpatrick had returned late from Mama Cheetah's where they'd celebrated with filet mignon and fresh asparagus the cash bonus Ron had won as February's Home Loan Champ. They'd dragged out dinner to calm Lila's fury that two of the tiles in the upstairs bath—where Ron now sawed a conical brush between his teeth—had popped free of their mastic. Ron's belly jiggled under the *Go Lobos!* T-shirt he liked to sleep in. The off-white tiles slanted up near him beside the toilet.

As they talked, their next-door neighbor, Manny Barnes, in sheepskin, robe, and sweats, was sneaking round the embankment toward the white Cadillac Escalade that Ron had parked in the driveway rather than the garage so as not to wake Lila when he left for breakfast. Lila stood now in her black, see-through wrap lighting four votive candles. They surrounded a soapstone sculpture squatting on the glass table near the TV. She had thumbed the switch on its electrical cord to start a trickle of water past two bonsai pines when Ron yelled out:

"Another's poppin', Lile; son of a peccary."

The hem of her wrap flapping, unveiling the skein of veins beginning to blue at the back of her knees, Lila ran barefoot across the blue pile that carpeted all twelve of the town houses dotting Plaza Hill, and stared in the direction of Ron's thrust forefinger. The eight-by-eight tile rose on one edge like a trap door. It stopped a couple of inches above its bed of yellow mastic.

With his left hand, Ron, gazing, hoisted his testicles against the bottom of his belly.

"Here comes another!" Lila cried.

His lips tight, her long jaw hanging, they goggled at what sounded like a pack rat gnawing through plasterboard as the edges of the tile facing the one just risen cracked their grout and broke free.

"Ron, make them stop!"

"Stop, you Comanche motherfuckers!"

The tile halted just above its mates. Ron slammed the heel of his cowhide slipper to it as if it were a giant miller moth, cracking it in two.

"What are you doing? Insurance has to see this. They won't believe this. How can this be happening?"

"We live on an Anasazi burial mound; the ancestors are strikin' back."

"Fuck." Lila swiped at her salt-and-pepper hair, yanked the black ribbon off her ponytail, and tossed it to the floor. Her hair fanned across her shoulders. "This goddamned town. Maybe I can stay married to you—don't bother lowering your eyebrows—but putting up with Maxine Morgan convincing us to buy this heap of shit? I'm heading back to Fort Worth. I mean it, Ron. I'm not your trophy wife. I'll drag us through a divorce that'll flatten you like that toothpaste."

"Lile, hon—"

"Watch that tile!"

The floor grate rattled as the furnace clicked back on. Lila squinched her eyes and wrinkled her nose at the sour musk.

"I love it when you steam. So does Prince." Ron pulled his T-shirt out and up to show her the small erection peeking over his testicles.

She brushed her palm across the rayon clinging to her drooping left breast and its ingrown nipple. "Maxine Morgan's ugly."

He threw the toothpaste to the counter, sending the box of floss clacking against the wall. "What are you accusin' me of? Better believe I noticed you smilin' every time neighbor Barnes mouthed off at the homeowners meetin' how he loves the way you've styled the boulders at the entrance to our compound, how you've chosen native I-forget-what—"

"Blue flax and Apache plume."

"—flax and Apache to plant this spring. I saw you take the chair next to his, babe. I noticed."

"Fuck you."

"One finger at me, three back at you. I partner real estate deals with Maxine Morgan for one reason—she hustles."

Lila snorted.

"Expert on human nature, treats clients like royalty, knows how to close, favors Los Alamos Mortgage. She'll make us richer than you ever imagined. You married the right cowboy, Lile, followed him here two years ago and you better stay put because when Bush quits diddlin' and launches this war, you're gonna see your Tom Mix haul commission checks home so big you can buy yourself and your music-festival galfriends a month of soirées to finger yourselves off listenin' to Bach or Beethoven or who-the-hell."

"You through yet?"

"No. I could care less if the tiles upstairs and all the ones downstairs break free and we have to hightail it to a motel while Vic Valdez — he should have stuck with carvin' santos — or the guy Barnes uses, or whatever Anglo or damned Hispanic we hire comes to glue 'em back down. Max found you and me and Manny Barnes and his gal these places for a lullaby, a mug a milk. Location, Lile. Views. Within a year we'll trade up for an acre in Wilderness Gate. Look at me, sweaty as a peccary dogged by hounds."

Sweat massed under his breasts and in the creases of his belly. Ron fingered his dangling penis and snuffed. "This night was sposed to be romantic. We've stuck it out a long time, Lile."

"Since you groped me in the pinafore Daddy bought for my seventh-grade birthday."

"Can't we make tonight work, hon?"

"Do I get my golden shower?"

"You'll bring me off the way I want?"

"If I can have my shower."

Ron turned and spat minty saliva into the sink. "I need to come somethin' awful. That breakfast I'm endurin' tomorrow involves a tenderfoot from Silicone Valley that Max's husband set us up with. The guy uses some lone wolf tax advisor in town named Ridley."

"Helen Ridley's husband? She helps me with publicity for the music festival."

"I dunno."

"Is she going to be there?"

"Ridley's wife?"

"Not Ridley's wife."

"Max isn't comin'," he lied.

"Good."

"Better use a larger towel than last time, babe."

"I bought a plastic cover and big fluffy flag I thought might turn you on."

"American flag? I dunno."

"You want your orgasm?"

"Gimme those." He stepped over the sprung tiles and threw his hands out, trying to reach her breasts. She jerked away.

"Wash that cute thing with soap. And wipe the sweat off your belly. And sprinkle on some aftershave."

He was upending the bottle of wintergreen when he heard noise crackling from the bedroom's TV. "What's that for?" he called, rubbing his palms and slapping his cheeks.

"When I switch on my vibrator."

"Vibrator?" As he left the bathroom, he saw headlights mow a path of yellow across the blinds. Who up here so late? Frowning at the crunch of tires on the dirt road, he crossed the rug to stand near Lila while she punched channel changes into the remote, after muting the sound.

"Vibrator you bet your butt. Anyhow, Patriots and Tomahawks and helicopter gunships and all this new talk about chemicals help me come."

He shuffled to the bed and tossed her lace-slipped pillows and stuffed animals to the floor. "Hey," he called over his shoulder. "We're goin' to war to get rid of Saddam's thugs and nukes and anthrax and sarin gas. We're goin' to war to give those twenty-four million sand niggers a shot at democracy. Not so squaws like you can get their rocks off watchin' the news."

"You don't care how we're staying safe from terrorism?"

"Right now, at this moment?"

"There's Fox News showing Stealth bombers loading up missiles. Aren't they beautiful?"

She went to her side of the bed and stooped. "Pull that spread, Ron, and scrunch the blanket back."

From under the bed frame she hauled up the beach towel, then unfurled its stars and stripes over the sheet.

He knuckled the towel; the plastic underneath gave the sheet a crinkly feel. Pulling his T-shirt over his balding head, he tossed it into a wicker chair. "Light level okay? I dimmed it in the bathroom."

"Perfecto. Nuts—a mouthwash ad. Lie still so I can play."

He felt his penis swell as his buttocks cratered the mattress. A tingling surged into testicles the size of Brazil nuts as she threw her black wrap onto the half dozen badgers and koala bears and pandas and lion cubs that lay at the base of the bedside table. Freeing a paper cup from the stack lying on its side in the drawer, she set it down and straddled his chest, facing his toes and the TV.

Her long strands of hair tickled his belly. He stared at the mole that swelled off her right shoulder as she ground her vulva against him. Attending for a moment the furnace's hum and the gurgle of the soapstone waterfall, he reached around her ribcage for breasts veined like the back of her knees, and shuddered as her fingers began to knead his testicles.

"Once my tits were good, weren't they, Big Shit? Remember how you used to suck to make the bud pop out?"

"Unh," he groaned, and his middle finger pushed into the hollow where her nipple hid. He saw the infant they never talked of, saw Lila press his tiny ears and re-guide the tiny lips to her right breast.

"They're loading Tomahawks under the wings of a Super Hornet on the Abraham Lincoln, Ron." One arm stiff against his thigh, she stopped grinding and began to milk his penis, spitting on her palm and sliding it up, releasing and beginning again near the loosening scrotum.

"It's workin', hon." He crimped his eyes, concentrating on the building heat.

"Little Prince is growing fast."

"Huh, huh, keep your promise, babe, do it."

"A flatbed's bringing a missile up I've never seen."

"Do it, Lile!"

His thighs twitched and his testicles ached as she released him and clambered onto her side, scrambling to bunch the edge of the towel into the hollow between her hip and the sheet. She lifted her head to take his glans into her mouth.

"Don't forget the jewels," he panted, arms flung from the fat spreading from his rib cage.

She freed her lips. "Stop telling me."

Sweat massed in the folds of his eyelids as he felt her fingers massage his testicles and stroke his inner thighs. She lowered her face to mouth his erection. Lucky Max's husband when she needs his money to add a cubicle to her office or remodel the office kitchen—no paper cup, Ron thought.

"Slow down," he gasped.

She licked the nerve as he'd taught her—the nerve Max teased to drive him berserk—and resumed squeezing his shaft, pressing the glans with her lips.

"Now!" he cried, releasing his own breasts, heavy as water balloons, and raising his right arm in salute.

Palming his testicles, she plunged down on the shaft, back up, down and back, until his semen massed for eruption. The ends of the hair she shampooed twice daily felt like feathers swishing across the tops of his thighs.

"Oh Jesus Christ and Paul Apostle, suck, don't stop, suck, suck, oh Judas Christ, oh." The wrinkles in his neck were soaked. "Uhhhhhhhh."

He arched his back, vising her head as the vasectomized liquid spurted toward her throat. When she strained to free her head, he relaxed his grip. She rolled over, grabbed the cup, spat into it, and clapped it on the table.

"I'm good?" she asked, chest heaving, voice throaty, turning her face toward him. The capillaries in her cheeks flamed. She pulled an edge of the towel around to wipe his forehead and neck.

"Oh yeah." He began to wheeze. His right hand squeezed his testicles.

"Do me now."

"Gimme a breather, Lile."

"You big shit." She reached for a pillow and plopped it against the headboard. She stroked her clitoris—longer than most (but be glad, a gynecologist had told her before marriage; she'd thought it deformed)—and stared at the catapult slinging an F-18 from the end of the carrier's deck. Between her other thumb and forefinger she rolled her nipple. Her chest stilled.

"Lie back," Ron growled, scooting off the bed to his knees.

She settled herself on the American flag's cotton nubs, legs dangling off either side of him. "Play with my tits," she murmured.

"I need balance to do this right. You play with 'em." Pushing his palms against the sheet and tucking his thumbs under her shoulder blades, he lowered his face to her gray nest of hair and found her clitoris. He drew his tongue's tip back and forth along the organ, so much longer than Max's; fussed with it like a cat, nipping, flicking; felt her hand slip under his forehead to join him.

"Good-O. Don't stop, Ronnie, please?"

He had trouble keeping his tongue connected because she had started revolving her pelvis. The ligature on the underside of his tongue smarted as if nicked with scissors.

"I've got to use my finger, babe." He rested his cheekbone on her thigh, gazing at his silver wedding band and its bits of turquoise.

"Come back, I'm almost there. Please, Ronnie?"

A few more swipes with his middle finger and he returned to licking and flicking the clit slick with fluid until the gaps between her moans shortened, as they had before Jonathan's birth. Her pelvis began to thrash. He bore down with his tongue until she screamed.

As awed now as he had been at their son's birth, he watched her fling her head. How was he going to dump Max? Christ Amighty, listen to those screams, look at Prince stretch. We'll start over, Lila, I swear it. Max can never have an orgasm anyhoo.

He bent to lick perspiration from the navel of this wife of thirty-eight years, massaging her nest with his palm until she quieted, her jaw hanging.

"Thank you, honeybunch, oh Lord."

"Lile, babe?" He pushed his testicles against his penis, wincing at how his heart galloped as he stood. "Let's do doggy."

"Your doctor didn't say only one spurt a night till you lose weight?" She rested a moment. "Another fib? You do it twice with that whore? And I put up with it." Her voice dropped to a murmur.

"There's no Max Morgan and me that way, Lile. I told you! I learned my lesson after Cowtown. Yes, the sawbones said one orgasm. But tonight I thought, Lila and I deserve more. Okay, we shouldn't."

"Right. Though I don't believe anything you say anymore. Good trophy wife." Leaning on her elbow, she swung her legs up and, knees squashing her breasts, rolled off the towel toward the headboard. "Come on up here."

His own breasts and belly jiggling, he climbed onto the mattress and lay on his back parallel to the stripes now warm and damp with lovemaking.

From the Fox newscaster she turned to face Ron on her knees, straight-arming the mattress with her fists on either side of his shoulders. Saliva wet her teeth and gold fillings—she'd cracked two molars after Jonathan's death at Fort Ord.

"Rise up, Lile, you're hurtin' me."

"Too bad. You ready?"

"I guess."

Raising her buttocks, she hunched forward, shaking the mattress with her knees and fists. He looked up into her matted vaginal nest, inhaling its salt, clenching his eyes like a boy expecting a slap, stiffening his shoulders.

"Piss on you, Ronald Kirkpatrick. Piss on that fat. Piss on treating me like shit. And piss on you for making me leave our beautiful Fort Worth home."

"That was your idea." Flinching as her hot urine splashed his face and chest, he pressed his lips together—that smell, more than sulphurous. He was trying to suck air through his nose when she cried out:

"Ronnie, green, it's green!" At that moment came a loud crrraaaak and a rumble like thunder at the rear of their house, below the upstairs sliding door. It was followed by what sounded like crockery hurled against the back wall that faced the downstairs deck.

"What was that? What's that smell? Get off me!" He wrenched his head to spit onto the towel.

"Something's wrong!"

"Who's throwin' things down there?"

"How should I know? Don't you care I hurt?"

"Where?"

"My snatch—call nine-one-one."

At last the crashing outside ended. Wet as a walrus, he heaved himself off the bed as she folded into a V. Green mottled the towel's white stripes and the sheet; the red seemed blistered black.

"Oh, Lord," she moaned, hugging her knees and rocking. "Something terrible is happening and worse downstairs and you stand there with your mouth open, squeezing your balls. The Lord's punishing us, Ronnie. We're crap and you're crappier than anybody. Do something."

Wheezing, he hurried into the bathroom, lifting his feet over the raised tiles into the shower end of the tub. He turned the faucet on cold, grabbed a washcloth, and, shivering, slapped the cloth to his chest, legs, and arms.

He dried off and wrapped the towel around him, then reached into the closet to pull his robe and blue Home Loan Champ cap from their hooks.

He was heading for the phone on her desk when he twisted to face her in the dimness. Across the TV screen, Super Hornets banked in unison, emitting white contrails. The soapstone waterfall gurgled, the four squat candles flickered in their hammered-silver bowls.

"Asparagus, Lile. We had asparagus for dinner. Take a laugh break."

He flipped the switch to light the stairs and lumbered down.

PULLING HIS RED KNIT CAP OVER HIS EARS, MANNY KNELT in the mid-March chill beside the left rear tire of Ron's new white 2003 Escalade. He winced as the gravel bit his skin. Lying in bed waiting, he'd heard Ron and Lila drive in; the tire's wall was still warm. As the light behind the glass blocks in their upstairs bathroom dimmed, a gibbous moon lit the American-flag decal darkening the rear window of the gleaming sixteen-footer.

Manny stiffened as a gust rattled the string of dried red chiles hanging from the front porch. The only other sound came from below his and Joyce's and the Kirkpatricks' town houses, shouts from the softball game on Baca Field. Proud he'd slipped downstairs without breaking Joyce's snoring, Manny swelled his lungs with a menthol-like whiff of the rabbitbrush that lined the Kirkpatricks' drive, and bent close to the tire.

Belching, he unscrewed the ridged cap of the air valve and laid it aside. From a pocket of the sheepskin coat over his robe and sweats, he pulled a long finishing nail and leaned to jam its head into the valve. He pinched his nostrils against the stale hiss, watching the Escalade's stack of brake and backup lights tilt and begin to sink.

The junipers and prickly pears fronting a town house on the dirt road's other side suddenly brightened from charcoal to lime green. Starting from the bottom of Plaza Hill, where the private neighborhood began, a crunching grew louder. It's nine-thirty, go to bed, he thought, and rolled to his side, scraping his left cheek.

Like a rattlesnake he wriggled to the front end of the listing Escalade. He tucked his lankness below the grille's five blades of chrome, which sparkled from the lamp that lit the Kirkpatricks' steps. He patted his cheek; blood made his fingertips sticky. Had he ripped his coat, he wondered?

Headlights jerked left and right as the Range Rover with its three-tiered, wraparound brush bar swerved across his view. Maxine Morgan's—he could see "Morgan Realty" on the door, an albino bobcat springing along the letters' tops.

The behemoth skidded and paused. Pressing his stomach to the gravel, Manny listened to the engine idling. He peeked past Ron's front tire as acid rose to his throat. In the moonlight the driver's window lowered with a hum and a fist flung a tiny bundle rolled up like a newspaper. It plopped near him. White smoke puffed from the tailpipe, another hum, and the SUV wove down the other side of the hill, rear lights waving.

What was she doing up here tonight driving drunk?

The pounding behind his eyes told Manny that he'd stopped breathing. He pursed his lips and blew out air, then eased out the gas that had built up in his colon so not to make a noise. Standing, he threw his elbows behind him to unkink his bony shoulders.

He stared at the white handkerchief or rag rubber-banded to hold some sort of cylinder from which wafted a stench of pepper sauce. Pinching his nose to keep from sneezing, he kicked the bundle toward the rabbitbrush, padded back to the Escalade's rear tire, and knelt again to finish his task.

Following the new hiss, the corner of the white bumper settled a few inches above the drive, curling back the mud flap as the trailer hitch thumped the gravel.

He screwed the valve cap tight and closed his eyes. Still on his knees, he arched backward and, shivering, steepled his fingers. To the first dirty-footed burkha-wrapped Iraqi clutching her infant, blasted to shreds by an American Tomahawk tagged for Saddam Hussein, I dedicate this hamstrung White Diamond Escalade, he whispered to himself.

Rising, he tasted the sweet salt of blood on his fingertips, then pressed them to the Escalade's fender. Blood sacrifice, fat Ron. He watched his breath pulse out.

With the toe of his moccasin he nudged the cloth-wrapped bundle out of the bushes onto the gravel, kicked it, and kept kicking until it rested beside the flat tire. He hurried around the piñon-strewn embankment that separated his and Joyce's town house from the Kirkpatricks'.

Except for the red-eyed surge protectors he'd bought to save his stereo equipment from lightning zaps, no light showed in the hallway. He climbed the stairs' thick blue pile. Crinkling his nose against the hot-pepper scent rising from his moccasin, he eased open the door he'd shut twenty minutes before, and peered at the bulge of Joyce, curled under the electric blanket in the far corner. Off the master bath he dumped sheepskin, robe, and red knit cap on the walk-in closet's floor.

Above the bed the moon lit two of Joyce's anti-war poems just accepted by *Cholla Review*; he had framed and decorated the typescripts with cholla spines and sunflower petals. He stood on his side of the bed and lifted to his nose his left moccasin, wondering whether to scrub it. She mumbled, "Hey, bud, where've you been?"

A foot shorter than he, Joyce sat up in the moonlight, and pulled the blanket around the top of her flannel nightgown. "What's that stink?"

Sighing, he sank to the mattress and told her; his gut hurt as though she were twisting a loop of his intestines with pliers.

"Knock it off, Manny! It's not your business what real estate games Maxine Morgan wants to play. Who do you think you are letting air from that tire, Mahatma Gandhi?" She jerked the electric blanket tighter around her shoulders. "I don't like what's happening since we moved to Santa Fe, bud."

"Meaning?" Pressing his lips against a belch, he raked the tips of his fingers through his short hair.

"Your games with women. Two years ago, after we signed the deal for this place. The lunch that Maxine Morgan and Ron bought us at the Great Books Cookhouse. I should have stayed alert."

"You're saying what?"

"How you spooned blackberry flan from her dish."

"What the hell, Boodie." It was the name he'd given her after she'd startled him, leaping around the corner like a blonde cricket at Sun Microsystems in Silicon Valley, where she'd edited Sun's employee newsletter.

The sharp sweetness of blackberries filled his mouth; again he saw Maxine widening those violet-smeared eyes at him.

"And telling Ron Kirkpatrick's wife at the homeowners' meeting how you love blue flax. You mean loved her unbuttoned blouse. She's an easy ten years older than us, Manny."

Tenderness swamped his insides. He loped around the foot of the bed, pulling Joyce's mop of blonde hair against his stomach. He felt her shoulders sag, and for the moment didn't care that she'd decided to let the hair of her armpits and legs grow.

"Boodie, it's your breasts I love, especially when you rub them on my cock and face."

"Your flirting scares me. So does wanting us to quit drafting marketing newsletters for Sun and Hewlett-Packard and Cisco. What are we supposed to do, live on the settlement from my divorce?"

"Chuck's diversified me into green stocks and municipals. I'm in good hands."

"You're as naïve as he is. He may be fine as your CPA, but with investments Chuck Ridley's a fool." She freed her small head from his grasp and pushed him away. He staggered to the wall—its rough plaster pricked his back. "Stocks are tanking, it's the deepest bear market in thirty years. We'll have to sell this place."

She clutched the sheet to wipe her eyes, then faced him. "We're planning marriage and a baby before I'm forty-five, aren't we? I should be ovulating midweek. Moving here makes me nervous. Okay, we got desperate. Christ, in every Bay Area garage some geek is lying on a cot scheming how to infect our lives with nanoelectronics. And I know your therapist suggested you go—don't stand so far away from me."

He crossed the four feet between them, plopped on the bed, and threw his sweatshirted arm around her waist. "We'll cut our spending, Boodie. I won't need to fly to San Jose for editorial meetings anymore. No hotel bills."

"Naïve. Hey, I'm tired, too, of grinding out newsletters. And I'm sick of writing poetry. What's the point? I told Allie at lunch today I want a life of muesli to prepare for the baby. But we can't afford muesli. Meanwhile, you stir up trouble next door and fantasize I don't know what about women."

"Enough, Boodie." He swallowed against another belch. His gut was crimping and, though clothed in sweats, he'd begun to shiver. The furnace must have quit for the night. "I gotta get my robe."

He was on his way to the closet when he heard her cry out.

"What's wrong?"

"It's that scrabbling noise again!"

"Switch on the lamp in your basket." He yanked his red-plaid robe off the closet floor. Now that a couple of journals wanted to publish her jeremiads, she planned to stop writing? With the Cheney-Rumsfeld-Wolfowitz axis of evil turning Christian fundamentalism into a world crusade, she and he needed to march, wave signs, and register Democrats to boot out the Bush cabinet next year. She needed to publish all the anti-war poems she could.

"Hear it?" She pointed above the water stain that darkened the wall between her poems. In the brown wool socks she slept in, she bounded from the bed and stood beside the night table, where her book of Sanskrit meditations lay.

"Seems the beast can't decide which poem to settle down over."

She mussed her blonde hair, laughing.

What a doll—why her patent-lawyer husband left her for a legal aide with two sons he couldn't imagine. Except that Joyce couldn't get pregnant by him. "If Stu decides not to march Sunday, maybe he'll come help find where the beast's wriggling through the tarpaper. I wonder what eye patch he'll wear this time?"

"Who knows—how can we sleep with that noise?"

"We can't. I want to show you something." He moved to the bookcase near the stairs, reached below her volumes on nutrition to where he kept his jazz CDs, and yanked out a three-ring binder. He padded to the tattered armchair that had been her father's near the sliding glass door that led to the lower roof, and flicked on the floor lamp.

"Come here." He patted the red wool plaid covering his thigh.

"I don't like this alpha-male habit you've developed since leaving the Valley."

"What habit?"

"Giving me orders."

"Sorry; you're right."

Her buttocks warmed his lap. "What happened to your cheek?" she asked, touching the rawness with two fingers.

"Hey, don't! I scraped it trying to scramble out of Maxine's high beams. Forget that. See this?" He flattened his hand against the binder's cover. "Chuck downloaded it: *Rebuilding America's Defenses*. Published in two thousand by a think tank called The Project for the New American Century. Paul Wolfowitz is a member.

"Seventy-six pages laying out why nothing is going to stop us from manhandling the Middle East. Does Bush believe Saddam has weapons of mass destruction? He knows Scott Ritter's UN team got rid of them in the mid-nineties. *Rebuilding America's Defenses* says we're going to force peace through economic globalization, backed by expanding military beachheads in the Middle East and Southeast Asia. Use designer weapons like nuclear bunker busters and mini bombs."

"Christ, Manny!"

"The Bush bunch wants to pummel the Axis of Evil, Saudi Arabia, and Pakistan into cobbling up American-style democracies. All it takes is persuading two billion followers of Islam to change their faith. Is that crazy? You and I have to do something."

"Like letting air from Ron's tire?"

"We ought to let air from the tires of all the American-flag gas-guzzlers in Santa Fe, cop us a slot on TV."

She jumped off his lap, clamping the light-blue flannel to her chest. "Who's crazy here? We left your stomach cramps from too much cranial mania back in Palo Alto. Didn't we? Count me out of your activist dreams, Manny."

He stiffened and shifted his eyes toward the glass door.

"What in the world?" Joyce whispered.

They listened to a loud snap, followed by a rattling and banging— rocks careening down the hill?

Throwing the binder to the carpet and tightening his sash, Manny heaved open the sliding glass door and closed it behind him. The din had stopped. Cold bit his cheeks and neck. Baca Field's floodlights had darkened. He stared at the moon, at Santa Fe's lights aproned below, and the glow rising over the Sandias from Albuquerque. Few SUVs or workers' trucks raced this late along Bishop's Lodge Road.

Manny rubbed his belly to quell its gurgling. Oh God, he begged, give me something meaningful to do. That little silver ring high up in Alexis's ear; me hoping she's bi. Why am I flirting again? Didn't losing my savings to three abortions cure me before I met Joyce? I have my life partner, don't I? "Praying to a God I don't believe cares—I must feel desperate," he muttered.

Shivering, he pulled open the slider. "Nothing to see except lights."

"It sounded worse than the racket the hot tub makes." She clicked off the floor lamp, then moved toward the bed and twisted the knob of her table lamp.

"That hot tub's a pain," Manny said in the moonlit dark. "Maintenance and chemicals run five hundred bucks a year and it leaks. Stu thinks the grinding means a blockage. Let's dump the whole system, Boodie—it's a capitalistic frill. No more stains, no more rats."

Kicking off his moccasins, he tossed his robe on the seat of the ladderback chair in the corner. He peeled off his sweats and Jockey shorts, stretched under the blanket, and threw a forearm over his eyes. "Everything's going to be fine," he murmured, worrying that tomorrow, after picking up a peace placard from Alexis at Chuck's office, he and Joyce must grind out April's *CEO Briefing*.

Joyce brought her knees up and faced him. "Hey, bud?"

"What?"

"I love our hot tub. I love to sit on the bench and soak when the plum branches above it wave. I like us to touch; I like you to touch me between my legs."

Her palm slid across his pelvis and settled on his testicles. Her thumb pressed his penis.

"I like it when we wrap each other in towels and come dripping up here to make love, Manny. Don't you? But we can't do it when you're overwrought and can't get hard."

"Tomorrow, Boodie. It's ten o'clock, I'm tired."

She retrieved her hand and flipped to her other side. He snuggled in close, genitals and belly pressing her buttocks. He hooked his arm around her waist to cup a breast, but her hair tickled his nose and he pulled away. He winced at the cramp of intestinal gas building—what a joke that he could leave stomach problems in California.

DRESS UP

"DEAR SANTA FE CLOUDSCAPE THAT KNOWS NOTHING OF war," Chuck Ridley whispered to no one.

Lying in bed in a violet silk pajama top, he shifted his eyes from the sky to the lawn glittering with frost. Ice warming to mush still gripped the tips of the weeping willow that shaded the pond whose installation Chuck's wife, Helen, had overseen last August.

Early this morning, schoolmates from Desert Prep had picked up Mark and Melodie—Chuck's and Helen's children—for a Saturday of skiing. Now the twins' pet llamas lay with forelegs folded near a scattering of hay in front of the stucco three-car garage. A breeze fluttered the wool on their harlequin flanks.

Feeling his penis stir, he twisted to face his wife of twenty years. Though she was one of five sisters, Chuck—the only child of a Santa Fe gynecologist—believed that population growth had become the world's primary sin and wanted no more children. The twins' birth in Greenwich Village through a cesarean section that took eight months to heal helped plead his case. Helen had had her tubes tied.

He had never reconciled himself to her decision, following the tubal, to crop her waterfall of hair into two-inch spikes. But now, curled under goose down with its embroidered jack-in-the-pulpit cover, she smelled like pancakes steaming. He gazed at the brown wisps spiraling down the back of her neck and pushed his lips against her bare shoulder.

"Ummm," she murmured. She shifted wide hips clad in the Indian-maiden loincloth which matched the fringed bra he'd bought her last summer at Indian Market.

"Guess what," he said, rising to his elbow. "We're alone." He thrust his genitals against the soft leather of her loincloth and bent to peck an earlobe.

She continued to gaze at the huge color photo on the wall, framed in birch, of their summer chalet outside Montpelier that they'd bought years before moving to Santa Fe. Three canoes floated beside the dock; the pond was ringed in beech and white pine. "Don't you have a business breakfast?"

"I do—renegade CPA, newborn investment advisor to the rich. First I'm meeting Alexis to see what figures she's come up with. Then Manny Barnes drops by to pick up a sign for tomorrow's march. Helen? Let's remember our anniversary early. Where'd you put those good-old-days clothes?"

"Give me a moment." She hoisted herself away from him, throwing her feet to the Navajo rug and pressing her eyelids. She rubbed fingertips across the washboard her forehead had become. "I want to go back full time, Charles. I don't mean New York City, I mean to Montpelier. Us four. Not just summers. Peonies in June and mosquitoes in July, leaves in October and for Christmas a yard full of carrot-nosed snowmen. I've tried to make this palace here home. But we live thirty-five miles from five hundred drums of nuclear waste. We came four years ago to care for your mother and now she's dead. My own parents are aging back in Hanover. I'd like to live less than two thousand miles away."

"It's a bad time for good ideas, Helen. My five stock-and-bond clients' portfolios fell eight percent the quarter ending in December; agreed, I'm just learning. But two major tax clients have left. They don't know what to make of my antiwar goings-on."

His eyes swept the vast bedroom, the Kurdistan rugs soaking up heat from the neoprene loops embedded in the concrete slab, the black spirals and sawtooths of a Dan Namingha acrylic that dominated the east wall, the trumpet-vine pot fountaining ricegrass which Helen had fired in the garage last month. In the corner sat the sofa of pleated calfskin they never used. Streaked and smudged because she couldn't find a workman with a ladder long enough for the slope outside, a picture window over the sofa showed the opera house and the piñon-green hills overlooking I-25.

"Too much violence in Santa Fe, Charles. That stabbing at Desert Prep last month felt like a final blow for me."

"It's no longer the town I grew up in, true. I'm also weary of this double life—" triple? he wondered, recalling how leafing though Alexis's gay-and-lesbian newsweekly yesterday triggered a surprise erection. "Let's talk later. Where are those new dress-ups you bought?"

"With the rest, of course."

Flinging back the comforter, he squinted against the seven-thirty sun sparkling off the screen of his laptop on the credenza. Embedded heat warmed his bare feet as he padded to the south wall across the long crack—jagged as Namingha's painted black lightning—that had separated the concrete slab.

The chest's scent of cedar greeted him. He peeled off his pajama top and tossed it onto the ottoman, then bent toward the paper-doll-like kachinas chiseled in the arched lid. He fumbled with the tumblers until he could pull the lock apart.

Bleach prickled his nose as he hoisted the lid and hauled out purchases from the store Helen had found last Saturday, smoothing back the preteen extra-large frock and boy's knickers he'd previously bought on-line that concealed more retro clothing.

"Catch." Over his shoulder he tossed a sheer, long-sleeved beige blouse with dahlia ruffles, a blue denim miniskirt, and a floppy hat whose brim flamed nasturtiums—all from the early 1980s. He rose and turned to Helen, who wasn't there.

"Anybody home?" he called, scratching the black stubble he'd decided to let grow—sideburns, no mustache, clipped horseshoe beard starting from the corners of his lips—better to ally himself with the City Different's peace activists.

Helen advanced from the bathroom in lime-green slippers and white terrycloth robe.

She glanced at his dangling penis. "You think this is going to work?"

"I do." But he wished he'd tweezed out the hairs on the shaft first; squirming at the sting often jump-started an erection. He squeezed his right eye tight—pain from last night's two hours in the den transferring figures from clients' tax workbooks into his laptop was assaulting his temple.

Moving to the bed, Helen plopped the felt hat onto her brown spikes of hair while he pushed his fists through the lawn-daisied sleeves of the man's shirt.

She had draped her robe over the hamper and was trying to snap the skirt tight when, right leg thrust into mustard-colored slacks, Chuck exclaimed, "No!"

"No?"

His penis swelled. "You wear the boy's. I'll wear the girl's." Though pain clawed its way down into his tongue, imaging the change unleashed a grin.

"What are you saying?"

"No one can see us—the kids' llamas, maybe. Get me a bra. I'll go find breasts." Yanking the pant leg free by its belled bottom and stripping off the shirt, he trotted across the room through the door along the heated, yard-square flagstones, down the hall past his den and Mark and Melodie's rooms and then into the kitchen, erection waving like a bowsprit.

From the cutting-board island came the odor of mangoes ripening in a yellow bowl Helen had fired in December. Wait; yesterday she said she found beefsteak tomatoes at Whole Foods for hamburgers tonight and salsa later.

He approached the refrigerator that dominated the maple-clad wall. A thousand dollars misspent to incise on it tiled macaws and halved papayas. Each tile bulged at a different slant; two looked about to tumble down. Hauling the door open, he spotted the tomatoes in their see-through bag. He reached in and rolled out two. What the hell was he about to do?

By the time he'd returned to the bedroom, the blood slamming his right eye had retreated like the blood from his penis—though when he saw Helen, it rose again. She sat at the bottom of the comforter, straight-arming the mattress to brace herself, a white lace bra slung over one knee. A small-billed cap slanted across her forehead. Her breasts plumped the buttoned green polyester shirt; the bells of her slacks pooled against the rug. She'd left the snap undone.

"Look," he smiled.

"Charles, those were for dinner. Do you really enjoy seeing me like this?"

"It's strange, but I do."

Advancing, goose bumps icing the back of his neck, he pushed the tomatoes against the black hairs on his nipples and turned. "See if they fit." Facing her, he waited for her fingers to snake around and press the cotton against the red fruit. The stub end of one bit his flesh. Their chill made him flinch, but what had become a full erection took charge. He stroked it while his left hand squeezed his testicles. "Hook me up."

Her fingers pulled the tomatoes tight; the catch clicked behind him.

He threw on the blouse and stepped into the miniskirt.

"How do I look?" From behind her he snatched the felt hat with its appliquéd nasturtiums, set it on his head, and adjusted its slant. "You're sexy. Why are you staring like you just swallowed a lizard?"

"I've . . ." She clutched her throat where it wrinkled, just under her chin. "I've never seen you with an erection like that."

He grinned, milking the shaft. A pearl of lubricant perched atop the glans. "How do you want me to go in?"

"I don't think I do." She faced him in the wool cap with a black button popping from its top while her left hand kept the men's slacks from collapsing. Her tongue circled her chapped lips. "I think what I want is to get out of these clothes and make us some breakfast. Pancakes with blueberries, I think. Are you hungry, Charles?"

"I am!" He lunged for her, knocking her cap sidewise, his own floppy hat sailing into her face as she pitched backward and he toppled onto her, smashing the tomatoes. Seeds and juice squished through the bra's lace to stain his blouse and squirted red rivulets across the comforter's jack-in-the-pulpits. Their hearts pummeled each other while the teeth along her undone zipper rasped the skin of his erection.

She batted the hat from her face. Her breath seared his neck, making the stubble prickle. "Get off me," she choked.

Drenched and gasping, he slithered to his knees. A gob of pulp cooled his forehead. His forearms pressed the comforter as he watched her rise.

She ran a palm across her eyes and stared at the red goo that smeared it. Gripping the waistband of the slacks, she grabbed her robe and hobbled along the blue, now crimson Zuni carpet into the bathroom.

When he heard the shower's splash, he pried off the miniskirt and lowered his buttocks onto the heap of clothes, leaning against the footboard, stenciled with the outlines of Toggenburg goats and shipped from Vermont with the headboard. He took his tumid penis and, setting his jaw, began to pump, squashed tomatoes bouncing against his chest. After a dozen strokes he groaned, arching his back to the onrush of semen that spurted into the green ruffles scalloping his wrist.

He waited for the tingle in his thighs to subside as the sounds of shower water stopped. With his forefinger he swiped a dollop of semen off his knee and licked the sweet pungency, blinking at the concrete slab's crack. He began to figure the cost of having it repaired. Three thousand dollars easy—the edges were crumbling. Three thousand? More like ten to jackhammer the concrete into chunks and replace the tubing. Plus a call to his lawyer to initiate a lawsuit.

He was reaching to undo the bra when Helen marched from the bathroom in her robe. Hair sleeked back and glistening, she stared at him but said nothing until she turned away.

"Twenty minutes if you want to eat."

"I'll catch something near the office." He wondered if she heard. All he wanted was to wander the lawn with the llamas, bask with them under the drifting clouds, whistle off flies.

Palms cupping the bra's soaked cotton, he blew out air and trudged to the bathroom where he dropped bra and the tomatoes into the sink.

——————

Five minutes down from upper Camino de Cruz Blanca, natty in a mohair turtleneck and hip-hugger black denims, Chuck mouthed the last of a poppy-seed bagel. He aimed for the driveway skirting his office at Palace and Otero, a renovated adobe perched on a mound garnished with hollyhocks to honor his mother. She had died three years before, following a head-on collision at Cerrillos and St. Michael's with a young woman high on heroin.

In the rear parking area Chuck spotted Alexis's mountain bike, handlebars spread like steer horns and leaning against the flaking trunk of a salt cedar.

Leaving his blue blazer folded over the passenger headrest, he shut the door of his Saab and hurried across the gravel with his laptop. Even at nine, the air smelled like a just-opened refrigerator. Cold chafed his ankles. The neighborhood's feral black-and-white cat, its ribcage prominent, slinked into the waving heads of sowthistle. On the back steps he wiped dust from his loafers with a handkerchief, plucked a spiderweb from the black grille that protected the door's window, and scratched his cheek.

"Good morning," he called, unlocking the door. Past Alexis's broad back he watched the just-leased Bloomberg Financial News System—by satellite from New York—run price/earnings ratios across one of its twin screens.

To bury his rage over how his mother had ended, two and a half years before he'd decided to update his CPA license, earned in New York City at Deloitte & Touche, and expand from calculating his and Helen's taxes to offering advice to others from an office near the Plaza. Soon he was also counseling investors.

Exploding a pink bubble of gum, his stocky assistant swiveled to face him. "Sorry," she smiled, chewing. "Oh my god." She jammed her knuckles to the braided skirt band above her pelvis.

Plopping the laptop on his desk, he stared with her at the mustard-colored, black-banded creature creeping from a hole below the copier. Last year a workman, laying planks for a new floor, had cut a board too short. The dozens of legs they saw scrabbling resembled the tentacles of sea anemones his son Mark had described in his seventh-grade midterm. Its head pincers opened and shut as it wound along the base of the replastered wall.

"Isn't it gorgeous?" Alexis pinched a bunch of brown hair behind her ear. "The thing's as long as my forearm."

"How do we get rid of it?"

"Hey, boss, you aren't scared? Look, it's squirming up toward the latillas." She popped another pink bubble as the centipede wriggled into the darkness between two debarked tree limbs.

"C'mon, toss that gum while we're talking."

"Sure." The wad pinged the metal bottom of the wastebasket. "Confer at the mogul's table?" She grabbed a sheaf of printouts from her desk.

He strode past, inhaling the scent that always moved him—of the sheets and pillowcases his mother hung out when he was growing up. Under her shaggy sweaters and calf-length skirts, did Alexis wear bras and panties soaked in sunshine?

He wondered what it was like biking into Santa Fe's quiet frenzy from Arroyo Hondo. Alexis lived with a woman named Baby who was even stockier than her who raised churro sheep and called Alexis "Sweetheart." Baby thought Alexis's stories works of genius, "which they aren't," she'd insisted the day before, as she and Chuck staple-gunned *Compassion for Iraqis* and *Stop the War Machine* to laths for tomorrow's march.

But Chuck had read one of Alexis's stories about a lesbian woman's fury at her father, the president of a Masonic Lodge, for keeping an adulterous tryst with a gay man in drag. He thought Baby right.

"Bring us some water, will you?" he called over his shoulder.

In the big room that opened onto a kitchen, Chuck glanced through the window at the still-blossomless hollyhocks. Sitting, he stared at the abstract by a former client looming on a windowless wall. Its pink and azure contortions told Chuck, This chaos is you, buddy, big time—half an hour ago you turned androgynous.

"Mrs. Morgan's gonna be there?" Alexis's contralto brought his gaze to her printouts as she set water on the table's mahogany planks.

"She is," he said, gulping. The cold water calmed him.

"She's a loose cannon."

"Can be."

"And the mortgage guy she uses?"

"There, too."

"They'll probably want Mr. Wilkes to buy residential, right?" Alexis asked.

"Good idea, you think?"

"The morning news says Bush is jetting to the Azores to meet Blair and Spain's prime minister. It's not a last-ditch brain-racking to find peace. It's a war council, all about oil and establishing a permanent military base, you and I know that."

"We do."

"Bloomberg shows personal bankruptcies up twenty percent in the same number of years, boss. A long-term treasury bond is paying under five percent, the lowest since the nineteen sixties."

"You know you already understand the blue-screened monster better than I do? After April fifteenth I'm going to start training you on our Lacerte Tax program, in case I get laid up."

"Sure, boss. Anyhow, you say to expect a crash if the war lengthens past a couple of months or we dictate democracy and the Iraqis balk."

" 'Balk' meaning they turn Iraq into a second Vietnam."

"That's a loud sigh."

He stared at her. "So what do I advise Bret Wilkes?"

"His portfolio looks like sixty percent blue chips, thirty percent municipals, and the rest liquid in Schwab's Value Added. His portfolio is down seventeen percent from this time last year—current value nearly a million bucks. But the prelim tax return you gave me shows an excess of business income. He needs a deduction."

He sighed again. "I better tell him to cash out three hundred thousand dollars and have Maxine find him income property that generates a net loss."

Watching him, Alexis took a fistful of hair and began chewing its ends. "Mr. Baca called yesterday. He's leaving his tax work here but moving his and his wife's portfolios to Murch Investments."

Chuck finished his water. Standing, he drifted to the picture window and stared at the dark-bellied clouds advancing above St. Francis Cathedral on the other side of the street. "Tell me, what's it like being gay?"

"Oh my god, awful until I met Baby. Okay now." She jumped from the black leather armchair and hurried to him, soft-soled boots soundless. The wool at one of her cuffs brushed his earlobe as she gave him a hug.

"Thanks, kiddo," Chuck whispered, closing his eyes.

"You look so sad." She let her arms dangle. "Do you . . . ?"

"Do I what?"

"Think you might be gay?"

"I don't know what I am. I do know I can't put up with corporation CEOs like Ken Lay of Enron who lie with the same gusto as Bush. Maybe I've been lying, too."

Slouching in an armchair, he threw his hands toward Alexis's research. "Who can believe this stuff when anything that promotes war passes as truth? I'm ashamed to be an American. Right now I'm ashamed to be me. Whoever that is."

"An honest man," she said, holding his eyes as she reseated herself.

"Aaahhh. Helen wants us to withdraw to Vermont."

"What? No, don't!" She pressed her breasts, then slid fingers garnished with silver rings below the table's edge. "Baby lived near Burlington. Except for the winters and the litter, she loved it."

"I'm staying put, don't worry. Driving down here, I got an idea you may like. You may not."

"Of course I'll like it. What is it?"

"No time now." Scratching his chin, he swept up her papers and pushed back his chair. "Go ahead and unwrap some more gum."

Through the computer room came a single knock at the rear door, then four. The braided silver ring high in Alexis's left ear jiggled as she frowned and turned her head.

"Manny Barnes," Chuck said. "He wants a placard."

"His girlfriend's my best friend."

"He's told me. Stay there, I'll let him in."

Swaddled in his gray sheepskin coat and red stocking cap, Manny stood stamping hiking boots on the stoop. "Late for a breakfast, can't talk," Chuck said, pulling the door wide. He gestured Manny inside, touching with his fingertips the sheepskin's ripped sleeve.

Manny unhooked the coat's loops and stuffed the cap in a pocket. He was wondering what Alexis would be wearing this morning, when she appeared around the bookcase blowing a pink bubble at him.

STOP YAPPING _____

IN HIS POINTY BLUE COWBOY BOOTS AND HOME LOAN Champ billed cap, Ron Kirkpatrick lumbered into the hotel lobby where Maxine Morgan sat—smelling like paint thinner—on one of the three Hopi-blanket upholstered benches facing the registration desk. Behind the counter ascended the mural that gave Hotel La Concha its name. The Spirit of Flamenco arched from a white oyster shell in an embroidered gold bodice and flouncing red skirt. Her right arm stretched toward the oaken ceiling; both hands gripped ivory castanets. Beside each ear an angel plucked a guitar.

"What in the name of Judas Christ did you bring Pixie for?" Ron growled.

From violet-smeared eyes Maxine squinted up under her swirl of black hair. White and red stripes snaked along the sleeves of her cashmere sweater, the rest of it a blue field of white stars. Gold hoops large as merry-go-round rings swung from her ears. No smile for Ron this morning.

"Shut up," she snapped at the black-faced Pekingese that, having sniffed Ron, had begun to yip and flap a tail still matted from his monthly carbolic-acid bath. The dog's pop eyes stared through a hut-like cage of red willow that perched on a red wooden wagon. A stars-and-stripes kerchief drooped from his neck.

"Why Pixie?" Maxine asked. "I need support. Which I have a feeling you're not going to give." Clearing her throat, from under the dark wool skirt she lifted one knee-length boot and settled it on the opposite knee.

"You been redecoratin'?" Ron asked.

"Hunh?"

"That smell."

"Turpentine, big boy. Balanchy's latest."

"It waters my eyes." The duck's bill of his cap dipped toward her. "Fuckin' why did you throw that note last night?"

"I didn't want to email it and I didn't feel like phoning. I figured you'd smell it when you came out to your car."

Face flat as Pixie's, long black hair fanned over his coat, a Native

American strode toward the restaurant's arched entrance. "Stupid," Ron muttered.

"Him?"

"You. What if Lila'd found it?"

"I was drunk."

He watched her larynx bob. "Move over."

Gripping the end of the bench, she tugged her buttocks to its end. He lowered his hulk beside her, unzipped a red polyester fleece with high collar and pinched cuffs, and peeled it from his back. Over his heart showed the badge, *Onward Christian Soldiers*, that a jeweler on the Plaza had fashioned for him the month before from turquoise and copper wire.

"Yip, yip."

"Quiet down, buddy." Ron waggled his pinkie through the cage's grid. "We've got business here."

Glancing at the mole that squatted like a bug on the bridge of Maxine's nose, he let his eyes drift with the hand he eased to her thigh.

She grabbed his wrist and set it on the rough blanket between them. "Didn't you read my note?"

"After Lila threw your Tabasco'd hankie and toilet paper tube in my face. I told her your 'Don't come over Thursday' meant that the regular meetin' she thinks we have with Giordy won't work next week because he's back to drinkin'."

"You're quick."

"What are you goin' to do about our tiles and the deck, Max?"

"Hunh?"

"The bathroom tiles are poppin'; last night the deck hightailed it down the hill."

"Rotten luck, big boy. I'll send Victor over."

"Lila's already called him. She's right, you sold us a piece of junk. Where's this new pigeon of yours?"

"Room service spilled latte on his slacks fifteen minutes ago."

"How do you know? You spend the night together?"

"Shovel your shit elsewhere, okay? He phoned me downstairs."

"How'd Giordy snag him?"

"Off our website. He collects petroglyphs."

"Saws them out of the rock?"

"No, dum-dum—collects motif sculpture, pottery, furniture, whatever. The funding flows from his security-software company in San Jose. Giordy's convinced him to buy a vacation hacienda here now, retire later. The usual."

She pressed her palm to her high forehead and clenched her eyes. "Look, I'm not saying you and I can't do deals together any longer, though that lard around your middle has become pretty unattractive. Mainly it's your wheezing that scares me. I can see Giordy driving home from Thursday poker to find you flopped in his bed with a heart attack."

Ron tugged his cap. "So that's why you flattened my tire? To say 'lose weight'?" The turquoise cinch on his bolo tie rose and fell over the green shirt snapped to his collarbone.

"Hunh?"

"Hunh? Hunh? When you threw the billet-doux sayin' don't come over Thursday night, did you let the air—"

"What air?"

"Yip, yip. Yip."

"Fermez la bouche, dog." Ron's stomach became a fist as he palmed his thighs and stood. "Watch you don't buy yourself a lawsuit, Max."

She threw her hands to her ears. "I didn't goddamn let any goddamn air out of your goddamn tire and quit harassing me." Her hands sunk to her skirt. "Maybe it bit into a nail. Though I did see some movement in the moonlight. Raccoon, maybe? Someone or something has it in for you, big boy."

"You."

"Not goddamn me. How'd you get to the hotel?"

"Lila's Mustang." He gazed at a stinkbug crawling onto the bench's arm, where it lifted its rear toward Maxine. She flung out her left hand, bearing a diamond-and-emerald engagement ring and platinum wedding ring. The insect tumbled to the flagstones.

Patting the black cotton candy of her hair, she jumped up. Her smile burst forth like sunrise. Ron stared where she looked toward the stairs curving to the right of the reception desk.

Down the green-and-red runners pranced a slight man with brushed-back brick-red hair, open-necked white shirt, faded jeans whose belt held a cell phone, and loafers without socks. As he approached, Ron saw blue veins webbing his ankles. He looked no older than forty.

"Chuck here yet?" he asked, breathless.

"We don't know what he looks like, partner." Ron advanced toward him. "Least I don't—she may." He jerked a cracked thumb back toward Maxine. "I'm Ron Kirkpatrick, Los Alamos Mortgage."

"Of course, by your cap." Stretching needle-thin lips into a grin, he shot out a small, freckled hand to squeeze Ron's paw. "Bret Wilkes." His fingernails were crescent moons. Ron held the blue-ice irises that lifted to his own until Bret broke Ron's grip and darted past him. "Hi, there, Mr. Raggedy Andy." Bret strummed the top of Pixie's cage. "We going to buy a place this morning?" He clamped Maxine's shoulders. "Did you and Giordy stay up all night sifting properties?"

"I didn't sleep much. I don't know about my husband."

Freckled forehead crinkling like the parchment frown of a nun, Bret turned to Ron. "This town, how I love this town, even more than last spring. And the Valley'll bounce back, don't you worry at all. I'm talking to fellows right now hatching DNA encryption systems that'll bury digital." He narrowed his eyes at Ron. "But I want a footprint here, you know? Santa Fe Institute, Los Alamos, the informatics boys, down I-twenty-five a ways the huge Intel fab, Sandia Labs, the university incubators, Kirtland Air Force Base. It's why I asked Mr. Chuck Ridley two years ago to take on some of my tax work. Jake, here he comes."

Jake? Ron faced the frescoed columns of the hotel's entrance. Kneeling maidens ground corn and scrubbed clothes as they supported an arch of mounted conquistadors in peaked helmets brandishing lances. Their silver and bronze dominated the Native American reds, yellows, and greens, which alkali from roof leaks had streaked white.

Oak doors twice as tall as Chuck hushed behind him as he hurried over the earth-tone-marbled flags. He'd pinned a white-on-black peace symbol to one lapel of his blazer. Though perspiration cooled him, burrs that had lodged in his black socks from taking a shortcut through puncturevine pricked his ankles. His feet hurt from the tasseled loafers he'd bought last weekend while Helen shopped for more good-old-days new-to-you clothes.

"Sorry," he breathed to Bret and Maxine, tonguing his lips. He addressed the double-chinned man in the mortgage cap. "I'm Chuck Ridley."

"Ron Kirkpatrick."

"Growing a beard, Chuck?" Bret asked.

"Camouflaging worry lines, but it itches." He scrabbled at his cheek.

"Let's go," blurted Maxine, grabbing the wagon's handle. "No poop, Pixie, no pee."

She led them toward the hotel's restaurant. Beside its dark iron chandeliers chained to vigas hung strings of red and green chiles. Daylight filtered through smudged skylights to bathe the room. Throughout, firefly lights twinkled on evergreen figs that soared from baskets as large as tumbleweeds.

"Ronald? Carry him?"

The dog's odor of carbolic acid had already overpowered the restaurant's usual fragrance of beans. Ron swallowed and cradled the wagon in his arms down three steps.

A goateed maitre d' dressed in black coat and broad red-and-green necktie, his ponytail swinging, beckoned them to the corner table Maxine had requested. From its center sprang a red-silk hibiscus in a tulip-shaped vase.

Guests filled half of the circular tables, all of which boasted hibiscus centerpieces. The fan-haired Native American who had passed them in the lobby slouched at a table near the entrance reading yesterday's *Wall Street Journal*. Amid the sounds of conversations and the clink of silverware against scalloped platters full of tortillas and eggs, Maxine, Bret, Ron, and Chuck pulled out oak armchairs and scraped them close.

"Shhhh," Maxine told Pixie, leaning down to rock the red wagon. From a woven-leather purse she extracted a Baggie bulging with kibble, then slid back the door of the cage. "Here, sweetie." She crooked her forefinger. "Waitress!"

A woman in black pantaloons, black crêpe-soled shoes, and a black blouse embroidered in red and green at the neck raised her chin in acknowledgment. Like most of the other waitresses she'd plaited her hair in a braid whose end flopped midway against her back. Balancing a tray of smeared plates and cups, she disappeared into the kitchen through stainless-steel doors.

Maxine moved her hand to Bret's forearm. "The help here is Hispanic. The lips are more like ours and the faces are not so fleshy as Native

American. You may recall from your earlier visit. Did you rest well?"

"I could have used another blanket."

Chuck caught himself wondering if Bret slept nude or in pajamas. He reached for the napkin peaked like a blue-linen tent, and spread it over his thigh. "We may get snow yet. Walking over I watched the clouds fusing."

"War clouds!" Ron exclaimed. "They told the Comanches when to arm."

"Really? Jake."

"Ron here."

"Jake's an expression," Bret explained.

"Ronald never knows what he's talking about. Where's that waitress?"

"Don't know what I'm talkin' about?" Ron glared at her over the hibiscus. "I know the sooner we suit up, war clouds or none, the sooner we teach those Iraqi sand niggers some respect."

Chuck noticed Ron's *Onward Christian Soldiers*. The throbbing returned to his right eye as his mind replayed Helen's march from the bathroom as he sloped against the footboard, the squashed tomatoes propped in his palms. He twitched, recalling how their juice dribbled down his belly.

"You with me, Bret? How do they feel in Silicone Valley? This damn dry air." The crack at the tip of Ron's thumb began to sting.

Before Bret could reply, their waitress appeared clutching what looked like a notebook computer. From under her elbow she dealt out menus garlanded in hibiscus blossoms. Her half dozen silver bracelets chimed as Pixie began to bark.

"Okay if I wait while you choose? We're filling up." She skipped back from the Pekingese. Her fragrance of sandalwood, added to Maxine's Turpentine and the remains of Pixie's bath, made Chuck blink. Through the mist he stared at the printed options wavering under *Breakfast*.

"Start me with a double Bloody Mary, two lime wedges, and a short glass of water for him," Maxine said. "Pixie, quiet down. Eggs Benedict, Christmas." She turned her shadowed eyes to Bret. "Christmas means red and green chile mixed—you may remember. See anything tempting?"

Not you, for sure, Ron fumed.

"The Southwestern Burrito looks lovely," Bret said, pinching half-lens glasses from his shirt and pushing them to his nose. He fingered the silver chain that disappeared down his chest.

"Red, green, or Christmas?" the waitress asked.

"I think the last."

Maxine cocked her head. "Con mucho gusto, señor."

The green-and-red bow at the base of the waitress's braid bobbed as she dipped her gaze to her computer, tapping its keys. "You?" she asked Ron.

"Huevos rancheros. Heavy on the cowboy beans and mucho red."

She turned to Chuck.

"Crunchy granola and bananas. Add plain yogurt if you can."

"You got it."

"No Christmas on that?" Bret laughed.

"Who's for coffee?" the waitress asked.

"I got mine upstairs between my legs. Mint tea will do me nicely."

"Cup runneth over," Maxine laughed. She began to cough.

A young Hispanic in baggy pants, hair shaved except at the top of his scalp, brought four fluted glasses of water.

"These people make good warriors," Ron said when the boy sauntered off. "My son was trainin' to be one. Hey, Bushie, get a move on. We want that black gold, boy. News this morning said Turkey still won't let us through." He jerked his head toward Chuck. "How you feel about this? That symbol on your blazer Anasazi or peacenik?"

Holding the big man's turtle eyes, Chuck said, "Preemption bothers me. We've thumbed our noses at more weapons inspections, we've told China and Russia and France and Germany to fly a kite. True, we need the oil, we use a fourth of the world's supply. My big concern is what happens after we level Nasiriyah and Baghdad. Have Donald Rumsfeld and Paul Wolfowitz developed a strategy for fighting the guerrillas who sabotage those pipelines we're going to re-open? Or the electrical grid we're going to repair or the water we plan to make potable? I doubt Iraqis want our democracy, I think Iraq is Arabic for Vietnam. So yes, this pin speaks for peace."

"Where's that drink?" Maxine muttered. With her left hand she fingered Pixie a few kibbles from her bag.

Licking the crack in his thumb, Ron swiveled toward Bret. "You a peacenik too?"

"Wars do happen. If I can make a profit, lovely. This morning, though, I'm here to buy property."

"You're neutral?"

"Yes, for now. Ten years ago when I was a data-security contractor in Kuwait, I smelled too many intestines spilling from both Christians and Muslims."

Eye pain pounding toward his tongue, Chuck reached for his laptop and opened it on his thighs. Hoping to quiet Ron, he spread paperwork between his silverware and the silk hibiscus.

"He wants to talk real estate, Ronald." Lowering her voice, Maxine faced Bret. "Ron's and his wife's son died in basic training at Fort Ord. A seagull that waddled into the mess hall startled a cook who spilled boiling water on Jonathan while he was scrubbing grease off the bricks under the stove. Two months later he died at Fort Benning from third-degree burns. I'll take that."

Tilting from her chair, Maxine grabbed the vodka and spiced tomato juice from the tray the waitress balanced on her palm. Glaring at Maxine, she grabbed the tray's edge and swung it to a square table set against the wainscoting.

While the waitress doled out plates, Maxine gulped half the Bloody Mary and cleaned her upper lip with her tongue. Glancing to her right, "Good," she began, "Chuck's brought a paper trail—ah, jeez, another stinkbug. Waitress! Climbing that table leg! Pixie: calm."

The Pekingese had straight-legged himself off the mat and knocked his skull against the cage's woven willow. He scuttled back and forth, yapping. With each bark his jaw dropped like a Chinese puppet's as the waitress, gripping the tray, strode to the side table to dislodge the insect with her shoe. Feelers and legs thrashed until she pile-drove her foot to the flagstones, squashing it.

"There's a long, black hair in my beans," Ron bellowed.

"Mister, I'm doing my very." The waitress rushed over Bret's cup, tea tag dangling, and Ron's coffee, then returned with Pixie's water. Sweeping up Ron's plate, she hurried toward the kitchen's swinging doors.

"Bring me another hair of the dog," Maxine called, brandishing her glass in her left hand. From the next table a blond man flanked by a woman in a yellow smock and a girl with a tattooed dagger slanting up her cheek stared.

Bret flicked up the underside of his wrist to consult his watch.

"Not one of your typical Santa Fe desayunos," Maxine simpered, leaning to pass the water glass into Pixie's cage. "You're looking for an acre and a half, pueblo style, Northside or in Las Campanas, right? Views and viga-and-latilla ceilings. Guest house for your daughter and baby girl if possible, expecting she'll want to repair her relationship with you. Looking to spend eight hundred thousand to a million two, Giordy says?"

Bret was nodding when a series of flute-like whistles issued from his hip. He unbuckled the leather holster, jerked out his cell phone, and thumb-flipped its cover. "Yes? Yep. Lovely." He swiveled his wrist again. "Probably half an hour, outermost. The Museum of Fine Arts? Okeydoke; jake."

"That was your husband," he told Maxine. "He wants to show me a couple of tin-shade lamps with little stick figures on horseback chasing horned toads."

"Good. I'll follow you, then we're gone. I've lined up four properties before lunch at Geronimo."

"Lunch?" Ron scowled. "I promised our manager—"

"Bret and me. Maybe I'll call you later. Chuck? What do your figures show? Oh, Ronald, your huevos smell fabulous. Scrumptious with salsa."

Emptying his lungs, Chuck rubbed the stubble on his cheek and, turning toward Bret, took in air. "Your preliminary tax return shows that from an investment standpoint, you should focus on income property; sorry about that, Bret. Perhaps take three hundred thousand from blue chips and look for office space or a fourplex."

Chuck realized that his feet were pumping out as much pain as his eye. His hand shook as he spooned up a slice of banana.

"Son of a peccary, Ridley, you think defense stocks aren't goin' to rock-and-roll? Build this man's portfolio fast, before we invade. Except for high-end restaurants and Canyon Road, commercial here is dead. Fourplexes? No way. High-end homes with views is what the real money wants in Santa Fe. Fort Worth, a different story. Agreed, Max? Say yes," he wheezed.

"Hunh? We could look at the Lofts, I guess. I know a fourplex priced to sell near the Unitarian Church—perhaps tomorrow. Monday or Tuesday we can study Chuck's figures if Bret can stay over. Bret?"

Like the rage Ron felt steaming up inside him, streamers of heat rose from the pink beans heaped next to the cheddar-topped eggs the waitress had clunked down before him. She returned to set Maxine's Bloody Mary on its coaster and left. To Ron, something still looked wrong with his eggs, but Bret's words broke his focus.

"Chuck's tax counsel the last couple of years has played nicely for me, though his stock picks the last six months have been iffy. I tell you what. Maybe I can let my CFO handle Valley appointments next week if the hotel here has an extra blanket and forgets room service." He spread a thin-lipped smile at Maxine.

Ron stabbed one of the eggs and sawed it open with his knife. He hoisted into his mouth a bite dripping yolk. Little of the hot, red-chile sting he'd expected accompanied the clicks his jaw made. He stared at Maxine, then Chuck, then Bret, then down at his plate. The cook had confettied his eggs green. He hated the mildness of green. Hispanic motherfucker.

Wheezing, he scraped his chair backward across the flagstones and stood, clutching the plate as though it held the cook's head. Rising on his toes, he hurled the plate onto Pixie's cage. It cracked, spattering beans, posole, salsa, and green-chile-speckled yellow over the terrified pet. The red-white-and-blue kerchief flapped as the Pekingese whipped his head back and forth and began to yowl like a black-masked cat.

Maxine bolted her drink, heaped hair tumbling to her forehead. Clapping a palm to one of the gold hoops swinging from her ears, she clutched the table's edge and dropped to her knees beside the red wagon.

All Chuck felt when he squeezed his eyes shut was the chill of beefsteak tomatoes.

Forehead crinkling, Bret leapt up, hand on his cell-phone holster.

Ron began blowing like a walrus. Striding past the gaping faces to the steps, behind him over Pixie's squalls he heard Max yell, "Let him go!" Twisting his head, he glimpsed not Bret Wilkes but the Native American pursuing, hair flapping behind him, *Wall Street Journal* rolled in a fist meatier than Ron's own.

DAMAGING MR. FIXIT _____

THROUGH THE CLOUDS MASSING THIS LATE SATURDAY morning, the sun turned Lila's cowgirl shirt and its mother-of-pearl buttons to warm peach. Lila had shampooed her shoulder-length hair, gathering its graying strands into a ponytail with peach-colored ribbon. Capillaries in her cheeks purpled the powder she applied. Though she often left her shirt open to show cleavage, this morning she also rubbed in Estée Lauder's honeysuckle-based Beyond Paradise—determined, given Ron's history in Fort Worth and, apparently, here, to attempt adultery herself before cellulite pocked her flesh in more places than just the backs of her thighs.

Try Manny Barnes? She stood now with Victor Valdez gazing at the tiles in the upstairs bath, convincing herself the stench of tobacco from his leather jacket turned her on.

Shorter by two inches than Lila, Victor raised dark eyes to hers. "Termites," he muttered, removing the black-rimmed glasses that hid his eyebrows and stuffing them into the pocket of a denim work shirt. His belly hid a leather belt holding up gabardine slacks pleated at the waist. Kneeling, he reached under one of the four raised tiles, pinching up a mix of dark specks and sawdust. With his other hand he stroked the tip of a handlebar mustache.

"Dry-wood termites, you've got 'em." He dropped the grains into his palm and pushed up the bill of a beige cap whose red band read *Proud To Be American*.

"Mr. Valdez," Lila said, sidling to him until her arm nudged his battered jacket. "Aren't you hot? Let me take that." His pocketed box of cigarettes pressed her hip as she reached for the jacket's collar.

Squinting at her with his right eye, he stumbled against the shelves that bore her towel-and-washcloth set imprinted with orange trumpet vine. "This powder? Cellulose. The black specks? Excrement. Your subfloor's riddled. All we—"

Turning to face him so that he could ogle her cleavage, Lila dipped toward the wastebasket. "Toss it in here, sir. And leave those tiles alone. I've left word with our insurance broker to send someone Monday with a camera." She thrust the green wastebasket at him.

He brushed off his palm above it as she flipped down the cover of the toilet bowl and, sitting, bent to pull her yellow skirt taut across her knees. "A terrible morning, Mr. Valdez. Mr. Kirkpatrick and I had a spat. Then Triple A came to patch his tire but couldn't find the nail—I've got to learn to tame that white elephant. My husband took my Mustang. I'm trapped here all day. Can you imagine? We left a four-thousand-foot home and stables in Fort Worth because the rich Muslim husband of Mr. Kirkpatrick's mistress sent him a note threatening his life. Muslims understand methods of torture, don't they?" Her fingers twiddled the humpbacked Kokopelli that hung on a silver chain playing his flute between her breasts.

"Who doesn't?" he murmured, turning to limp toward the bathroom's doorway. The soles of his alligator-skin boots clacked on the tiles. "You have other problems I can help with?"

"Mr. Kirkpatrick may be having an affair right now with a woman you know," she risked.

He twisted toward her.

"An affair with the realtor who sold us this heap of shit."

Victor formed an O with his lips. He yanked the bill of his cap down over his forehead, now a mass of ruts. "About Mrs. Morgan I know nothing," he said, "except she steers work my way. I'll bring you a bid on these tiles Monday. They all need to come up. On the phone you mentioned a downstairs deck?" He shoved his glasses back onto his hawk nose.

"In a minute. That patriotic slogan on your cap, your limp—I notice these things. Have you served the U S of A, Mr. Valdez?"

"I sure have. We fought for a democracy in Vietnam and ended up with sixty thousand Americans dead and a country full of Commies. The steel ankle's a gift from that screw-up."

"And what do you think this new war will accomplish?" She fingered an end of the ribbon securing her ponytail.

Raising one arm to brace himself against the bathroom wall, he stared at her. "We got the firepower in self-propelled howitzers and GPS-guided bombs to end this mess in two months, maybe less. Are we gonna add billions more to the billion bucks a month we're throwing into Afghanistan to try for democracy in Iraq?"

"You speak in depth, sir."

"No way our dollars were going to work in Nam. Mrs. Kirkpatrick? I need to be home to fix lunch for Mom by twelve thirty."

"Let's go see that deck." She stood and smoothed her skirt over her hips, smiling at him.

From under Victor's cap, black ringlets jiggled down his neck as he turned and started across the blue carpet, the right side of his body dipping with each step. A yard from the doorway leading to the landing, he twisted his head to her. "Tell me something." He peered through his glasses, breathing hard. "Are you—?" But she'd been glancing to the side to see if she'd picked the stuffed panda off the carpet after her fight with Ron, and squashed her breasts against Victor's back.

"Oh!" she exclaimed, slapping her right cheek. "I was checking the bed, I didn't realize you'd stopped."

"The hell you didn't, lady. You want it bad, don't you? All drenched in that perfume." He grabbed both her cheeks and rammed his lips to hers. His belt buckle pressed her belly.

Panting, she threw her arms around his neck. "Slowly, sir. It's my first time out of wedlock." Her arms went slack and she backed away. "You take care of your mother? What a good man! Will you come back later? I want to savor you." Reaching to cup his erection, she laughed to see his eyes bulge behind his glasses.

Biting a hair straggling from his mustache, he pirouetted from her, throwing the shrapnel-blasted ankle toward the landing, and smacked his temple on the doorjamb.

"Unnhhh," he groaned and staggered.

"Oh, my dear! The skin's broken." She grabbed her desk chair and wheeled it to him. "I'll go get a washcloth."

Blinking at her, he lowered himself to the cushion and gazed at the palm he brought down from the purpling bulge. Lifting his buttocks, he hauled a handkerchief from his rear pocket, wiping off the blood and grasping his genitals.

Lila rushed back. Kneeling, she squeezed the cold washcloth against the wound as drops of water dribbled down his neck. "Can you walk?" she asked, rising.

He nodded and stood. She took his elbow and hung on to the banister as they headed down toward the living room's faux-elkskin sofa and two padded armchairs. A beanbag ottoman upholstered in scarlet vinyl squatted in front of each.

"I need you whole, sir," Lila said, watching his buttocks sway under the leather jacket, feeling her vulva wet her black lace bikini. Might small talk comfort him? "Do you think our drought will bring out the millers early this spring? I hate it when they swarm."

He paused beside a cabinet across whose doors cavalry raced toward a painted adobe labeled *The Alamo*. Next to it a cigar-store Indian capped by a red-and-yellow war bonnet guarded Ron's home office. One of the yellow feathers had snapped. "I gotta pee," Victor blurted.

"Of course you do. You'll find talcumed towels to your right."

Massaging the breast with the ingrown nipple, Lila moved to French doors opening on the remainder of the deck that the crosshatched two-by-fours still supported. She peered out at the redwood boards strewn like pickup sticks among the junipers and piñons that rose from the greenbelt. The post that had propped the deck's outer corner lay broken across a coil of garden hose. Her rattan lounge tilted against a clutch of rabbitbrush. At the base of a Russian olive, its gray leaves fluttering, gleamed a shard of her Chinese urn. "Fuck," she exploded, anger occluding the buzz that had tickled her vagina. A couple of cottontails, backs arching, scampered under a juniper. The air smelled of trucks and SUVs whooshing along Bishop's Lodge Road. Snow patched faraway Mount Baldy and the Ski Basin closer by.

She had just spotted the snapped half of Manny and Joyce's plum tree pointing like a barbed arrow across the railing guarding their hot tub when Manny appeared in a black vest and long-sleeved plaid shirt. He cinched the lariat of his hat as he strode around the tub sunk in its small deck, fifteen feet from what remained of the Kirkpatricks' deck. Joyce followed Manny out the door in leather thongs, nubby skirt and sweater matching her blonde mop of hair.

Behind Lila came Victor's voice, "What've you got here?"

Lila pulled open one of the glass doors. "Not as cold as I imagined — look at this mess."

She waggled her fingers at Manny and Joyce but only Manny waved back. Joyce had thrust her pelvis forward and stood scowling at the severed treetop attached to the rest of its trunk by a strip of bark.

"Termites or could be dry rot," Victor muttered as Lila snaked her arm around his thick waist. "Depends on whether—"

"This was my favorite tree," Joyce yelled over the drainage ditch, dammed since last night by Lila's glass-topped table and its bent-in-two umbrella. A few new-growth leaves fluttered from the plum's nearest branch as Joyce jerked its top upright. "What do you plan to do about this?"

"What do I plan to do? Nothing. Go splint it back. Or buy another one. It's not my fault." Lila glanced at the boulders and buffalo grass exposed by the ripped-away two-by-sixes, and taking Victor with her, backed two paces across the remaining planks to lean against the living room's stucco wall.

"Not your fault?" Joyce called out.

"The screws in the metal anchors must have loosened, Boodie." Manny dropped a long arm around her shoulder. "An act of God."

"Take your arm off me. That's no act of god. She loaded it with too much trash. You come home late from breakfast with my friend and expect me to have finished our newsletter and now stand here excusing this person's need to load her deck with trash? Bug off."

"Good idea," Lila shouted. "Crawl into your holes. Embarrassing my husband and I with your *Make Love Not War* bumper stickers. That was one of you let air from his tire? C'mon, Mr. Valdez, let's go."

Clenching her teeth, Lila pushed Victor sideways into the living room and drove the brass handle down to lock the doors. She grabbed the looped bronze lariats of one of the stand lamps flanking the sofa. "I need you to love me to tears, sir. Now and after lunch. Come on." Undoing her shirt's second mother-of-pearl button, she started past him for the stairs. "That furnace is supposed to shut off when it gets this warm." She looked over her shoulder. "Why are you standing there?"

Jamming his fists into his pleated gabardines, he shifted from boot to boot. "I have to use the little boy's room."

"Again? Drench that bruise, will you?"

"The problem is not the bruise."

She narrowed her eyes. "Have you a prostate situation?"

His eyelashes fluttered. The graying tips of his mustache bounced as he shook his head. "Pee-tee es dee."

"Pee tee . . ."

"Post-traumatic stress disorder. From Nam.

"You poor man!" The lust Lila had conjured for this moment drained as though her bladder had opened and her own hot pee was coursing down her thighs.

Outside, an electronic horse whinnied.

"Car horn!" Lila cried. "He's back."

Jerking his hands from his pockets, Victor lurched past the cigar-store Indian, rounded the corner, and slammed himself behind the bathroom door.

PEACE

ACTIVISTS ALL OVER THE WORLD CHOSE NOON ON SUNDAY as the time to vent their outrage at George W. Bush's resolve to press war on Iraq. "I do God's bidding," the papers quoted him. "Saddam Hussein and his sons must go."

In Baghdad, 8,000 Iraqis brandished Kalashnikov rifles while torching American and Israeli flags. Crowds jammed Madrid chanting insults to Bush and Spain's prime minister, José María Aznar. Romans and Milanesi watched flaming effigies of Colin Powell and Donald Rumsfeld flutter from gibbets. In faraway Jakarta, Muslims hurled coffin-crammed likenesses of George and Laura Bush into the bay.

Among 300 other protesters, an hour before noon on the southeast corner of Santa Fe's Railyard Park, Manny and Alexis stood shivering, awaiting Chuck's arrival. The three had agreed to meet at the bus stop opposite Whole Foods Market, where Alexis chained her mountain bike, and where SUVs now dipped across speed humps under the cloud mass. Along Cerrillos Road, the roar of pickup trucks, refrigerated semitrailers, flatbeds hauling hay, motorcycles, and low-riding Chevies dulled the chatter of those waiting to march westward toward the platform that United for Peace & Justice had built.

A gust whipped Alexis's red tassel and sent a dust devil past a clot of homeless men huddled at the base of one of the park's massive Chinese elms. Smoke from their cigarettes twisted skyward. One man lay on his back on the dirt, sandwiched between the folds of a cardboard refrigerator case. Near him lay a mountainous, dirty-white dog.

Manny had not been able to move his bowels this morning, and the din from traffic was transforming his skull into a drum. Even so, he reached out to squeeze Alexis's broad shoulder with his mitten. "Aren't you glad to be doing something positive? Tax season must be driving you and Chuck crazy—I haven't even started filling in my workbook for him. Look at this crowd. I wish Joyce weren't still upset."

As he lurched toward a concrete picnic table, a man balancing a poled sign reading *Get a Hobby, Donald Rumsfeld* brushed Manny's hip. Three other men and two women, seated at the table and bundled to their noses, waved him on.

In the vermillion scarf that Baby had woven for her thirty-sixth birthday the month before, Alexis gazed up to give Manny a quick smile. "Upset? What about?"

"My asking you for breakfast yesterday. She had to rough out the Hewlett-Packard *Briefing* by herself." He hoped Alexis couldn't hear his intestines gurgling.

Sidestepping from Manny's hand, Alexis bumped a teenager wound in cellophane imprinted with blue stars and red stripes. A shorter length of cellophane made up her blue-and-red turban. The girl's lip rings shook as she brandished her cardboard *Do Not Bomb Children* in Alexis's face. Her other hand gripped a loop of clothesline, whose far end held a long-haired sheltie panting beside her ankles.

"I wish Chuck would hurry," Alexis muttered. "He's always late. Manny, listen, I want us to get clear—oh, that's disgusting."

He turned to follow her stare. Ten feet away, at a bus stop whose canopy resembled a rusted calla lily, other activists were shrinking from the bearer of *Get a Hobby, Donald Rumsfeld.* He and the five from the picnic table who had joined him gripped bottles of what looked like castor oil, which four of them were swigging. Two bent vomiting in front of their boots. Manny watched the mess dribbling into the gutter.

The wind swirled the shoulder-length gray hair of a bareheaded fat man with a cell phone clamped to his ear. He swiveled his face as though estimating the crowd's size.

From far away came the bleat of a siren that swelled and shrank as its decibels grew. A blue pickup sprouting an aluminum ladder leaped past Whole Foods and veered toward the curb fronting Nails by Annette to make way for two squad cars' winking lights.

The remaining four protesters were now retching. They directed their mouths to spray a peace symbol into the rough circle of spewed yellow and green gobbets.

"Not Tibetan sand painting," Manny commented.

"I'm uncomfortable with your standing so close to me, Manny." Alexis leaned away, clothespinning her nose between gloved thumb and forefinger against the stench wafting from the bus stop.

Out of the white car lettered *Police* in red capitals jumped two men, and out of the white car behind it jumped a woman and a man, *SFPD* appliquéd to their shoulders. They handcuffed the six vomiters and hustled them, three and three, into the cars' back seats. Across the peace symbol, *Get a Hobby, Donald Rumsfeld* lay soaking up their outflow.

"Some of you grab pails of water from the market there," shouted the long-haired fat man, holding his phone away from his face.

Manny started threading his way toward the sidewalk past prairie-dog mounds when Alexis caught his arm. "We need to talk."

He looked down at her—churro scarf flaming across her jacket, blue and yellow leather diamonds checkering her boots—and wished he could hug her against him.

"I don't get it," Alexis squawked above the noise. She tugged a wisp of brown hair from under her cap and yanked it. "Yes, I love blintzes, and no, I won't do it again. You think I'm available, Manny? I'm a gay woman and committed. What can be whirling in that macho mind of yours? Joyce is my friend."

He could not recall ever seeing her forehead furrowed so deeply. She raised her fist to her mouth and begin chewing one of her silver rings. The nausea of constipation coupled with shame and headache, made him feel like retching his own peace symbol on the brown puffs of aster that rose between his boots. Beyond Alexis, the homeless man lying beside the elm unfolded his cardboard and pushed to his knees. So did the dog.

"She's my friend, too," Manny breathed. "I'm not in a good space right now."

"No kidding. Hey, boss, boss!" From a jacket pocket she pulled a stick of bubble gum and began to unwrap it.

"Thanks for giving me the bumper sticker website," Manny added, though she'd turned to wave at Chuck. "I put a rush on a hundred yesterday afternoon."

He winced as his stomach threw up a belch and acid, followed by another and another. Alexis paid no attention. Clutching against his pea jacket three signs stapled to stakes, Chuck elbowed his way through the milling bodies. He stepped around what looked less like a human in rags than a crusted fruit dropped from one of the locust trees lining the drainage ditch that bisected the park.

"Here, here!" Alexis shouted and blew a bubble as large as a frog's cheek.

"I got held up," Chuck panted. A Russian cap of fake fur made him seem taller than Alexis. "I wanted to bring Mark and Melodie but Helen refused. She read an editorial in *The New Mexican* this morning on how rallies become riots. I yelled at her, damn it." He paused and sniffed. "Someone sick?"

"Six protesters swallowed castor oil by the bus stop."

"Why?"

"A vomit-in against invasion. Here comes the bucket brigade."

"Can't see," said Chuck, rising on his toes. "Oh, yeah. Listen, even though Alexis and I have to work this afternoon, I'm so glad we three came. Here's your sign, kiddo." He handed Alexis *Compassion for Iraqis*. "Manny, how about this *Stop the War Machine*? I'll carry *No Blood for Oil*."

Manny stiffened as he felt three soft fingertips of Chuck's glove dimple his cheek. He drew back as, staring at Chuck, Alexis pulled a tuft of hair from beneath her tasseled cap, tugging the ends into her mouth. Chuck opened his lips to speak but clamped them shut.

"How did the La Concha breakfast with Wilkes go yesterday?" Alexis asked.

"I can't hear, too noisy." The stubble on Chuck's chin felt as if ants were scurrying across it.

"Bret Wilkes, the breakfast. How'd it go?"

"We'll know tomorrow or Tuesday. Bret and Maxine Morgan are coming to see us after looking at properties yesterday and maybe today. The mortgage guy made an ass of himself so I doubt we'll have to deal with him."

"Yeah?"

"Big time." Chuck raised his voice. "Before this crowd starts marching, I want to plant an idea with you two. Well, damn, there's Michael Plotkin and his wife hoisting placards. *Defoliate the Bushes*; good. Maybe now besides doing their taxes they'll let me buy them green." Chuck raised his *No Blood for Oil* and waggled it in their direction.

"What's your idea?" Alexis asked, moving close. "I told Manny your wife wants to go live in Vermont."

"She does. I don't. But I've decided to stop learning the blue-chips game. I can't support our defense effort any longer. I'm thinking of renaming my company New Mexicans Thrive, maybe franchise it later to other states. Helping businesses with publicity—Manny, that's where you and Joyce fit in. Finding clients appropriate investments is where you come in, Alexis. Microloans, school bonds, low-cost housing bonds, alternative energy. And I'll concentrate on taxes."

"Let's go," barked a man in a shaggy coat and beard. Manny glanced back to see the tops of two orange socks blooming from his side pocket. His *Visualize Whirled Peas* banner fluttered between two poles.

Two ravens swooshed off the branch of a nearby salt cedar encircled by bales of hay, their wings rustling like silk. Feeling in memory the fingertips of Chuck's glove, Manny stepped forward with the crowd. How long had it been since he'd touched Joyce, or she him, with that kind of gentleness? He couldn't recall a man ever touching him that way.

Someone began to sing "We Shall Overcome." Others grabbed the words as they funneled onto a ten-foot-wide swath of dirt paralleling Cerrillos Road on one side and the locust-lined drainage ditch and railroad tracks on the other. They trampled mounds the prairie dogs had built, scuffling beer cans and bottles into the rodents' homes, singing their way toward Alarid Street—police cars blocked it at both ends. Beyond the asphalt sat a train's red caboose and the speaker's wooden platform.

Manny jumped as Alexis burst a bubble of gum. The jostling and fumes swelled the pounding in his head. He twisted as a horn blared from a pickup whose floodlights paraded like periscopes across the top of its cab. He was staring at its bumper sticker, *Saddamize Hussein,* when fingers clawed his arm.

The hand belonged to one of the homeless men he'd seen huddled at the base of the elm twenty yards away. Two of his teeth were as black as his fingernails, two were gone. With his white dog he shuffled along in a dark blue serape from which flapped shreds of wool. Below a dirty red kilt, his calves showed scabs that disappeared into a left boot and right bootless sock. On his back hung a bedroll and two clanging pots; behind him he dragged a green garbage bag bulging with boxes. Braided into cornrows, his brown hair seemed sections of rope. He smelled of cigars.

One of the dog's mud-splattered ears flopped near Manny's belt. The animal smelled like pickles.

"Mister?" the man rasped, releasing Manny's sheepskin and showing a streaked palm. "To stock up for the war?"

"Scare off," Manny breathed.

The crowd had paused.

From under a concrete table overlooking the drainage ditch, two men in rags and a woman unwound themselves from blankets and stood. The thinner man, head wrapped in gunnysack, looked blind—his companion, gripping his elbow, placed a white cane in his fist. The woman grabbed a guitar off the table's bench. Manny watched them push toward him and Alexis and Chuck and the beggar in the dark blue serape.

The crowd started up again, passing the bleached skulls hooked to Tin-Nee-Ann Trading Company's adobe walls on the other side of Cerrillos. A gust iced the earlobe peeking from Manny's stocking cap. Belching, he felt Chuck wedge between him and the black-toothed beggar as the woman and two men in rags wobbled close—the blind man's eyes looked like egg whites. Handing the guitar to the blind man's guide, the woman shoved out a palm that seemed more cow pie than flesh.

"For you and you; you, too," Chuck muttered, hauling ones and fives from his wallet. The blind man began to flail with one arm.

"What's wrong with that guy?" a girl called.

"Get him into a shower!" someone else cried.

The man humpbacking the bedroll and pots who'd first accosted Manny slunk away dragging his garbage bag, followed by his dog and the woman. But the blind man turbaned in gunnysack stayed. So did his guide; he'd strapped the guitar to his back, his navel exposed under the torn white shirt, his feet bound in rug strips.

"Jesus, boss, that was beautiful," Alexis whispered.

It was, Manny thought. From far in front, he heard a loudspeaker bark words he could not understand. As amplified trumpets and tubas succeeded them, a scene from his high school days in Southern California filled his aching head. While learning to drive, he'd spotted a hitchhiker at the beginning of an on-ramp. He'd started to brake when his father snapped from the passenger seat, "Step on it, Manning. You don't need to complicate my life."

Over heads to the right Manny glimpsed the cottonwood towering beside Benny's El Palacio restaurant. Was he going to have to bolt for the men's room? His gut churned; he could feel the pressure on his sphincter build, though when he tested, only gas emerged.

"Music lover," Alexis shouted at him from behind, "how do you like those tubas?"

Most of the crowd had spilled onto the lot west of Alarid, where a yellow banner proclaimed that presidential candidate Dennis Kucinich would be keynoting. Manny and Chuck and Alexis stood on Alarid's east side, blocked by a white car near St. Elizabeth's Shelter and another where Alarid ended at Cerrillos. The squad cars idled, their lights revolving as indigents lolled on the steps of St. E's and on sheets of cardboard in the buffalo grass nearby. Band music whirled out of loudspeakers near the red caboose.

Feeling Chuck's hand press his shoulder, Manny turned toward shouts coming from their right. Out of El Palacio's wooden door tumbled three men, two of them swarthy in fedoras and beards. The third was moonfaced, a tuft of blond hair sprouting below his lip. Down the steps they wove onto the dusty path, cheering and guffawing and punching each other until they spotted, near a clump of rabbitbrush, a young man and older woman squatting. Nearby, stained pillows banked a scarred brown suitcase lying on its side.

The woman's gray hair fell in sheets to her lap as she fingered the holes of a wooden flute, blowing crosswise near its end. Half her age, the man— a boil swelling his neck—sang with chin lifted toward the lowest branch of the cottonwood, whose trunk braced their backs.

"Hey, lookee," the moonfaced man called out, rattling the seedpods of sunflowers as he clomped from the path over an empty bottle of Jack Daniels to reach the pair.

Alexis spit her gum into a tangle of nettles and took Chuck's arm.

"What a crowd!" a voice blared from the two distant loudspeakers. "I'm Frank Davis of United for Peace and Justice. We have with us four-term US Representative Dennis Kucinich, author of the proposed Cabinet-level Department of Peace and first among Democratic candidates to oppose Bush's push for war."

Two TV crews with video cameras lugged their tripods closer.

When Manny saw the moonfaced man's companions follow, he broke from Chuck and Alexis. One boot crunched a cigarette box, the other cracked a heap of chicken bones.

"Manny, don't," Alexis called.

"Thanks so much," blared Kucinich's amplified tenor. "As we gather, squads of Nighthawks eighty-two hundred miles away hone their nighttime bombing maneuvers from our US base in Qatar."

"You fellows, leave those two alone," Manny growled, smelling tequila or mescal on the three men's breaths.

"Yeah?" asked the moonfaced man. "Trash needs hauling." He turned to the pair. "Go play that in Iraq. Benny don't need you spooking his clientele."

Heart thumping the notebook in his breast pocket, Manny took a step, then stopped as the moonfaced man kicked his boot up against the shoulder of the singer, who toppled back. The woman clutched her flute; Manny saw blood caking the cracks in her chapped knuckles.

Under their black fedoras, the two swarthy men glared at Manny as the taller one, beard and facial hair black as a chimney sweep's, thrust his right hand into the pocket of his slacks.

"Beat it, you thugs," Manny heard himself say.

One eye of the moonfaced man began to blink. "Yeah? Watch this." Spinning, he lifted his boot again, shoved the woman onto her side, then wheeled to lunge at Manny. He drove a fist low into his gut, collapsing Manny's lungs. Sure he must puke or shit, Manny cocked his right arm and aimed a roundhouse at the man's head. His fist struck bone; his knuckles seemed to spurt fire as the moonfaced man's companions rushed forward and Manny careened sideways into the dirt.

His head throbbed and his belly wanted to split open. The cheek he'd scraped on the Kirkpatricks' drive two nights before flamed. Squinting, he saw a long blade glint above him. But the long-bearded man who'd guided the blind one raised his guitar by its neck and smashed it against the temple of the moonfaced man, who folded to his knees.

The crowd crushed in on the three drunks, trapping them. One of the TV crews fought close; Manny glimpsed the camera's red eye flash on. Kucinich's voice no longer swept Alarid Street—instead, a whistle shrieked. Crouching, Chuck took Manny's face in his hands and told him that Alexis had run for the police.

"Are you badly hurt?" asked the reporter from Channel 4, thrusting her mic like a rapier at Manny.

"Chuck," he bleated. "Get me to the restaurant. I'm about to soil my shorts."

The old woman with the matted waves of hair righted herself, urging the beginning of "Yankee Doodle Dandy" from her flute. From a clump of snakeweed the young man stuttered, "Father—and I—went—down to camp . . ."

"The splintered guitar you'll see in a moment just made beautiful music by saving a man's life," the reporter intoned to the camera.

In spite of himself, Manny began to chortle, which made his gut twist. As Chuck grabbed his elbow and stood, hoisting Manny's bony frame, his black-stubbled face began trembling and his chapped lips stretched open. From the strain? Or was he laughing, too? Manny couldn't tell.

MAYBE TOMORROW _____

AS THE ALUMINUM WIND CHIMES JANGLED OUT BY THE hot tub, Joyce prowled the carpet braless in a blue-and-brown plaid skirt and blue sweatshirt imprinted with a photo of the art museum at Stanford University. She moved from Manny's stereo equipment stacked against the living room's wall to the bookshelves that guarded the door to the guest room. Her mukluks and the brown socks wrinkling to her calves seemed made for a woman taller than the five feet of frustration pacing here, biting her lip.

Stu Fisher plucked a fold of his own gray sweatshirt off his belly and relaxed into the armchair's cushions From the patch covering his left eye, a taped black-and-white print of Buddha gazed at her distress. "Look," Stu said, "Manny phoned, didn't he? He said he was okay, said the cops released him. You've got a hero on your hands."

"Knock it off, Stu. Manny's just another alpha male. His best pal is a deaf, Dumbo-eared, oversexed old muckraker named Dirk Pellington, who makes trouble in a broken-down casita up off Acequia Madre. Maybe you know him."

"I see his notices posted next to mine at Lorenzo's Grocery, trolling for women to help him work his vegetable garden."

Rumpling her hair, Joyce blinked at the younger man slouched beside her father's oak hat rack.

"What are you staring at?" Stu pulled his ponytail to the front of his gray sweatshirt.

"Buddha," she exclaimed and lurched toward him.

"Uh-oh." His fingertips hit his forehead.

She gripped the muscles massed above his collarbone, inhaling the scent of sawdust in his light brown hair. "Talk to Manny! He thinks you can fix anything, Stu—the hole some rat's gnawing between our solar panels, that grinding the hot tub's been making. But can you fix him? His stomach is bad again."

"Bad stomach?"

"Talk to him, will you?" She straightened. "His CPA and Dirk have been egging him into peace activism. Christ, activism's not peaceful.

Peaceful means serene, and he's not. This war hype is wrecking our life."

"Bush seems to think we can turn Iraq democratic."

"And you?"

"The man's bonkers. Firing the Iraqi military will only throw goons with AK-forty-sevens into the streets."

"And all the sit-ins and marches are just another kind of violence—oh, god, here he is."

The automatic garage door rattled up and clunked to a halt. Stu pressed his hands to his knees and stood as Joyce pulled at one of the monarch-butterfly earrings Manny had bought in Pacific Grove in January to celebrate their third year together. She stepped toward the kitchen and stopped.

A bony finger reached around the laundry room's jamb to punch on the fluorescent light. Yanking off his stocking cap, Manny clumped across the *Mental Health Center* welcome mat Joyce had bought at the flea market. He shrugged out of the sheepskin; its left sleeve, now ripped from shoulder to wrist, sprouted curlicues of wool. He dropped it to the gray tiles. "What's going on with you two?"

"Christ, bud, look at you."

"I thought you and Buddha'd be up on the roof, Stu."

Stu licked a chapped lower lip. "Not yet."

Joyce moved toward the dining table that stood in an alcove facing Sun and Moon mountains. "It's too dark in here." She switched on the lights over the table. Three crows sailed past the window. Their squawks sounded like choking.

"I could use some soup," Manny muttered.

"Don't you want to lie down? Maybe first dab hydrogen peroxide on that bruise."

"Don't tell me what to do. Forget fixing the soup. I'll do it."

"Stay put, bud."

"Fine. Add toast, will you? And a major glass of water." Wincing, Manny lowered himself to a corner of the long cushion that covered the alcove's bench. As Joyce padded in front of him on her way to the kitchen, he grabbed her forearm. "How glad are you that I'm here?"

"Let go of me, Manny."

As she shook her arm free, he felt a belch rising. Her butterfly earrings flashed.

"A daddy longlegs in the sink."

"Smash it," he snapped.

"Of course I won't smash it."

"Scald it, then."

She reached in the cabinet, tore off a sheet from the notepad by the wall phone beside the four-color calendar of Carmel gardens, and carried the thrashing three-inch legs to the front door in a water glass.

When she returned, Stu was asking, "So the dude with the guitar saved your ass?"

"Him and the crowd and the cops. The skinhead did me a favor with his fist—threw me a laxative." His guffaw felt like another fist.

"You make it to a men's room?"

"Barely. Those sons of bitches. I'd have loved to slash their tires." He jerked his head up. "Stu?"

Joyce took a can opener from the drawer as the refrigerator door hissed closed.

"Yeah?"

"Help me plaster the peace stickers I'm having rushed from back east to the bumper of every SUV we can find, will you? Wednesday or Thursday after dark? Minimum fumes."

The can opener's crunching stopped. Watching Joyce stare at him, Manny visualized the blonde hairs lengthening in her armpits and noticed glimmering on her calves.

"Stu?"

"I don't know."

"She's obviously been talking to you. What else has she been doing?"

"I'm outta here," Stu said, grabbing his tool belt and fat-bellied electric drill off the bench's cushion.

"Sit down, Stu! Apologize to him, Manny."

"I'll pay you."

"Stu, reason with him."

"We'll get TV coverage. I'm probably already on the news."

Joyce whisked out a jar of honey and kicked the pantry door closed. Steam rose from the aluminum pot she'd set on the front burner. "Didn't this morning teach you anything, Manny?"

"It sure did—gave me something to live for. Chuck's starting a new business to help small New Mexico companies thumb their noses at this country's military-industrial complex. He wants you and me and Alexis in on the ground floor."

"You and Allie? That's it, I'm . . ."

The blare of the wall phone stopped her.

"Leave it," Manny snarled. "It's your mother's Sunday check-in. You're going to do what?"

"Walk." She hoisted the receiver and slapped her palm to the mic. "Finish your own lunch. Hello?"

Stu lowered himself to the bench as Manny strode to the stove, his heart pummeling.

"Yes. Really? Very nice of you. I will. I don't know his plans but I'll tell him. What?"

Manny's thighs felt like mud. He poured the bubbling black bean soup into one of Helen Ridley's bowls, glazed stags chasing does through brushstroked grass.

"All right." Joyce hung up. She asked Stu to make room for her in the alcove. "Another female with the hots for bud."

"Not Mom, I gather."

"Your friend next door."

"My friend? Obvious from what she screamed at us yesterday? Reeling with her arm around some guy with a Pancho Villa mustache." Manny turned his buttocks toward the cabinet to ease out a fart and opened the door to the toaster-oven.

"This afternoon she likes the *Make Love Not War* on our bumpers." Joyce retuned her voice into a falsetto. "'We'll make love all day and save war for special. And please thank Manny again for helping my friend and I tomorrow with next summer's music-festival theme of world peace. Our old director quit and our new director just hates the publicity we okayed last fall.'"

Buddha jiggled with Stu's laughter.

"Lila no speak so good," Joyce said from the side of her mouth. "Now she promises to have her insurance pay for that railing I showed you."

Manny carried his soup and silverware and honey-drenched toast to the free end of the table where *Sunset: The Magazine of Western Living* still lay open to the article on Half Moon Bay hiking trails that Joyce had been reading at breakfast. He returned to gulp more water, came back, and sat.

"I don't care about the railing. I want my plum back."

Manny slurped his soup, keeping his head bent.

"Salt cedar would grow fast," Stu offered.

"That weed? I want my pink blossoms and purple fruit. That cut is purpling, bud. Don't go over there tomorrow. Please?"

Manny raised Helen Ridley's bowl; each bob of his Adam's apple felt like a stuck bone. Tearing free a bite of toast, he reached for Stu's tool belt. "Let's go look at what's staining that wall upstairs and get rid of the rat. Did you bring steel wool to stuff in the holes?"

"Yeah I did."

Manny turned to Joyce. "Did you clean up last night's raccoon shit?"

_____

"If it shits again, you're bagging it."

"Hey, Boodie, relax." Under the water Manny fingered the few black hairs on his chest.

"Easy for you."

In the bromine-sanitized churning, they sat on the tub's opposite benches soaking up its heat while scarves of steam fluttered toward the nearly full moon. Joyce's brown terrycloth robe and Manny's red plaid hung on hooks screwed into the stucco wall. The wind chimes hung quiet.

Like steel teeth the nozzles spewing water began grinding again. She jumped as, sighing, Manny punched the neoprene seal that covered the on/off button. The foaming subsided.

"This is good, Boodie. So okay, let's have Stu repair this capitalistic toy. Thanks for working with him while I slept. There's nothing going on between you two, right?"

"That's right."

"I guess I owe you both an apology." He fondled his penis, felt it thicken, and leaned forward. Under the water's placid surface he reached across to settle his right hand on her knee—smooth as a ball, unlike her legs.

"You should still be in bed." She lifted his hand off by the wrist.

"When does Stu come back?"

"Tomorrow. He needs a special wrench to open the inlet to the roof panels to find where the antifreeze is leaking. He said he'll also check the gaskets of this tub's pump and blower. To get some quiet to proof the April H-P newsletter, I made him leave. Then Mother called."

"Every Sunday after lunch. What's her news?"

"Dad's boyfriend has testicular cancer. She wants to visit us, Manny."

"Why? She hates me."

"She's trying not to, that's why she wants to come. And she misses me. And this war talk frightens her. She'll like you fine once we're married."

"I need time to find out how committed you are to promoting peace, Boodie."

"You already know what I'm committed to: loving you, living quietly, eating natural food. I won't slap stickers on SUVs, if that's what you're getting at."

"Stu never said if he'd help."

"He wouldn't tell me, either. If you and I split up, bud, what's your plan? Talking Allie into leaving Baby? Maybe she'll do bumper stickers with you."

He was silent a moment. "How are we going to change the government's warmongering without activism?"

"We aren't going to change anything, activism or not."

"That's too defeatist for me."

"Commiserate with your pal Dirk. Or go into business with your CPA. Or ask my best friend to dinner."

"Enough, Boodie, okay?" This time when he reached for her knee, she left his hand where it lay.

"Let's go get some sleep."

"You don't want to see if I'm on the evening news?"

"No."

Rain or snow seemed immanent; the sky had gone black and a gathering mist was scattering the lights of the town houses that dropped toward Baca Field.

"What a horrible way to end a horrible day."

"At least you're not in the hospital yet."

He filled his lungs with steam. "Last week I bought a box of the spearmint rubbers you like."

"I doubt I'm up for it, Manny."

"You don't think our ritual might help?"

She said nothing as, gripping the edge of the fiberglass, she scampered out and shuffled into her leather thongs. Grateful for the ache that spread from the base of his penis, he watched her breasts wobble before they disappeared into the robe she swept down from its hook.

He hoisted his bones into the cold air, grabbed his own robe, and wrapped his arms around her from behind. Cupping her breasts, he pushed his cheek against her wet mop of hair, fitting his testicles into her buttocks' cleavage. His penis reached full erection against her lower back.

She freed herself to open the outside door to the guest room they had converted into an office. He turned to roll the tub's foam cover away from the snapped-off plum that arrowed through a gash in the railing. Lowering the cover to the tub, he followed her inside. She passed through the far door into the living room and up the stairs.

He entered the bathroom as she headed for the bed. He came out naked. Unscrewing the top of a bottle of sandalwood oil, he approached her, testicles slapping the insides of his thighs. Warm air billowing from the floor register sounded like her Honda Accord fast-idling. Over the bed gaped the vertical crack Stu had opened between the two brass hooks where her antiwar poems had hung. Was she really abandoning the literary life? The exposed copper pipe glimmered; no scrabbling rodent sounded inside the wall.

She lay curled under the electric blanket facing the Zuni basket and its lamp on her bedside table. He flicked on two night-lights next to the TV and started a CD of the Brubeck Quartet playing in Monterey. "Twist onto your back, Boodie." He strode close to peel away the covers. "I want to suck your nipples."

Setting the oil on the table whose drawer contained the new box of condoms, he climbed up to kneel beside her. "Don't touch me yet," he said. "I'm about to fire."

Flipping from her belly, she raised an arm and settled it along her ribs. Her blue eyes gazed at the ceiling as he closed his own and bent toward her chest. How he loved to roll the puckered nipples back and forth between his lips. Bracing himself on spread fingers, relishing the torment advancing from his groin, he reached with his free hand for the blonde softness of her vulva.

She wrenched her shoulders aside. He jerked open his lids to see her shaking her head. "Manny." She plopped his hand onto the sheet. "It's not working."

He squeezed his erection and leaned back on his haunches, listening to his belly gurgle.

She rolled to her edge of the bed and stooped for her brown terrycloth. Straightening, she grabbed the paperback of Sanskrit meditations. "All I can see is you hoisting signs with Allie this morning, and tomorrow nibbling canapes with Lila Kirkpatrick and your CPA's wife. I'm sleeping downstairs; I can't live like this. I said we can't change anything, but something has to. It's raining, by the way."

"HOW'D YOU GET IN HERE?"

Pixie whimpered under the oval glass table in Maxine's office where she and Bret Wilkes faced each other, poring over house specs. No more tail-wagging to greet Ron Kirkpatrick—corseted in red-white-and-blue knit, the black-faced Pekingese turned and slunk across Maxine's Navajo rug to quiver against the wall under her desk.

Glancing over her shoulder to see where the pet had fled, Maxine swung her face back. Her larynx bobbed as she growled, "How'd you get past Jennifer?" Over the pantsuit with its flaring lilac collar she had pulled a hooded sweatshirt lettered *Range Rover*. Her curly black hair was twisted into a topknot held by a blue-and-green band.

Over his half-lens reading glasses Bret spotted Ron filling Maxine's doorway. He gripped the back of his neck and stood.

"Jen and I're friends, for Judas's sake," Ron exclaimed, blue *Home Loan Champ* cap askew. "I've done some research that you and your Silicone Valley pal there will be glad to see. Plus I wanted to thank you both for pryin' that big Indian off me yesterday. Bastard bruised my ribs."

"Ronald, do you really think I'm going to use Los Alamos Mortgage ever again? The vet had to flush green chile from Pixie's eyes."

"My manager says we'll give you a ninety percent commercial loan at five and a quarter. You can't beat that anywhere, Max. If you do, we'll match it. We decided Ridley's right. Anyhoo, now you have the option. Expectin' rain?"

"Hunh?"

Bret eased himself into the red leather chair studded with brass. He began to finger the filigree chain glinting among the hairs curling up from his white, poplin shirt.

Wondering if she'd spent yesterday afternoon wrestling Wilkes back into his hotel bed, hoping for an orgasm at last, Ron pointed to the galvanized tub that filled a corner beside a bonzai saguaro onto whose spines Maxine had stuck notices proclaiming her awards: *Santa Fe Broker of the Year; Chairwoman, Buckaroo Ball; May Day Queen, New Mexico Vietnam Vets; Beloved Adopted Daughter of Northern Pueblo Elders*. Above the tub the plaster spiraled down in yellow strips.

"Can't Victor fix that ceilin'? Been lookin' like sheep guts since last summer's monsoons. The man should've stuck to carvin' santos; he told Lila termites are chewin' up our subfloor. Termites? Who's ever seen a termite in Santa Fe?"

Maxine grabbed Bret's wrist, limp on the table's glass top. "It's going to snow tonight, Ronald. Snow or rain. Do you notice how I'm keeping my voice down? I'm asking you to leave now. Go away, Ronald. Do you understand?"

Wilkes must get those nails manicured once a week, Ron thought. He shifted his boots; his feet felt like steamed rutabagas. "My manager expects some kind of answer, Max." He tilted his big head. "Professional courtesy," he smiled, staring down at her violet-shadowed eyes, which began to narrow.

"No!" Propelling her chair back so fast it toppled over, studs rapping the gray-swirled tiles, Maxine straightened her sweatshirted arms. "Get it, dum-dum? No! No again! No city realtor is going to use you once I say what you pulled. Jennifer!" she shouted. "Get in here!" She bent forward, coughing, and gripped the table's edge.

Squeezing the blood from his lips, Bret left his chair to right hers.

In the doorway, Ron twisted to see the gangly Jennifer come clacking in red jumper and gold boots past the realtors' cubicles. He felt his wheezing begin, but worse, felt a jab like heartburn beneath his breastbone as a bullet of pain raced down his inner left arm. Listing against the jamb, "Expect a lawsuit, Max," he gasped. "Giordy isn't goin' to like what he learns." Drops of sweat squeezed onto his forehead.

"Get out!"

"Trade me for my lawyer." The ache in his arm receded as he lurched toward Jennifer, waving her back.

She pushed open the half door to the reception area, frowning above her glasses as he wheezed, "I do enjoy that scent, darlin'. Like summer lupine outside Cowtown." He turned the glass knob, over which Victor had carved a bobcat springing along black script reading *Morgan Realty*.

"Jennifer!" Maxine called behind him as he shouldered his way into the cold.

The air bit the folds of his neck. From a pocket of his red polyester fleece he tugged elkskin driving gloves. Across the dirt lot he picked his way past the dark mounds of gophers, staring at a pair of squinty eyes and flattened ears that popped into view. They sprang back down.

He'd parked his white Escalade next to Maxine's golden Range Rover—both sixteen-footers, though her headlights and rear lamps sported stone guards and a three-tiered wraparound brush bar that blackened her grille. How he'd love to scratch his penknife through the lacquer, spelling out *Mortgaged to Ronald K.*

Before beeping his door open, he massaged his left arm; the pain had left the flesh tender. With a handkerchief he dried his forehead. He'd better phone the sawbones—that attack in Max's office felt like someone had clothespinned his windpipe. And he'd better show Lila how to drive this beauty, should they be headin' out and the bullet of pain struck again.

Who the hell let air from his rear tire Friday night? Manny the peacenik? Manny's gal? Max still seemed most probable—another of her lies. He pressed his sole to the pedal. The 345-horsepower V8 roared, passenger-side tailpipe scaring up a dust devil as he skidded right onto Washington toward Plaza Hill.

———————

"I don't care if the founders are peaceniks, this Karamel Sutra is delish," Lila said, lapping the last of the tawny sweetness from her spoon and biting off a crescent of gingersnap. "Are we really moving back to Fort Worth, Ronnie?" The flicker from three votive candles on the dining table made the gold filling on the left side of her mouth gleam.

"Returnin' to our kind, where the black gold flows and this cowboy knows how to leverage its use—twenty million barrels a day."

Outside, next door, Manny and Joyce inhaled steam from the hot tub while Ron and Lila lingered over plates smeared with the remains of rainbow trout and seared zucchini. The wind had died down; moonlight turned the cloud bank into a choppy pewter sea.

"You like my perfume, Big Shit?"

"Surely do."

"It's called Beyond Paradise." Snug in her black velvet robe emblazoned with prancing ponies, sashed around the black-lace bikini and rayon wrap,

Lila sat blinking at the candles' tongues of flame. Across the living room a loose splinter clicked against a leg of Ron's remember-the-Alamo cabinet as the furnace forced warmth through the grate underneath.

"I can't hardly deal with what's been happening, Ronnie. First you frighten me about the chest pain, then you show me how to drive that white elephant of yours. You mix tequila martinis and lock yourself in the guest room—then burst out with a headache saying we're putting this shithole up for sale."

In tapered corduroys and the blue-wool shirt he'd worn to Maxine's office, Ron pushed from the table, uncorking his split-end thumb from between his lips. "We're through with Santa Fe peckerheads, kemo sabe."

"Are we really returning to the Trinity River and T-bones at Zippy's Grill? Aren't you scared?"

"Of Zippy?" He started rubbing his ribs as though scrubbing shirts on a washboard.

"Two years ago Massoud Khafi threatened your life, if you recall."

"Forget it, babe. My old office called last month. Veronica dumped Humpty Dumpty Khafi for an Anglo horse trader who owns majority interest in our convention center."

"Here?"

"*Our* convention center—Cowtown's."

"You never told me that. Do they want to rehire you?"

"Asked me to take over the Arlington branch." He wiggled his toes. Judas Christ, these fleece-lined slippers felt good.

"Well, call them back, Ronnie!" She began massaging her breast with the ingrown nipple.

"It's my plan, Lile, hon." He reached across the raffia mat to squeeze her hand.

"Ouch."

"Want to reassure you there'll be no more Max—"

"I knew it!" She jerked her hand away. "You *have* been fooling with her."

"Hugged her once a couple of months ago. I still feel awful 'bout it, don't you fret."

"You haven't been seeing her Thursday nights? That's not what the note meant she threw on our drive?"

"I told you, we met with Giordy on business Thursday nights but I guess he's hittin' the bottle."

"Why?"

"How should I know? Maybe he's begun suspectin' Max of sleepin' around. No more huggin' for me except Miss Lila K. You know what else? I'm goin' to email Humpty Dumpty an apology and propose a business deal. He scouts the stockyards district, I rustle loans for an office park: live-and-work lofts, fitness complex, rec center, tennis courts, big-ass pool. I been ruminatin' it for years."

"Dad and your folks will be thrilled—but how will it feel with Jonathan not there?"

"Let's keep sharin' truths tonight, okay? Jonathan hightailed it into the infantry because he couldn't stand our squabblin' over my messin' with the Anglo squaw of a Shiite billionaire. Now you and I are gonna make amends."

"We are? How?"

"By returnin' in harmony to where Jonathan was born."

"Big Shit? I need to make an amend to you. This tenement may not sell for a while. If Maxine Morgan stops you from getting work, we'll have to eat into savings or I'll have to find a job."

"No way you gotta work, babe."

"We need cash to fix this rattrap up, Ronnie. And I don't want to use Victor Valdez, even though he does take care of his mother."

"The hell with that. The man's incompetent."

"Not what I'm getting at. If you hadn't rushed home from La Concha yesterday, I would no longer be your trophy wife."

Ron withdrew his hand as if hers was the head of a prairie rattler. "You and that Hispanic creep?" He started to wheeze and turned to stare past the three votive candles at the blackness outside.

"I needed to hurt you for Veronica, for Maxine Morgan, for Lord knows who else. But He sent you home early and I thank Him."

For a few moments they sat silent, Ron's chest heaving, Lila twisting her robe against her thigh. He dragged his spoon through the melted Karamel Sutra as his heart tried to thump itself loose from her confession.

"Ronnie? Make love to me? Not like two nights ago, no piddle. A love pact asking the Lord to forgive us."

"I dunno," he wheezed, marveling how she could turn his thoughts sexy faster than he could cut a mortgage deal.

"I'll ride you, honeybunch, or you go in behind so you don't have to strain. You don't even have to lick me. I hate what that bitch is putting us through. If you get sick from this morning's humiliation and I have to work—but what can I do? I can't type. Maybe I could hostess at La Posada or Mama Cheetah's." She snaked her right hand between the billows of her robe and pressed her vulva, dimpling the bikini's warming cotton.

"Already gave a big No to that one. What we're gonna do is find us a barracuda to rip away Maxine Morgan's grin. Gonna show this town before we vamoose how she and Giordy mislead tenderfeet into buyin' junk property." He hoisted his buttocks off the dining chair's wickerwork and re-settled them. "I'll detail how she sexually harassed me, I'll talk about Wilkes. When the papers print it up, Giordy'll can her like the garbage she is."

The tip of an erection rammed the lower edge of his belt as he watched Lila's shoulder gyrate. Round and round, her fingers wadded hot lace into her vagina. "Me, too," she panted. "I'm going to find a way to punish the bitch for trying to split you and I up from forty years of being together, after you first groped me in seventh grade. Leave that runny mess be, Big Shit."

With her free hand she pushed the glass dish from him and shoved back her chair. "Let's go watch war news in the living room while we stroke each other."

"Why down here?"

"No popping tiles, honeybunch."

"Can I watch you use that vibrator?"

"Sure you can. You want to see me use my twenty-four-karat ben wa balls, too?"

"Your what?" He began to rub his Little Prince through the dark corduroy.

"Gold-plated balls in a rubber I stuff in my snatch to tease it."

"Yeah, yeah, bring those, too."

"Trophy wife," she giggled. She rose and skipped past his wooden Indian sprouting red and yellow feathers, one of them broken. "Turn that news on." The rope soles of her slippers slapped the tiles as she hurried toward the stairs.

When she returned, Ron had unzipped his fly and was kneading his erection and testicles over briefs patterned with the green ovals of prickly pear, careful not to come. Light glinted off his scalp from one of the looped bronze lariats that served as stand lamps at the ends of the sofa.

"Colin Powell reports that Uday and Qusay contact Al-Qaida's chief hatchetman—Jordan's Abu Musab al-Zarqawi—daily," intoned NBC's local anchorman, peering out at them through black-rimmed glasses. His face glowed as brightly as the brass buttons on his checked coat.

"Good news?" Lila asked, approaching the sofa's faux elkskin back. She dropped onto a cushion her panda, lubricant-slick vibrator, and two ben wa balls knotted in a condom. She leaned forward to wind her robed arms around Ron, cupping the blue wool that covered his flab. "Get your hand off that dick, Ronnie."

"You stink of somethin' I want more of."

"Gargled twice and re-drenched myself in Paradise, sir. Mr. Valdez will never know how good I get. Turn that sound up—look how ugly those guys are."

"Al-Zarqawi has plotted poisoning Rome's water with botulin, assassinating the UN delegate to Somalia, and blowing up a kindergarten in Saint Petersburg with an ambulance laden with canisters of hydrogen. Some say Saddam's secular tyranny and al-Qaida's religious tyranny don't mix. Colin Powell says they do mix, to our detriment."

"I want to see the missiles, not murdered children. " The capillaries in Lila's cheeks flamed as she rounded one of the lariat lamps. As she grabbed her sex tools from the cushion, her elbow tumbled the panda onto the carpet. She laid her body on Ron's so that one of the sofa's arms cushioned her head and the backs of her knees pressed his thighs. "Twist those balls in, Big Shit. I'm sopping."

Yanking open the lapels of her robe, she massaged breasts veined like river maps flopping to either side. Ron pinched up the cherry-colored condom by its knot. He was staring at the glistening, battery-powered vibrator resting on her belly—curved shaft knobbed like a gourd, polypropylene testicles larger than kiwifruits—when she exclaimed, "That's our neighbor! Manny's supposed to be over here with Helen Ridley tomorrow."

"Yeah? Why? That's him all right."

"To help with music publicity."

Weaving through the crowd, the cameraman zoomed in on Manny doubled over in the dirt, the hem of his red stocking cap blinding one eye. "Son of a peccary. That's Ridley kneelin'. He looks like a Russki in that fur hat. Who's the hag playin' a flute and that bozo clutchin' the smashed guitar? Hey, you sure my stuffin' these into you won't hurt?"

"I'll do it, honeybunch. They work faster anyways when I stand." Straight-arming herself upright, she grabbed the glistening condom and whispered, "Watch this, Little Prince, with your one good eye." Legs spread, she rotated the balls between gray-bristled lips until only the knot showed. "Oh, Lord," she groaned, corkscrewing her hips and pressing her vulva with her palms. "You want to see the vibrator work?"

It had rolled to the carpet.

"With those things in you?"

"I want to turn my lord and master on, make his doctor-ordered one-orgasm-a-night the hugest he's ever had."

"Do it," he breathed, staring at her swaying breasts. The TV screen clicked into blackness as he stabbed the remote's button to off. He tugged testicles and penis past the zipper into the furnace-warmed air.

He began to stroke, watching the arteries fatten that wormed up his shaft. "Hey, babe, forget the vibrator, look what I got hog-tied and squealin'."

"Strip, Big Shit, and get yourself down and dirty." She dropped to her hands and knees, facing him on the carpet.

Ron started freeing his shirt buttons. "What's that noise? Sounds like a bunch of woodpeckers. More tiles goin'?"

"Rain, honeybunch, sweet rain. Hear the coyotes singing?"

He hoisted his buttocks to let her haul his slacks off by the legs. Scooting from the cushion, he slid to one of the carpet's zigguratted blue-mesa motifs.

Lila crawled toward him, clutching her panda. "You want me on top or doggy, Ronnie?"

She dropped the stuffed pet. Using her fists as stabilizers, rejoicing in the hive the ben wa balls were stirring up inside her, she leaned between Ron's legs and raised her head like a mama bear sniffing.

He closed his eyes, inhaling her scents of honeysuckle and the aftermath of mouthwash. He felt his own breasts jiggle as her hands held his cheeks and her lips mashed his own. Suddenly he realized that the eyes he gazed at behind shut lids were not Lila's but Maxine Morgan's, shadowed in violet.

Lila pulled back and waited on her knees. "Do what, master?"

"KEEP THE CHATTER DOWN, LILE, I'M TRYIN' TO FIND US the right lawyer. I've enough trouble here with the squirrels battlin' the motherfuckin' jays."

"Your language, Ronald; please."

"Yeah, sorry, babe."

In cowhide slippers that hugged his ankles, blue sweatpants, and loose-fitting maroon shirt—happily exhausted from last night's orgasms and to hell with what the doctor warned—Ron grinned at Manny and Helen Ridley in the living room.

"Hi there, Manny. Hi, there, whoever." With a clack he shut himself back into his home office.

On the slopes of Plaza Hill, the sparse snow that ended last night's rain had already melted. Midmorning clouds were breaking into silver-bellied shapes jigsawing themselves around a board of blue. Images shifted in a steady wind that kept juniper and piñon branches shaking.

Its ripped left arm crisscrossed with Stu's yellow-and-black safety tape, Manny's sheepskin lay flopped on one of the beanbag ottomans. He sat stooped on the sofa beside Helen, who had draped herself in a black silk blouse and black, calf-length skirt festooned with mariposa lilies. Lila faced them in a pale blue blouse fringed at the hem and cuffs and buttoned to her collarbone. She'd chosen J. Lo's Glow, hinting of musk and soap, to honor last night's revel on the rug and this morning's resolve to air fresh thoughts about next summer's music festival publicity.

On the barnwood coffee table rested last year's festival program guide, newspaper clippings, an orange pot of tea, a plate of whole-wheat wafers mounded with salmon paste, and a couple of pads of yellow-lined paper. Manny held a third pad on his knees.

"I have to apologize for my husband's language. He didn't sleep well," Lila lied. "The rain. Helen, more tea?" Lila's palm drifted to the breast with the ingrown nipple.

"No thanks. I want to hear Manny talk more about his poster idea. But don't you hurt from yesterday, Manny? Even though it's tax season,

Charles couldn't leave bed until nine—and no one hit him. That bruise on your cheek looks raw."

"It'll heal. My stomach hurts and my knuckles smart." He brought his hand to his mouth to muffle a belch, and winced at the upthrust of acid.

"I read about your protecting that homeless mother and son in *The New Mexican* this morning."

"My husband and me, too," Lila said. "A brave gesture even to conservatives like we straddling the far side of the fence. But show us what you've been sketching."

Ron's tone, and now Lila's, reassured Manny that neither suspected him of letting air from the Escalade's tire. Sorry Lila had buttoned off her cleavage, he turned to Helen. The gelled brown spikes of her hair seemed at odds with her blouse's softness. "Take a look. It seems a natural for the festival's theme of peace: players from around the world."

He raised the pad, on which six stick figures seated in a circle held scribbles intended to be seen as instruments.

"Does the beard and robe mean Muslim?" Lila asked. "I'm not sure a Muslim's appropriate. Perhaps a Sikh? We have those in Santa Fe, don't we? He'll need a white turban. May we add a gal playing the oboe? Mama played first oboe in Fort Worth. Her passion for it is why I help out here, though I don't care much for classical music. Growing up, I loathed it."

The doorbell clanged. "Oh!" she cried, tugging the end of her ponytail. "I forgot to tell Ron about the insurance person. I must remember to keep my voice low. Manny, do you like my stress-relief tea? Gingerroot's the secret. Excuse me."

Tummy bulging in her beltless jeans, Lila marched past Ron's wooden Indian toward the front door. The soles of her boots smacked the entryway's sandy-red quarry tiles. She twisted the dead bolt free and yanked the door wide. "Oh Lord, you."

Shorter by a couple of inches and stinking of the unfiltered Camel jutting from below his handlebar mustache, Victor waited in baggy gabardines. His left temple bore a Band-Aid, his right hand a white envelope. As the string of dried chiles rattled above him, he scowled at Lila behind black-rimmed glasses and jerked down the bill of his beige cap whose red band read, *Proud To Be American.*

"You said bring on over estimates this morning. My camera's in the truck."

"Camera?"

"Photos for use at Home Depot. Your husband's out, right?" He winked. "Hel-*lo*, there." The tips of his handlebar wiggled as he reached to grip her forearm.

"People are here and he's here too." She shook her arm free and shrank away, shuddering. "A lot has changed; we're selling this place as fast as we can. Give me the envelope. I need to shut this door now. It's cold."

Narrowing his eyes, Victor pinched his cigarette and reddened the ash. Turning his face from her, he blew out smoke. "I thought at least we'd be able to talk, you know? Plus I need to use your little boy's room."

She wrinkled her nose. "That pee-tee es dee thing?"

"From Nam, yeah."

Lila's stomach felt as if it would throw up if she had to watch his mustache twitch any longer. "Leave that outside." She pointed to his Camel.

The limp-induced cluck-clack of his alligator-skin boots followed the noise of Lila's white ones. She hurried into the living room. "A workman with estimates—I told him to come back later," she lied to Helen and Manny. "He needs to use the powder room. Can I see that drawing again?" Tossing Victor's envelope into a wicker wastebasket, she paused beside one of the lariat stand lamps.

The salmon-pasted wafers were making Manny's stomach gurgle. Embarrassed, he gulped some tea before tearing his sketch off the pad. For all her efforts at camouflage—raccoon mascara, blazing lip gloss—Lila seemed unable to hide the veins webbing her cheeks.

She gazed at his stick figures. "I'm picturing Hispanic with guitar, Native American with his flute, Oriental and gongs, a nigra with his drums of course, let's say Sikh playing whatever Sikhs play. Can you research that, Helen? And Mama from the dead tooting her oboe. A one-world sextet; bravo, Manny."

"Goodbye, Mr. Valdez!" she cried.

The front door slammed.

"Son of a peccary, what was that?" Ron wheezed, pushing his own door wide.

"The tile and deck workman. I forgot he was bringing estimates."

"Valdez?"

"Yes, but he's gone. We'll be quiet now, Ronnie. Do your good work."

"Pretty damn difficult." The breeze from the door Ron hauled shut cooled Manny's face.

"We better speed this up," Lila breathed, taking the chair upholstered in purple corduroy imprinted with cowboy hats. "Helen, can you turn Manny's idea into a watercolor to show our new director next week? He's this side of frantic." Her palms flew to her breasts. "Oh, and I just got our motto. 'Make a joyful noise, all ye lands.' "

"Psalms," Manny said. His gut began to cramp. He drained his cup of tea and poured more.

"I knew you'd know." The two fillings lurking in the corners of her mouth gleamed. "Helen, am I on the right tracks?"

"I suppose." Licking her lips, Helen took Manny's drawing and reached for a wafer. Her neck wrinkles bunched as she chewed.

"You don't seem very enthusiastic."

"I'm worn out. One of Charles's clients left for Murch Investments last week. My husband going on that peace march yesterday and what happened to Manny and all this war gossip is grinding me down."

"Us, too." Lila picked at the fringes of a cuff. "I guess I better tell you, Ronald and I are returning to Fort Worth. He don't care but between you and I, being so close to the war work at Los Alamos is keeping me from sleeping," she lied. "We're putting this place up for sale."

Manny stared at her. The heel of his left moccasin began tapping the carpet and an urge to curse the Bush cabinet kick-started his heart into a round of push-ups. As his lips parted, Helen exclaimed, "I'm leaving, too! The twins and I are going to winterize our place in Vermont."

"And not your husband?" Lila asked.

"He's staying put," Manny said.

Helen's dark eyebrows flew up. "How do you know that? He hasn't told me that." From a beaded purse she extracted a tube of menthol jelly, twisted its bottom, and scrubbed her lips.

"Crap, I'm sorry. He told Alexis and me at the peace demo." Manny raked the sides of his head. "Colin Powell says our diplomacy at the UN ends at midnight tonight—we're going to invade. War to stop war? Come with me to the Plaza at six thirty for the candlelight vigil, will you both? My computer's *New York Times* predicts seven thousand vigils tonight in a hundred and thirty-nine countries. Will you come?"

Helen's spikes of hair shimmied as she stared at his sketch. "I hate crowds, Manny."

"Lila, will you?"

Smiling only with the left side of her mouth, salt-and-pepper ponytail swishing, she said, "I have to support my husband."

The doorbell clanged again. Frowning, she stood up, smoothing her palms along her hips. "Insurance person this time for sure. We must, must, must keep our voices low."

Fuck and shit, she exclaimed to herself, seeing the mud Victor had streaked across the tiles. She yanked the door open to a redhead in a small-lapelled jacket, beige slacks, and low-heeled black shoes. Taller even than Lila, the young woman shoved a business card at her. Her elbow pinned a metal clipboard to her ribs and over one shoulder hung a black patent-leather purse. Over the other hung a digital camera.

"Come in, it's blowing," Lila whispered, taking the card. "*Rita Fergus.* The cleaning women will be here this afternoon but please remove your shoes anyway, Rita, you see this mud? We've got to talk quietly, my husband's on edge. Shut in his office for now, thank the Lord. Oh, you've got nylons on—hold on, I'll bring something."

She dashed upstairs, hurried back down carrying her pink-and-orange polyester slippers, and swung into the living room. "We must take photos of the bad tiles upstairs, two more popped last night. Then"—gesturing toward the French doors—"photos of where the deck was until Friday night. Let's hope Mr. Kirkpatrick doesn't have another fit."

As Lila and Rita tramped up toward the master bath, Manny turned to Helen. "I blew it," he said. "Maybe Chuck's changed his mind. Scared off, wants to be with you—all the time, I mean—because he'd miss the children."

"Charles and I see the world through different lenses, Manny. I need to change it into art to stay balanced. He may need to change himself, I don't know. I think he still enjoys the accounting work. The twins and I can live cheaply in Montpelier." She paused. "In fact, we all could." With a forefinger she waggled the tiny chimes hanging from her right earlobe.

"Do you like the sound?" Her sad smile forced his gaze down.

Both stiffened at the yelp that escaped from under Ron's door.

"Did Chuck tell you anything about the business breakfast at La Concha Saturday?" Manny thrust his thumb in the direction of Ron's office. "Apparently he made an ass of himself."

"I was upset, I didn't listen. Something about dumping pinto beans on the realtor's dog."

Chuckling, Manny muffled a belch with the back of his hand. "Our realtor called earlier asking if a client could drop over this afternoon. Bret Wilkes from Silicon Valley. Where we're from. He wants to pick our brains about living in Santa Fe."

"Maybe we'll use her to list our home, too, because I'm going to need money to upgrade the summer place in Vermont."

They turned toward the Alamo cabinet as Ron burst from his office, face flushed. "Where's Lila?"

"Upstairs with the claims adjuster," Helen answered.

"We've got to muzzle that damn bell. Tell her to rustle herself in here."

"Now?"

"No, no, what she's doin' is crucial. Though I guess maybe, if she dawdles. I have big news." From his sweatpants pocket he pulled a pocket watch. "Give her five minutes." He closed the door.

From the upper landing came "Remember to lower our voices," then the thud of Lila's boot soles on the stairs' blue pile. Manny hoisted himself from the cushion and strode close. Good-looker behind Lila, he observed, wondering if, when loosened, the tucked red hair would fall to her waist. "Ron wants to see you," he said, nose tingling at Lila's bittersweet scent. "He says he has news."

"What kind of news?"

"Big, he says."

"Oh, jeez—Rita? Can you snap the outside mess on your own? Take your shoes, I don't want to dirty up those slippers. Past the sofa and out the glass doors. Don't fall off, please."

"Ronnie?" She examined a knot in his door's tongue-and-groove slats.

"That you?"

"Who else?"

"Enter."

She swung the door in.

"Close it tight, babe."

In front of the massive rolltop desk—topped by a black-and-white of Ron grimacing in a crouch with the rest of his high school football team—he swiveled to face her, then turned his gaze toward the window which looked out on a small deck. "I'm about to hightail it upstairs for my thirty-eight and exterminate those peckerheads."

They stared at the piñon jays shouldering each other off the tray of sunflower seeds jutting from the wall. Huddled on the deck's railing, tail swishing and ebony eyes glowing, a squirrel clicked its teeth at their squawks. Suddenly a jay flapped up and swooped six inches from the squirrel's back, sending it scampering down one of the railing's white posts.

"Like our gunships are goin' to start pickin' off those sand niggers, I'm guessin' by midweek," Ron said.

"Look at that tangle of cobwebs on your track light. Let me tell the cleaning women to come in here this afternoon, okay?"

"I don't like spics messin' my space, Lile. I'll broom them out myself."

"So what's your news?"

"C'mere, sexy." Maroon shirt billowing, he threw his arms out. She stepped close and he pressed the fringes of her collar to her shoulder bones. "Tomorrow Max Morgan wants to buy me lunch."

She jerked from his grasp. "And you said no way, José."

"No way I said no way, José. She wants to make up, Lile. Doesn't want Giordy knowin' what I know. No barracuda for us. No lawsuit. We don't have to move."

Staggering against the door, Lila felt as if she were spiraling up toward the ceiling. "Don't have to move? I thought we wanted to move. What about last night's pact and all that good loving?"

"Judas Christ, hon, no way I'm makin' love with anyone but you. What I spect this means, only sposin' until we lunch tomorrow, is that she understands that ropin' with this cowboy is the smartest decision she can make. You and me gonna be wealthier than your pretty head ever dreamed."

"I don't want to be wealthy, I want to go home! I'll kill the bitch," Lila warbled, wagging a forefinger at Ron. "You, too." Grabbing the glass knob, she spun it, yanked the door wide, and lurched into the living room.

Camera in hand, Rita was letting in cold air from the remnant of the big deck. Lila spotted the pink-and-orange slippers parked beside a leg of the coffee table. She watched, trembling, as Rita headed toward her, smiling and tracking rainwater across the rug's pile.

"Are you all right?" Helen asked, rising. Her red-blossomed skirt swirled.

"No," said Lila, "I'm not."

"Let me help you," Manny offered as his intestines crimped and his stomach squirted acid.

"That vigil tonight," she said to him. "I'm coming with you." Under the powder her cheeks flamed.

"I have the photos, Mrs. Kirkpatrick; I'll be in touch." Securing the clipboard under her elbow, Rita started for the front door, leaving a trail of muddy prints.

Manny guided Lila to the armchair. When she grabbed the top button of her blouse, it ripped off. She flung it to the carpet before undoing the second button, exposing her cleavage and the hunchbacked Kokopelli fluting on his chain.

Again the bell clanged.

"I'll get it," Helen said. She bent to grasp Manny's sketch. Taking his jacket from the ottoman, he hurried after her toward the door. Rita backed onto a stair to let them pass.

"Stop, all of you! This is my house. I open my own doors." Leaping up, Lila was about to round the coffee table when her knee struck the tray holding the canapes, spinning it to the carpet. She turned to goggle at the overturned, salmon-smeared wafers, then pivoted and loped past her guests.

The brass thumb latch wouldn't budge. She yanked at it until she noticed that she'd slotted the dead bolt.

"What's the ruckus now?" Ron cried, charging from his office.

Lila pulled the bolt free and twisted the knob.

On the doormat Victor had muddied stood big-boned Frances, her sunken cheeks pocked, and little Pilar grinning gold. Frances clutched the yellow handle of a broom, Pilar a mop. A plastic bottle of all-purpose cleaner and degreaser nested among rags in a green pail at their feet. Victor's unfiltered cigarette lay nearby.

"Perdón a nos, señora Kirkpatrick, por viniendo tres horas temprano pero no puedia nos evitarlo. Es okay?" Frances asked.

"I don't know what you're blabbing about, but sure, why not, come in, come on in." Lila sawed her bare forearms across her breasts and tossed her head, ponytail flapping. Turning, over her shoulder she beckoned them to follow.

"Thanks," she said to Helen and Manny. "Thank you," she said to Rita, who stayed rooted to the first step of the inside staircase. To Ron, who stood blinking beside his cigar-store Indian, she said, "I'm going shopping, yes, I'm going shopping. And I'm taking your new Escalade solo."

Forgetting to ask for keys, forgetting she wore no coat, forgetting that the cleaning women's van no doubt was blocking the drive again, Lila marched into the laundry room and swept open the inside door to the garage.

BRET WILKES RANG THE BELL ON MONDAY AT ABOUT THREE. A black Stetson sporting a partridge feather shielded most of his brick-red hair.

Manny opened the door to the man's high-pitched "Zeet!" and lower-down "Kew-kew," repeated fast. Bret turned to face him, lips stretched in a bloodless grin, and flipped up the collar of his camel-hair coat. A gust rattled leaves against the tendrils of clematis webbing the porch's white trellis.

"You've got yourself a dark-eyed junco there." Bret extended his arms, then pushed a forefinger to his lips. Twisting his chin, he called again three times, "Zeet! Kew-kew." From the top of the embankment came the junco's reply.

"We've got the Oregon race in the Bay Area," Bret said. "You've got the Southern Rockies here; that up there must be a Gray-head. More flying down from Canada soon. Another month, they'll be calling all over the place—spring starts Friday."

Before Manny could ask him in, Bret's blue-ice eyes fastened on his own. "Jake, I appreciate this!"

"Manny Barnes, Bret." Manny's teeth started chattering. "Come meet my partner, Joyce." In his plaid wool shirt, his torso shook as he stepped aside to let Bret pass, noting the shorter man's bare ankles rising from loafers and disappearing into a pair of creased Levi's.

"I'm glad, when Maxine phoned, that Joyce could say we'd be happy to see you. Apologies for the hammering. A guy is fixing the railing guarding our hot tub. Let me take that."

Bret wriggled out of his camel-hair.

"Some shirt," Manny said, inhaling Bret's lime cologne. A scraggly goat, a turtle with human limbs, a cow with a man's face, what looked like a roadrunner, and a pair of rattlesnakes scrambled through greenery across Bret's knit-collared pullover.

"Jake."

"Jake?"

"An expression I use—Dad's nickname for my sister." Bret outstretched his arms toward Manny. "Rock art and birdcalls cheer me up when peddling data-security software gets too old."

Joyce approached them from the kitchen in black-soled flats. "Hello. I'm Joyce Hunt."

Though she usually left her small breasts unsupported, today a brassiere accented them beneath the blue-and-white shirt she'd tucked in. A white leather skirt sculpted her buttocks. "May I fix you a glass of our local root beer? Sarsaparilla and licorice; no preservatives. At seven thousand feet we're supposed to drink a lot of liquid to curb energy drain. Sometimes it works."

"Lovely; I'll try it." The freckles on Bret's cheeks rose with his smile.

"Manny?"

"Water, no ice." He arched his back to relieve the pain that had settled in his lower spine since helping Helen and Lila with music publicity this morning. Twenty-four hours had passed since he'd been able to move his bowels.

At the rasp of Stu's circular saw, Manny ran over to slam the guest-room door. On his return he punched the CD player into releasing Claude Bolling's *Suite for Flute and Jazz Piano.* Grabbing his water from the tray Joyce carried, he hunched himself into the rocking chair against the window overlooking the pedestaled bird bath on the large deck. Bret settled on the sofa near him and leaned for the root beer Joyce brought. Nearby sat the March issue of *Sunset,* which she'd opened to the cover article on double-dug Bay Area gardens.

Manny coughed to stanch the rise of stomach acid. "Maxine Morgan says you're thinking of leaving the Valley? We got out two years ago."

The guest-room door creaked before Bret could respond. Stu emerged in a gray sweatshirt sprinkled with sawdust, jeans ripped at the knees, and ankle-high basketball shoes. Today the photo of a cholla's magenta blossom graced his eye patch. "Manny? Can I borrow you a minute? I can make the new railing any height you like."

Joyce jumped from the navy-blue armchair she'd sunk into. "I'll take care of it, Manny. You and Mr. Wilkes talk." She hurried across the carpet and disappeared behind Stu's swinging ponytail.

Manny gripped the base of his skull to quell the growing ache. The furnace clicked on.

"That's some eye patch," Bret laughed. "Does everybody turn creative here?"

"Stu put his eye out stealing the neighbor's roses for his girlfriend a few months before we arrived here. What draws you to Santa Fe?"

Bret narrowed his eyes. "It's not a pretty story, but I'm going to level with you." He bent to massage an ankle. "In Oakland, about the time you left, I met a girl named Hisi who'd slipped away from her folks in Taos Pueblo to get an abortion. I fell for her hard and ended up bankrolling the procedure. Her mother's brother had knocked her up. It's Hisi who taught me how to talk to birds. Early last year she moved in—which really freaked out my twenty-year-old and her husband. Both became Christian fundamentalists after he lost a leg fighting in Somalia. Finally, Angie brought my granddaughter over to meet Hisi this January. Carl slapped her around pretty bad when they got home.

"My thinking is to shift my company's operations to Santa Fe so Angie can dump Carl before I kill the prick and move her and little Carla in with me. But what about Hisi? I doubt she dares to return to northern New Mexico. I hope to god she isn't hiding another pregnancy. Her waist seems to be thickening."

Manny watched Bret's freckled forehead pleat. To counteract a sudden onrush of dizziness, he pushed his forearms against the rocking chair's. Joyce's father gay, his own a suicide, Bret concocting unlikely sanctuary for his daughter and granddaughter—was Manny truly looking forward to fatherhood? He doubted Joyce would give him the chance now.

"Really good brew," Bret said, draining his glass and swiping his lips with the heel of his thumb.

"Where have you been looking for property?" Manny managed as the purple-pink bruise below his left cheekbone began to buzz.

"Saturday Maxine and I lit out for Las Campanas." Why is he wincing? Manny wondered as Bret continued. "Those two Arnold Palmer eighteen-holers are jaw-droppers. This morning we went back for second peek at a hacienda with a nice garden casita near the clubhouse. But the woman's starting to make me nervous."

The guest-room door swung open. Behind Joyce, Stu lugged his saw, tool belt, and yellow-bellied drill to the stair landing and up.

Bret stood until Joyce lowered herself into the armchair. "Tell me how you two feel about this Kirkpatrick fellow."

"He's pretty much a neocon, and we're . . ." Manny swallowed as his gut bunched like a fist.

". . . totally against this war, although he and I differ on what to do about it. Manny marches, I meditate." Joyce crossed her legs at the knees; the blonde hairs on her calves and thighs glistened. "The Kirkpatricks are for do it quick. At least Ron is. What his wife wants I haven't a clue. She's a nutcase, though Manny thinks otherwise."

"Oh?"

"War jitters are straining their marriage," Manny whispered.

"In his nibs' favor," blurted Joyce, flipping her thumb toward Manny.

Bret grasped an arm of the sofa. "Perhaps I better leave?"

"Don't, please." The pressure from Manny's gut became unbearable. "You'll have to excuse me a minute." Unfolding himself, he moved toward the bathroom as though carrying a sack of cement on his forearms.

Joyce uncrossed her legs. "Manny's suffering a lot of intestinal trouble. I guess it's obvious we're both on edge." She leaned forward. "What are your views on this preemption business?"

"Okeydoke. Last night I finally had time to watch the news. It seems clear that Saddam Hussein will soon figure out how to bully us with his nuclear and chemical warheads. Or use operatives to sneak nukes in suitcases or satchels packed with anthrax through customs. In two months Baghdad will hit a hundred and fifteen degrees by mid-afternoon. Yep, I've been against preemption, but maybe we better move fast, UN backing or no UN."

"Donald Rumsfeld doublespeak, Mr. Wilkes. Those trailer trucks Colin Powell showed the UN aren't mobile weapons labs, they produce hydrogen for weather-observation balloons. Turn on public radio's Democracy Now for what's true—here comes Manny. I need to check our worker's progress." Rumpling her blonde mop, she rose and charged past Bret.

Watching her hips swing, Manny emerged from the bathroom, sure today she'd dressed like a whore to inveigle Stu, despite what she'd said last night in the hot tub. Though his ass continued to sting, at least, by straining, he had been able to empty his colon. Thanking the God that he doubted gave a damn and shaking his head to clear it, he said to Bret, "Let's go get some air."

He strode over the entryway's flags to the closet, grabbed their coats, and, padding in moccasins across the carpet, yanked open one of the French doors to the big deck. "Those bare ankles may go numb," he said over his shoulder.

"I've got varicose veins; cold stops the pain. Does that nasty cut smart?"

"Not so much. I fell yesterday marching for peace."

Gripping the low stucco wall, Manny filled his lungs. Clouds hid the Ski Basin's lift sixteen miles north but Mount Baldy, nearer by, gleamed in light snow. On the other side of the living room the aluminum chimes jangled. He shivered as gusts iced his ears—he'd forgotten his cap.

Behind him came a sudden "Chewink."

Bret eased beside him, peering over the gate and down the slate steps. "There, beside that scalloped bath by the dead piñon, hopping backward—you see it? Your spotted male towhee. Pish, pish," he called. "Chewink."

The rufus-flanked bird with the salt-and-pepper wing bar froze, then cocked its hangman's head.

"Pish, pish, pish," Bret coaxed.

The red eye stared; the bill opened. "Chewink?"

"Chewink," Bret replied. "Pish, pish."

Isn't that what we're all doing? Calling out? Manny thought.

The towhee bent to peck among the stones surrounding the basin that Joyce filled every day at dawn.

"It's going after your juniper berries. Or maybe leftover grass seeds," Bret said.

"When it warms up, we spend evenings outside watching flickers and ground doves come to drink. Once in a while we see mule deer. At the end of Canyon Road—three miles that way beside the river—is the Audubon Center: a hundred and thirty-five acres of bird-watching."

"Jake, I wish I lived here now." Bret wrapped his arms around his coat and, lifting one loafer and then the other, stamped the redwood two-by-sixes. "Listen, do you know another realtor?" He licked his lower lip. The nightmare of fending off Maxine in his hotel room late Saturday afternoon made him shudder. "I think your fellow next door is out of the picture, but dealing with Maxine's mood swings is rough enough. Can you believe she told me she married her husband because he could outplay her at poker?

I guess she met him dealing blackjack at the casino he owned in Vegas. Myself, I hate to lose him. He knows where the petroglyphs are and the best buys in rock-art furnishings."

The rough stucco prickled Manny's palms. He slapped one to the sheepskin where his heart had begun to pound, spooning again that bite of Maxine's blackberry flan two years ago as she and Ron and Joyce and he lunched at the Great Books Cookhouse. Had she no sexual effect on Bret? Manny felt his cock push his khakis as he said, "Better than anyone we met, Maxine knows where to buy. But you're going to find shoddy construction—new or old—everywhere here."

"Chuck invited me up for drinks tonight to see a Grand Canyon crack in his and Helen's bedroom and to watch tiles fall off their kitchen wall."

"Santa Fe has other negatives," Manny said. "Workers pouring out of Mexico don't speak English, twenty miles north of here there's more heroin per capita than anywhere in the country, public education sucks, and we have the same percentage of homeless teens as San Francisco." Goddamn it, he thought, was Joyce still upstairs with Stu? He arched his back to quell the pain in his lower spine.

"Bret? I'm glad this weather shrinks your veins, but my feet are turning to bricks."

Abandoning the view of St. John's College tucked into hills beyond the Cross of the Martyrs, which brooded over the downtown offices of *The New Mexican*, Manny pivoted and depressed the brass handle of one of the French doors.

"Our dear Maxine showed me a marketing newsletter that you and Joyce put together for Cisco," Bret said, clicking the latch behind him. "Do you two do it long-distance no problem?"

Trembling in the furnace's warmth like a hound shaking off water, Manny threw his coat into the rocking chair. "I fly back once a month. But even with all of Santa Fe's troubles, I hate leaving anytime. So I'm searching for a way to make a living staying put."

"Hey, Manny, we've found the leak," Stu called as Joyce trailed him down the stairs. "I've got to hit Empire Builders for solder; I'll be back tomorrow morning to wrap up. Joyce said to stash my saw and drill under your bed."

Manny strode to the cabinet that held his stereo equipment and punched the power off, breaking the flute's cadenza. "You going to help me with those bumper stickers, Stuboy?"

"Not sure yet, buddy. But I'll be at the vigil tonight. How about you?"

"Bet your life."

The glossy photo of the magenta cactus blossom Stu had taped to his patch glinted as he turned toward the entryway. Hammer and wrench swinging from his tool belt, he grabbed a scarred leather jacket from a hanger in the cloak closet and exited.

Manny's gut seethed; Stu seemed to have moved in. He stared at Joyce, who stood hugging the stuccoed post on the bottom landing and frowning.

"I've been thinking that getting along might be easier if we all wore flowered eye patches," Bret said. Still in his camel-hair, he flipped his wrist to consult his watch. "Jake, my hour's gone. You have a newsletter to email and I need to wash and scurry up to the Ridleys'. Before I fly home, let's talk about you two people doing some marketing for me. It would give me an excuse to hurry back."

Joyce's frown disappeared.

Manny rubbed his lower spine with his knuckles. "I'm not sure we'll have time, Bret. Chuck wants us to help him jump-start an advisory company. He thinks refusing to buy goods from the big chains will let New Mexico businesses flower."

"Chuck Ridley's cracked in the head." Joyce lowered herself to a carpeted stair and planted her cheekbones on her fists, gazing at the two men.

"Iffy, you think?" Massaging his neck, Bret frowned. "Maybe so, though his tax advice has been outstanding. As really it should be—he left Deloitte and Touche in New York a senior partner."

"Probably fired him."

"They didn't fire him, Joyce."

"I'll quiz him tonight. Or maybe tomorrow, after we decide what to do about me buying a house."

"Maybe I'll see you at his office," Manny said.

"Lovely. How about you two letting me treat for dinner afterward?"

"Boodie?"

"I'll sleep on it."

Bret rounded the sofa and clacked onto the entryway flags, red hair bouncing. He turned toward Joyce. "Cheer up, you." Waving to Manny over his shoulder, he took his Stetson and pushed open the door.

"Zeet! Kew-kew," he whistled and leaned into the cold, flicking the door shut with his elbow.

TOO MANY COOKS

THE CLEATS OF HER HIKING BOOTS SMACKED THE SIDEWALK as, under cleared skies, she hurried toward the restaurant tucked between the card shop and Nattie's Footwear just north of the Plaza.

Posts bristling with flakes of blue paint held up the one-story adobe arcade. Brown pods trembled from a troop of thorned New Mexican locusts that rose from circles of brick fronting the street. Snug in heavy sweatpants to protect her from the wind, Joyce flipped up the collar of her quilted jacket and pulled its elastic cuffs taut.

She yanked open the door lettered *Great Books Cookhouse*, wondering if scorpions still fed on each other back by the bathroom. Like she and Manny now were. They ate here last in November, rhapsodizing over their planned late-May wedding at Allie's and Baby's, surrounded by Baby's sweet lilac. That was the same day, she recalled, that Colin Powell had cajoled the UN Security Council into authorizing the use of force against Iraq for that country's failure to reveal weapons of mass destruction.

Bathed in the restaurant's fruity scents of merlot and chardonnay, Alexis sat in a long, braided, blue-and-scarlet skirt beside a glass table displaying menus, hands in her lap.

"Here I am," she rasped as the door hushed shut. Her shoulders, covered in a rough wool turtleneck, swung toward Joyce. "What's up?" She rose.

"In a minute," Joyce frowned, glancing at the jowly man, hunched in a white shirt buttoned to his throat, who bustled up to them from the main room. Gray wisps like a clown's angled off his head; gray hairs sprouted from his ears.

Farley, owner of the Cookhouse, had earlier taught at St. John's College, two miles east. After his wife left following his affair with a freshman, and his father, a former US ambassador to Cypress, died a year later, Farley used his inheritance to fund the Cookhouse. His son served as chef de cuisine; St. John's undergraduates served as waiters.

"Two, ladies?" Farley arced Joyce's hooded jacket onto a peg behind Alexis.

Over bricks set in sand, scabbed white by alkalai precipitating from groundwater, they filed past the oaken bar. Customers filled two of ten tables draped in blue linen. Track halogens lit the spines of books central to the curriculum at St. John's, written by the West's strongest thinkers—from Homer to Einstein—placed on high shelves that formed a frieze around the plaster-walled room.

Between two windows facing the locust trees hung a blackboard the size of a card table. On it Farley had scrawled today's food for thought: *It is NOT better for people to get all that they want—Heraclitus.* He seated Joyce and Alexis at right angles beneath it.

"Leaks everywhere from Sunday night's rain," Farley said, handing them menus and nodding toward one of the sills, along which lay a twisted dish towel. "Enjoy."

"Want to talk now?" The silver rings on Alexis's right fingers glinted as she pulled strands of brown hair from behind an ear and twisted their ends. She glanced up as a young man in a white cook's apron, lanky like Manny but afflicted with pimples, stood by.

"Drinks, ladies?"

"Raspberry Zinger," Joyce said.

"Excuse me?"

She raised her voice above the chatter. "Raspberry Zinger tea, if you have it."

"Here's hoping," said the undergraduate as he swiveled toward Alexis.

"Water with ice for me."

"Good to see you again, my lady."

When he left, Alexis leaned forward. "Well?"

"What's going on between you and Manny?"

"Not a damn thing."

"He's bringing up your name too often, Allie."

Blinking at her, Alexis guffawed. "Joyce. Why should I have passed up a couple of breakfast blintzes with Manny on Saturday? The next morning at the peace march I rammed it home to him that I'm committed to Baby.

"That was true when you and I lunched last. At the moment I'm feeling awful. No problem that Baby's never been an activist, but this past weekend she glued herself to Fox News and babbled like a neocon. 'You know, Alex,' she said last night, 'Saddam has stockpiled enough botulin to paralyze the lungs of millions of women. You better rethink your position.'"

Joyce stared at her a moment. "That's exactly what I'm doing. Last night after Manny drove off to the vigil with his candle, I sat on the toilet upstairs and cried for half an hour. This morning I took my temperature; I'm ovulating and thinking 'to hell with it, head on back to Palo Alto. Your mother's there and so is your gynecologist.' Allie, it's not only you Manny's making passes at—he spent yesterday morning with Helen Ridley and our neighbor, Lila Kirkpatrick."

Joyce's right palm crept to the buttoned cardigan covering her belly.

"Chuck told me Helen said Kirkpatrick rattled his wife yesterday with some kind of bad news," Alexis said.

"He would. Did Lila get to the vigil? Manny said zilch afterward and I didn't ask."

"A tall woman with a ponytail and caked makeup?"

Joyce nodded.

"She yelled something at Manny and left before the singing started. Oh, he introduced me to your handyman. I loved that eye patch, the rifle broken across *Just Say No*?"

"Earlier it was a cholla blossom. Manny thinks Stu and I have something going."

"Do you?"

"Knock it off, Allie. At dinner he accused me of dressing like a prostitute to turn Stu on. It's Manny I wanted to turn on. This damn war—what a disaster everything is."

The pimpled waiter squeaked close in crepe-soled shoes. "Zinger?" He set a blue pot and red foil bag on a saucer. "And water for my lady, lots of ice. You'd like to order?"

"We haven't looked yet," Joyce said, towsling her blonde mop of hair.

"I'll try anon."

Joyce lifted the cardboard menu. "Does he smell to you like steamed spinach? Christ!"

"What?"

"That's our realtor coming in."

"Mrs. Morgan lunches here a lot."

"See the guy trailing her in glasses with the Pancho Villa handlebar?"

"Yeah?"

"Saturday, Lila Kirkpatrick had her arm around his waist on what used to be her deck. Is everyone on the make around here except me?"

A Celtic cross jeweled in green swinging across her breast, Maxine held the door for Victor before marching forward in patent leather boots. She'd fluffed her black curls into a storm cloud. Gold hoops swung from her ears.

Farley took the trench coat Maxine handed him and led her to a table near Joyce and Alexis. Joyce returned her wave with one less frantic, overhearing Victor ask Farley, "Where's the little boy's room?" He limped past the bar toward an alcove where a terrarium sat.

Upon delivering the Bloody Mary that Maxine had asked Farley for, the waiter turned to Joyce. "I can recommend the Nietzsche Duckling with Polenta. My own favorite is Flannery O'Connor Hot Pepper Stew for this cold day in high-mesa hell."

"You don't like Santa Fe?"

"No."

"Me neither. I'll take the Spinoza Grilled Chicken Niçoise," Joyce said.

"I guess I'll try the St. Anselm Veggie Soup."

"Anon, ladies." The undergraduate bowed and squeaked off, scratching his neck.

Joyce leaned sideways to whisper, "That perfume Maxine Morgan's wearing is making me gag."

"Sugared roadkill. Listen, you okay about Manny and me? Because I want to bring something up myself."

"What?"

"Hold on."

Out of the dark, dipping to the right in stained slacks, Victor cluck-clacked across the bricks. Frowning at Joyce as if trying to place her, he bent his red-banded *Proud To Be American* cap toward Maxine.

"You know what he's got back there?" Victor asked her.

"The scorpions?"

"How about that sign he's hung over them?"

"So what? Farley's food is superb and his liquor's only a block from the office."

"Obviously he's never faced a slant aiming a stolen M-sixteen at your huevos. If you want me, I'm pulling tile at Kirkpatrick's after I fix Mom's lunch. Plus I need to take some photos for rebuilding the deck."

"Uh-oh," exclaimed Joyce. Her boot kicked the table's pedestal. "Here comes our big-ass neighbor."

As Victor limped toward the table holding menus just inside the door, Ron strode through in a broad-brimmed straw hat. He threw it and his red polyester fleece onto a peg and, grinning, lumbered into the main room. Waving off Farley, he nodded at Victor as they passed.

Joyce and Ron traded smiles before he lowered himself into the webbed-steel chair facing Maxine. By now Farley had filled all ten tables except the one that separated Ron and Maxine from Alexis and Joyce. Acoustical ceiling tiles and the rough plaster of the walls minimized the din.

Joyce sipped her Zinger and set her elbows on the blue linen. "You wanted your turn."

"Who is he?"

"Lila Kirkpatrick's neocon mate."

"Oh, man." Alexis fumbled the ring that pierced the top of her ear. "I bet he's the one Chuck told me dumped cowboy beans onto Mrs. Morgan's dog. Anyway—what you said on the phone about giving up poetry. That piece you read me Friday—water nymphs or dryads or whatever they are wheedling Donald Rumsfeld to change the part in his hair from right to left to calm him? It's perfect, Joyce."

"But Manny's pounding the drum for peace has deadened my heart. I don't want to write anymore."

Alexis placed her own right hand over the balled fist of Joyce's left. "Has Manny said anything about the new venture Chuck is dreaming up? To stay in accounting but jettison big-league stock picks in favor of showing New Mexico businesses how to turn a profit? He thinks you can help."

They raised their eyes to the steam drifting from the vegetable soup the waiter brought for Alexis. Also on his tray perched a tequila martini in a funnel-shaped glass for Ron, and a second, lime-crowned Bloody Mary for Maxine. First he set down the soup and Joyce's chicken salad.

As Alexis removed her hand, Joyce startled at a vision of herself undressed, Allie kneeling above her and rolling her turtleneck up and off, heavy breasts swinging above Joyce's face.

"We have to work late again on tax stuff," Alexis said. "Mrs. Morgan's bringing a client over in an hour to decide what kind of property he should buy. The guy you hosted yesterday, Bret Wilkes. And I think Manny is bringing us his two-thousand-two workbook. March and April are so busy, Chuck says we'll have to wait until after the fifteenth to brainstorm his new idea."

"Bret Wilkes is paying for dinner tonight to talk Manny and me into writing marketing pieces for him. He's my choice for adding to our income, Allie. I think Chuck is as much a nutcase as our neighbor's wife. Manny's investments are tanking."

"Oh, jeez, I'm sorry!" The waiter's high voice shot across the intervening table.

"Dumb-shit kid!" Ron cried.

"I'll grab a towel. I'm sure Farley will okay wine for you on the house."

"Indeed Farley will," Farley called, charging over. Tequila had splotched Ron's chinos and darkened a pointy toe of one of his neon-blue boots. "Farley pays your cleaning bill as well."

"Why do bad things happen when we're together, Max?" Ron righted his glass.

"Going to change, big boy."

Grabbing the wine list, Ron muscled away his chair and stood as the waiter brought rags. Farley bent to furl the linen from the webbed-steel tabletop as the waiter sopped up what had not already trickled down between the bricks.

He returned with a dry tablecloth, silverware rolled in napkins, and a fresh martini. "May I accept your order?" He smoothed the blue cloth with his free hand.

"Need to enjoy these drinks, kemo sabe." Downing the martini in three gulps, Ron handed him the glass by its stem. "Bring me another so I can lope along with my ropin' partner here. And rustle us up a bottle of one of these Smokin' Loon merlots."

"Yes, sir."

"Son of a peccary, Max, you do smell preferable to that paint thinner you were wearin' three days ago." He stared at the split end of his thumb. "Damn dry air!"

"This one's called Beaver, Ronald." She traced her lips with her tongue. "New from Saint Grêve. I thought you might like it."

"Surely do. You watch the news last night?"

She shook her head.

"Bushie plans to give Americans one-and-a-half billion to straighten up Iraq. Foreigners need not apply. Seed money for jump-startin' more fat cats into buyin' second homes in Santa Fe, no?"

"Pixie's still mad at you, Ronald. You need to bring him a treat."

"Oh?" Ron swigged his martini.

The brown mole on the bridge of her nose bobbed. "Like two nights from now while Giordy's at his poker. Victor has promised to lose as usual so Giordy'll stay late. You know our gate code."

"Should by now—I figured maybe that's why you called. I could use some lovin'. Lila's gone wacko. She tried to drive off in the Escalade without keys and last night she ran off to some Plaza peacenik confab."

"Victor says you and she want to sell your place."

"Not gonna happen unless you leave Giordy. What's he, pushin' eighty?"

Two orgasms Sunday and hardening again? You middle-aged stud, Ron thought, Little Prince stretching along his thigh.

"Let's see how much money you can help me make, big boy. Muchas gracias, by the way, for the phone call this morning from your client three years back, Dirk Pellington." She fisted her second Bloody Mary in her left hand and took it half down, then fixed Ron with a watery stare.

"I'm still kinda wonderin' if you weren't the one let air outta my tire," he wheezed.

"Not going to say it another time, Ronald."

He twitched as pain grabbed muscle under his breastbone and sent a lit match down his left arm, deflating his erection.

"What's good?" he managed to ask the waiter bearing two goblets and the fifth of Smoking Loon.

"You may want to try Nietzsche Duckling, on special today with polenta."

"Yeah." He thrust his thumb toward the silk shirt that glistened between the lapels of his deerskin jacket. "Max, you?" He clamped his eyes shut, wheezing.

"You okay?"

"Little heartburn."

"Let's hope that's all it is. Caesar salad for me. Throw some pine nuts into it."

"Yes, indeed." The waiter set the goblets on the cloth and poured them a third full. The dark wine frothed and settled, spreading a whiff of cherries.

"Gotta go potty, Max."

"Steer clear of the cannibals." She upended her Bloody Mary.

Ron lurched past Alexis and Joyce and past a trio of law partners he knew, lunching in suits and vests. He wove his way down the bar toward the *Men and Women* stick figures stenciled blue on two doors.

To his right, a purple radiance tinged the dark alcove. Capped by a black lid under which hung three long ultraviolet bulbs, the terrarium, large as a hope chest, sat on a bare wood table. Maybe a dozen hairy desert scorpions glowed greenish-blue, though Ron didn't pause to count, the tip of his penis stung so. The big five-inchers lurked half under rocks or stalked each other across sand, stingers arced over their backs ready to strike. Like red-hot leeches, suction cups held heat lamps to the terrarium's end walls. One giant, the hairs on its back jerking, was shredding another's belly with its pedipalps. Suspended by chains screwed to the latilla ceiling, the wooden sign read *We Kill for Capitalism, They Kill for Food.*

Heartburn before he ate? He'd better make that appointment with the sawbones soon. As Ron's urine reddened the water below (had Lila cooked beets? he couldn't recall), in the main room Joyce speared an anchovy fillet to a parsleyed slice of potato.

"Maybe your boss's new idea will work," she said. "But it's Manny I'm worried about. His belching sent me downstairs again last night. After bringing you tax papers this afternoon, he's driving up to his dried-out old Dumbo-eared friend's shack to talk him into slapping peace stickers on SUVs. I don't know if Stu's going to do it, too. Promise you won't, Allie. Promise?"

"If you promise not to abandon poetry."

"I'll try," came her sputtered reply.

Above Alexis's broad shoulders Joyce watched Ron emerge from the dark to roll like a barge back along the bar. Negotiating the narrows created by two tables, he lowered his bulk to face Maxine. His teeth gleamed like dice as he pulled her wrist close and kissed a knuckle of her middle finger, next to her wedding ring.

"Look, Allie, above their neocon hearts, her embroidered flags and his *Onward Christian Soldiers*. Those two can't wait to celebrate our spring fling of blowing up civilians in the hunt for warheads that no longer exist. Warheads that Saddam produced with technology we gave him. Hans Blix urges more inspections? He could as well be speaking Sanskrit."

With her left hand, Maxine poured Ron's goblet full as the waiter trotted close to deposit Ron's duck and polenta and her salad spattered with nuts. "The Smoking Loon pleases?" he asked, straightening.

They nodded. When he turned, she plunged the tip of her forefinger into her mouth, then pointed it across the table. "Lean close, big boy, I'm going to make you crazy. After Bret and I looked at property Saturday I asked to see his room. 'Hey,' I said, and ran my fingers through all that red hair. One thing led to another—you should see his ding-dong, a donkey's on a spaniel. 'Tie me up,' I told him. He starts whimpering about some live-in Native Amerian pussy and hauls on his jeans before I can pull out a condom. 'Grow up, Ding-Dong!' I yelled. Preemption isn't the only thing he's soft on."

Her larynx rose as she gulped a mouthful of wine. "So what if I've lost him as a client? I wish I were a man, I'd help more women catch fire than Pixie heats fleas. One day you're going to figure how to treat me to my own explosion, Ronald."

His turtle eyes narrowed. "Your place this afternoon."

"Giordy's home at three."

"Hotel room, then."

"Can't use Giordy's war hammock."

"War hammock?"

"A surprise I've been saving for you. Besides, I'm supposed to meet Bret at Ridley's."

"Tonight!"

"Property consultation with your old client, Pellington."

"Right now then, bitch."

"Hunh?"

Draining his goblet, Ron pushed from the table. Deerskin fringes swaying, he wriggled between the blackboard and table corner to clamp Maxine's piled curls between both palms. "You and me, Max. Now!"

"Sit down, Ronald." She seized the ends of his fingers.

"What's the trouble here?" Farley called, hurrying across the splotched bricks.

"No trouble, Farley. Let's see if he'll return to his chair."

Nearby conversations dwindled; a noodle flopped off a tuft of Farley's hair. He cupped Ron's elbow.

"Nobody manhandles me, Comanche motherfucker." Glistening in sweat, fingers wrapped around the waist of the half-empty goblet, Ron goggled down at the hunched-over proprietor.

"Ronald, not another scene!"

"Let's go do it, Max."

Farley ran toward the wall phone behind the bar, across which a waitress and two waiters in white aprons stared.

"Okay, we'll go do it. Put the bottle down, I'm right behind you." She forced the heel of his hand to the blue linen.

He loosened his grip on the wine as she shoved the meaty small of his back. As he stumbled toward the table full of menus, she unsnapped the green purse bouncing at the end of its shoulder strap, snatched her wallet, and tossed a hundred-dollar bill onto her lettuce.

"Give me your car keys," she hissed, pushing. From the pegs she grabbed her trench coat and his sombrero and red fleece.

Her belly pressing his kidneys, they turned the corner toward the front door.

"I'm going, too, Allie. I can't swallow," Joyce whispered. "I'll be sick if I don't lie down."

HALF AN HOUR AFTER THE WALK BACK TO CHUCK'S ADOBE office from the Great Books Cookhouse, Alexis rose from the Bloomberg's twin screens to find a couple of extra-strength Tylenols. The front door being pushed open stopped her. Manny ducked under the lintel in red stocking cap and sheepskin, its left arm patched in Stu's yellow-and-black safety tape.

"Goddamnit, Manny, I just swallowed my gum." Alexis tucked a sheaf of brown hair behind her ear.

"Bringing my tax workbook; I'm late to see a friend." He raised his fist to muffle a belch.

"Did Joyce go to bed?"

"In her clothes. She said Kirkpatrick went nuts an hour ago."

Alexis rolled her eyes. "That cut on your cheek looks like it's scabbing. You want a glass of water? Mr. Wilkes said to snag you a moment if you showed up. He's in there with Chuck."

"All right," Manny sighed. "No ice in the water. Thanks."

"The cold pipe sprang a leak and every plumber I've called said expect two weeks' delay because it's not an emergency. I'll pour hot and plunk in a few cubes." Alexis pulled a fresh plug of bubble gum from her blue-and-scarlet skirt. The paper crackled when she untwisted it.

She preceded him across the oak planks in soft-soled boots checkered with blue-and-yellow diamonds. As she turned the door's handle, he asked, "You want to help me plaster peace stickers on SUVs tomorrow or Thursday?"

She whipped around. His eyes flicked to her breasts swelling the turtleneck that Baby had knitted in three shades of green, then back to her face.

"I told you again last night to cool it, Manny. Stop pissing me off." She opened to the conference room and marched into the kitchen down a path of damp hand towels spread along the tiles. Manny followed.

The stubble growing around Chuck's lips and covering his chin had begun to look like soot. This afternoon he wore a leather vest over a shiny blue shirt that flickered under the ceiling fluorescents. From a leather armchair he waved hello above his laptop. Through one of the black-barred windows, shadowed by the cathedral's tower, blossomless hollyhocks trembled over their mound that fronted Palace at Otero.

Bret leaped up in a cuffed shirt sporting white daisies. "Howdy, Manny! Are we on for dinner?"

From the holster at his belt, which secured khakis whose creases seemed just pressed, commenced a series of flute-like whistles. Bret hoisted the phone and thumb-flipped the cover. "Oh, hi." He pressed his lips together.

Manny leaned forward, straight-arming a joint in the mogul table's mahogany to brace himself, as Alexis brought water floating a couple of ice cubes. Jaw working her gum, she set the glass beside his hand, retreated past the black-framed abstract painting of pinks and azures, and closed the door behind her.

Bret returned his phone to its holster. "Dear Maxine," he said to Chuck. "Calling from I can't imagine where—close by, somebody was chainsawing wood. She says she has a headache and can't meet us."

He turned to Manny. "That's not a problem. Chuck and I had a long talk last night. The woman scares me. I'm backing off buying a hacienda or commercial till I can figure out how to move Hisi here with my daughter and Carla. But I've decided to invest in Chuck's New Mexicans Thrive. My company'll fly him out to learn the growth-forecasting program we offer our encryption clients. So, Jake! Dinner tonight? I may head home tomorrow."

Nausea from a colon suddenly desperate to empty itself made Manny press the tabletop with both palms as stomach acid burned his throat. "Joyce says she'd like to." He gulped the tepid water.

"Lovely! My hotel, six-thirty outermost?"

"Sure."

Chuck raked his chin. "This beard feels like fire ants. "You watch the morning news, Manny?"

He shook his head, "Chuck, I've got to go."

"Bush says we assault Iraq in the next forty-eight hours, even if Saddam and his sons leave."

"I figured." Manny arched his spine, pressing it with the back of his hand.

"The Dow gained two-hundred-and-eighty-two points. Traders bet invasion won't disrupt the flow of oil. Rumsfeld says invasion has nothing to do with oil; what garbage. Four years ago Saddam bought himself a US coffin by starting to trade in euros instead of dollars."

The dizziness Manny felt yesterday returned—he squirmed to check his gut's insistence. As he stepped toward the door, Chuck bolted off his chair, the flaps of his vest fluttering like sails, and gripped the bones of Manny's shoulders. "Even if Bret isn't one hundred percent sure that preemption assures disaster, building small businesses here excites him. Listen to him tonight, okay?"

"I will." Manny pulled from Chuck's grasp. Reaching the conference room's door, he swung it wide, and hurried toward the bathroom.

Colon emptied and anus stinging, though his bladder had refused to void, he picked up his sheepskin by one elbow from Chuck's desk. "Listen, Alexis?"

She swiveled to face him as numbers flitted like confetti around the Bloomberg's blue screens. A pink bubble grew from her lips and thinned.

"You won't hear me ask anything more of you."

She sucked the bubble in and scraped its remnants from her upper lip with the nail of her little finger. "Relax, Manny. Look how your left arm's trembling."

———————

Joyce work for Chuck? Meeting with Bret at La Concha this evening seemed a joke.

Manny gunned his year-old, half-gas, half-electric Toyota Prius toward Canyon Road. At the white cross and plastic flowers he turned right, then left onto Acequia Madre, and right onto Don Miguel. Following the news on KSFR, Bruch's *Kol Nidre* adagio for cello and orchestra helped slow his breathing. He decided to stop for milk to soothe his stomach.

Lined in Chinese elms and an occasional Russian olive, Don Miguel rose through a mix of shacks and remodels. Lorenzo's Grocery perched ahead on a high corner a couple of blocks from Dirk's. Past columns of mortared stone buttressing a retaining wall, Manny swung right into the grocery's parking lot, where he spotted what looked like Stu's pickup. Having to confront Stu after listening to Joyce babble on with him earlier this morning made Manny's chest muscles bunch.

At the tires' crunch on gravel, a black, unclipped poodle thrust its nose out of the truck's half-open window.

Manny yanked his knit cap over his ears. He read Stu's notice tacked to the bulletin board under the store's porch roof: *If you need a dog nursed back to health that's been shot, run down, or poisoned, call 982-4224.* Below fluttered notices of garage sales and, in the bottom corner, Dirk's plea pinned in a transparent Baggie:

WORKERS WANTED FOR COMMUNITY GARDEN
See Dirk up Don Miguel Place or call 982-9338

Manny pulled open the outside screen and pushed at the inner door— *No Restrooms* lettered on its glass.

Pausing under a string of red chiles to adjust his eyes, in the murk he spotted Stu's ponytail. He stood in a blue denim jacket reading *The New Mexican* near the filigreed cash register. Lorenzo's sister, Gloria, mannish gray hair slicked back, hunched behind the oaken counter. The air smelled of tamales heating in the toaster oven near her. Clomping across chipped linoleum, Manny passed below the cross of wired-together cottonwood branches that dangled high under a couple of flyspecked fluorescent bulbs. In the back room, near the washer and dryer, Lorenzo worked at his desk.

Pain wrung Manny's bladder as he opened the glass door of the oak-trimmed refrigerator and extracted a half pint of milk. Expanding his lungs, he headed toward the warming tamales.

The morning's dandelion still gilded the patch over Stu's left eye as he threw back his shoulders. "What brings you up here?"

"A writer pal of mine, Dirk Pellington, lives around the corner."

"I've seen his notice. Look at this." Stu hoisted the newspaper's front page to Manny's gaze. *Bush Calls Preemption God's Will.*

Mounted above on the wall, a moth-eaten elk's head, jaw drooping, gazed down at them glass-eyed. Nearby, the portable generator that delivered cold to the refrigerator hummed *om.* Manny handed a dollar bill to Gloria as he said to Stu, "You took your saw and drill?"

"What?"

"Pulled them out from under our bed?"

"What do you think, Manny?" Scratching his forehead, Stu reached across his denim to knead the muscle topping his left shoulder.

"What I think is that lately you and Joyce follow each other around far too much."

"You're as bonkers as Bush, you know that? As a matter of fact, I planned to call you this afternoon to say forget my helping with peace stickers, I don't want to stir up trouble between you and Joyce. Besides, car fumes cloud my good eye."

"Crap on that. Where I have in mind, cars will be parked for the night. Don't lie to me, Stuboy. Yesterday and this morning I saw how she dressed for you."

Behind the counter, round-backed Gloria rose and called, "Oye, Lorenzo, vente paca," her cheeks crinkling like dried peaches.

With his free hand Manny grabbed Stu's sleeve, sending the newspaper spilling onto the linoleum.

"Avolar, malquidos!" The balding old man stormed past the drier lifting both arms, his white shirt rolled to the elbows as he rushed between wooden shelves of chips and soaps and cereals, little cans of asparagus and fruit salad.

Releasing Stu, Manny snatched his milk and hurried under red chiles back out to the store's front porch.

———————

Minutes later, Manny swerved into Don Miguel Place past the *Dead End* sign, gulping down the last of the milk. A Mexican hairless sprang yipping from a pile of lumber and beer cans as the dust boiled up behind the hybrid sedan. Ahead he saw brown smoke feathering above Dirk's roof, which was dotted with loose bricks.

Opposite the two-room casita, beneath cottonwood branches shading a blue-gated adobe hacienda, stood two pickups whose bumpers read *Fuck Iraq*. Along the west border of Dirk's own ample lot, last year's hips of yellow roses spread across a chain-link fence. A rusting stovepipe pierced the rain-wrinkled tar paper that slanted toward the porch's plywood overhang. Under this sat a ladderback chair. Two plywood shutters painted green shielded the casita against July monsoons, infrequent in recent years.

Manny slowed onto the dirt and stopped beside one of the metal poles strung with lengths of clothesline flapping in the wind. Near Dirk's Olds 98 low-rider, both rear fenders dented, waited a sparkling BMW convertible, its top up. Below the old man, clad in his usual white bib overalls over red flannel long johns, knelt a woman wrapped in a coat whose back displayed an embroidered golden bull. A matador's hat studded in gold topped her black hair. She straightened as Manny unfolded himself from the Prius.

Abishag, Dirk's tabby, slunk between two beds of soil mounded for vegetables and shored in granite riprap. She headed toward her litter box, stationed between the ladderback and a half cord of split oak.

The sun lit Dirk's white stubble as he waved, hair blowing like rice grass.

"So you'll help Saturday get the deer fencing up before the chard shows?" Dirk growled to the woman. "Don't wear those rags. Bring a spade and heavy gloves; we've two more beds to raise up." He extended a liver-spotted hand, pumping hers as if it could add water to the morning's drizzle. "Here's my young friend Manny—gotta split."

Though his bladder ached and the tip of his penis stung, Manny relaxed as Dirk's arm dropped across his shoulders. Among the homes slanting north up the foothills, the descending sun turned distant patches of snow the color of Dirk's hair. He propelled Manny toward the porch, where Abishag had hidden her tail beneath her belly.

"I'll be right out," Manny said, preceding him into the living room, which smelled of smoke and fish. The warped pine floor creaked as he turned into Dirk's bedroom, past the stove's fire twinkling behind its glass doors. An acrylic painting of a scarlet sky filled with ebony crosses hung askew over a headboard fashioned of scimitars, which Dirk had collected while serving as Middle Eastern correspondent for *The New York Times*. The hollow onyx pedestal of a table lamp glowed from the bulb inside it. Pressing his genitals, Manny hurried into the tiny bathroom.

He emerged in a few moments. "Who was she?" he asked in a normal voice, assuming Dirk was using his hearing aid. He pulled off his cap and coat. Dirk stood at the kitchen's chipped-enamel sink which divided the Formica counter lining the wall. A gust whistled north through cracks where two unwashed windows didn't meet their sills. Through a third, Manny watched a quartet of aspen Dirk had planted among tangles of tumbleweed and sowthistle bend like fish poles.

Having followed the men in, Abishag moved from a green dish daubed with bits of sardine to a pile of back copies of the *Times*. They draped the base of a floor lamp in the shape of an anorexic mermaid that Dirk had shipped from Yemen. Under a shade woven from eel skins, a bulb lustered the patch on Abishag's back where Dirk had said a feral cat clawed away her fur.

Dirk's eyes crinkled under wild brows as from the kitchen he proffered Manny an unopened tin of sardines.

Manny nodded, yelling this time, "Who was she?" He sank into a tangerine-colored chair, from whose arms dangled various lengths of thread. His knees rose to his breastbone.

"Another snappy eastside dresser joining our efforts to make Don Miguel Place organically self-sufficient. Who else?"

"How long before she stays the night?"

Standing with his back to Manny, Dirk twisted the handle of a can opener.

"How long before she stays the night?" Manny, annoyed, shouted.

Dirk looked over his shoulder. "A couple of weeks; guessing. Not your business. Coffee?"

"My stomach won't take it," he shouted. "Water, no ice." He thrust his fist to his mouth to suppress a belch, glancing at the black-and-white photograph looming askew that showed dunes rippling across the White Sands Missile Range. On them Dirk had thumbtacked cutouts of women's rouged lips.

You old lecher, Manny thought, dropping his gaze to the half-inch crack between a couple of planks.

"Blast the bitches!" Dirk grabbed a red-mesh flyswatter and slapped the sink's enamel. He whirled to lunge at the back window's turquoise frame.

"What's going on?" shouted Manny.

"Millers showing up early this year. The grubs fatten on roots and warm under the floorboards. Got her—blast, there's another." Tossing the swatter into the sink, he jumped and clapped his hands. "Missed. I'm dumping this place."

The moth smacked the pink wallpaper, livened with minueting ladies in hoopskirts and gentlemen in doublets that Dirk had left alone when he moved in. It spiraled toward the latilla ceiling.

"Screw in your Songbird," Manny shouted.

"You came to talk."

"I've got to."

Dirk brought over sardines and Norwegian crackers, returned to the kitchen, and brought back coffee and water. Setting them on a bench, he plopped into a corner of the divan upholstered in red, yellow, and blue carpeting. Abishag leaped to his lap.

He pinched out a disposable, ninety-day hearing aid from the breast pocket of his overalls, secured his white curls with the heel of his hand, thumb-twisted the device into one of his jug ears, and pushed its plastic stem. "If I'm in luck, next time you'll need to head down to the Bosque del Apache, where I'll be explaining cranes and coyote willows to the ecologically starved. I'm buying myself a house trailer. The realtor my mortgage broker suggests is coming over later to say what kind of money this rattrap might bring me."

"No way I'm going to let you leave here, Dirk." Manny forked a sardine onto a hexagon of cracker. Its head and tail flopped over the edges.

"What's the trouble, sport? That's some bruise scabbing over."

"I fell during a peace march. Two days earlier I fell on my neocon neighbor's driveway while letting air out of his tire. What's the trouble? Women, work, and war." He stuffed his cap into one of the sheepskin's pockets and, bending forward, shrugged out of it. "I think Joyce and I are breaking up."

"Why?"

"My activism riles her and she says writing activist poems is pointless. I've started eying other women, even her gay best friend. I want to fuck them all."

"The world's a henhouse, sport."

"But I'm nuts about Joyce—last week I thought I was coming over today to ask you to be my best man this spring. She had wanted to get pregnant before the wedding. Now all she wants to do is meditate."

"Good for her."

"You don't meditate."

"Haven't reached that level of grace, sport." He rapped the buckle on the bib strap that covered his heart. "I'm still priapic. She's good in bed?"

"She's the best when we're feeling okay."

"Then sweet-talk her; I wish I were as lucky. Baiting an endless string of women makes me bughouse. Damn millers, they're too early!"

Hurling Abishag onto the planks, Dirk ran for his swatter. He hopped to a folding stool's black rubber footrest, curled his fingers around its stainless-steel handle, and backhanded a latilla.

"Gotcha!"

Manny watched the gray corpse drop, the dust on its wings glittering. It sizzled when it hit the stove's black top. He lifted a buttock to let out gas.

"What about work?" Dirk asked, resettling on the divan.

"I can't stand this flying back to Silicon Valley once a month, trading technobabble with engineers. I have appointments there next week and I can't bring myself even to organize interview questions. My CPA in Santa Fe wants to start a company showing local businesses how to succeed through sound accounting practices, green investments, and publicity. He's asked Joyce and me to join him but Joyce thinks the idea's crazy."

Dirk thumbed his straps as Abishag climbed up, whiskers as white as his. "Doubt it's going to earn you enough to live on, sport. New Mexico chuckles at forward thinking."

"I want us to sell our town house and move into something smaller."

"With a baby?"

"People do. Anyway, it's a pipe dream. Joyce is going back to the Bay Area, I can feel it."

"Maybe, maybe not. Keep working your newsletters is my advice. What else?"

"War."

"War's endless—and I boot you out in five minutes. I need to soak the dirt from my pores before that realtor gets here."

Manny pressed a palm to his belly to quell the intestinal pain. "The news on the way over said our first objective is Basra's oilfields. Does anyone still believe the reason Bush wants to invade is to make Iraq safe for democracy?"

"How should I know who believes what? God tells Bush what to believe. The truth is, we males are all hardwired to fight because it turns women on. Quick story. An anthropologist in the Congo interviewed two tribes of aborigines who rip each other open with the fire-hardened tips of limbs from mahogany trees. These bozos have plenty of land, plenty of food. So why do they practice mayhem? One explained it. 'The more enemies I kill, the prettier girl I get.' "

Dirk slid a crackerless sardine headfirst onto his tongue. "Me, I'm moving south to the Bosque. I'm betting your Joyce will have your baby, I've seen how you two are together. Don't end up bitter like me, bedding needy women and waiting for a prostate to metastasize."

"You told me the cancer was in remission!"

"This month it is."

Manny stared at the gray eyes, liver spots at their corners, that gazed back at him from under Dirk's white curls. "Will you help me slap peace slogans on neocon bumpers tomorrow night or the next?"

Yanking its stem, Dirk twisted the Songbird free and dropped it into his breast pocket. He smoothed a palm along the white bush on his chin. "Like everyone, aren't you, Manny? Can't listen, can't learn. Look, two millers crawling up between the floorboards next to those combat boots of yours."

THE SONGBIRD WAS SNUG IN HIS EAR, AND AT THE CRUNCH of tires, Dirk rolled up a shade to peer at the woman who slowed her golden Range Rover next to his Olds 98. As she emerged in a navy wool pantsuit, he marveled at the tumble of black curls held by a blue ribbon over her high forehead. Mussing his own white curls, still damp from the shower, he hauled on a heavy, red-and-black plaid coat and scurried for the door.

"Hiyuh, Morgan Realty," he called, trading the casita's warmth for the chill of the porch. "It's going on dark soon, so let's eyeball the grounds first." A gust started the ladderback rocking as he tramped in rubber boots between the vegetable beds.

The south wind carried to him the woman's sweet peppery scent. He noted the big, lozenge-shaped diamond on the ring finger of the hand gripping her black, faux-lizard briefcase. She removed her dark glasses. "Maxine Morgan, Mr. Pellington. I'm glad Mr. Kirkpatrick made this meeting happen. Quite a piece of property you have here."

"Unh." He jerked his head at the squealing in his ear.

"Something wrong?" She shivered and cleared her throat.

"My hearing's bad. Reported too many atrocities in the Middle East for *The New York Times*, I guess. This doodad squeaks when the seal breaks— there." He stopped jiggling the hearing aid.

"So now you garden and hang your clothes out to dry."

He watched her larynx bob, her violet-smeared eyes scrunching as if in pain.

"You got it. I'll show you the back forty." Grasping her elbow, Dirk led her along the chain-link fence festooned with orange-hued rose hips to view the four aspens rising among tumbleweeds and sowthistle. A split-rail fence separated his lot from the neighbor's garage to the north.

"If you can't get me a decent price, I'm bringing in geese and a goat. Maybe I'll shoot the mule deer that wander in. I'm set on becoming self-sufficient."

"That I believe. Can we go in? I'm a little under the weather."

"Want to help me grow community vegetables out front?"

"Right now no time, but you're kind to ask. Look at those twigs blow."

"Clue me in to what that flag on your lapel means," he called over his shoulder, kicking away the cottonwood branches that had skittered across the lane.

"That I wish I could be one of the men"—she coughed—"about to better things in Iraq."

"There'll be women going over, too."

"I'm used to thinking men for jobs like this."

He came up beside her on the two thicknesses of plywood that served as a porch.

"Might you have a Tums handy, Mr. Pellington?"

"I believe I do." Feeling himself quiver at the closeness of her scent, he held the door as she scraped the soles of her black boots on the sisal mat.

"Oh!" she gasped, knocking over one of the pails he'd set out to catch the leaks.

He clapped the door shut and threw his mackinaw over the upholstered arm of the tangerine-colored chair. "My roof leaks. Like to down that Tums with a glass of wine?"

"Not just now. Your artworks, they're all hung crooked. Those lips on the sand dunes . . . "

"I call it *Air Force Wives Bless White Sands Missile Range*."

"Oh? And that lamp with the snakeskin shade?"

"Yemeni Department of Antiquities dredged the original from two hundred BC out of the Red Sea. The shade's shellacked eel skins."

"Eel skins . . . all this pink wallpaper . . ."

"Wallpaper came with the place."

"It's a little upsetting."

"Go ahead and sit."

He left for the bathroom. Opening her briefcase on the wooden bench, she moved to the stove to warm, staring at the miller that lay on its back, fried wings furled.

"Here you go." He placed a mint-green tablet in her palm—to his fingertips, her flesh felt like ice—and handed her a blue glass filled with water. "Excuse me."

Clopping across the planks, he grabbed the swatter and, hurrying back, whacked the spine of *War and Peace* which sat with other classics on war in a waist-high bookcase fashioned of wrought iron. A foot-high stack of magazines topped by *The Nation* leaned against it.

Maxine lurched toward the card table he used for dining as Abishag lit out from under it toward the bedroom.

"What was that?" she cried.

"Abishag."

"Abishag?"

"Abishag the Shunammite, King David's comforter. My cat's about as old as she was."

"Not your cat—what you smashed."

"Damn millers are coming up out of the floorboards."

"But it's too soon for them."

"Not in this wreck it isn't."

The sun had set; outside the kitchen window the light glowed orange. He stared at her open lips. "What do you think I might snare for this hovel?"

When her breathing had slowed, she lowered herself to the brightly carpeted divan he'd bought before flying home for the last time five years ago from Kuwait. Past the sills of the south windows, a gust fluttered the corner of the listing-form she propped in the cover of her briefcase. "You've maybe . . . a quarter acre?" she asked, blinking.

"I believe it's a bit over." He smoothed the white stubble on his chin and throat, watching her.

"Any title complications or easements?"

His cheeks jiggled as he shook his head.

"Well, Mr. Pellington, up off Acequia Madre here, your land alone could bring up to four hundred thousand. Especially if we use Mr. Kirkpatrick. He and I should have no trouble finding you a qualified buyer—who, I should tell you, may want to tear your home down—"

"I would."

"Even so, I think we'll list at four-seventy-five, maybe go to four-ninety-five K."

"Sounds like I need to be grateful that the realtor who helped me buy three years ago bit the dust and Ron sent you."

Squinting at him, Maxine mopped her forehead with the back of her hand, shoring up the pile of curls. "Tell me about your mortgage." She pulled an aluminum clipboard and pen from the briefcase, inserted the listing form, and began to write. Her lavender lip gloss and nail polish glittered under the mermaid lamp's shade.

"Adjustable, maybe two hundred thousand to pay off. Which makes it seem that, after your commission, you and Ron might hand me a check for at least that?"

"It sounds about right. I'm assuming you're an artist, Mr. Pellington?" Maxine kept her eyes on the form.

"Mostly I'm a failed do-gooder; I hang all this art crooked to show that nothing works. This war you think'll free oppressed Muslims? Not a prayer. It'll help Al Qaeda recruit more thugs. And may unleash the Armageddon that fundamentalist Christians believe'll whisk their leader back from the skies to the Temple Mount in Jerusalem.

"The only good I know to do anymore is to mind my own business, Mrs. Morgan. If you and Ron can free me up two-hundred grand, I'm going to scamper south with my pension to the Bosque del Apache. Even though I just found out that twenty miles north of there, New Mexico Tech's Energetic Materials Center invents our own country's weapons of mass destruction, I'm buying myself a trailer. I want to learn to listen to the red-winged blackbird, the Rio, to thunder—to coyotes howling. Start making amends for being born a human being."

Her left hand pushing up her blue-ribboned curls, Maxine lay the clipboard across her thighs, staring at the elderly man sunk in the armchair nearby. Her lips began to twitch as Abishag padded back from the bedroom and jumped up onto Dirk's lap. Drops gathering in the corners of Maxine's eyes soon formed violet rivulets. She mopped one with the heel of her palm. "I wish I could tag along with you. Everything in my life is complicated and wrong. I slept all afternoon to be fresh, and look at me."

Her torso shuddered, sending the clipboard and pen clattering to the floor. She unsnapped her shoulder bag and pinched out a tissue, smearing mascara over her cheeks as she dabbed her eyes. Gripping her temples, she hunched forward; her trembling increased.

"Come with me," Dirk said, rising.

"Hunh?"

"For now, you're lying down." He walked to the stove, swung open the glass door, and tossed in two splits of oak from the jumble laid on tar paper nearby.

"For a minute?"

"As long as you like. I'll fix us soup and crackers and a few sardines."

"I think not for me."

He moved close and took her hands. "Up you get."

Keeping her chin close to her throat, she lifted her dark pupils to his gray ones. Though he spied a miller wriggling out between two boards, he let it be and led her into the bedroom, where the pedestal of the onyx table lamp glowed.

"Lie here," he commanded in a quiet voice, patting the queen-sized mattress, nostrils flaring at the faint scent of smoldering oak and her own sweetened pepper.

The scimitar headboard creaked as she lowered her back to the madras spread, woven in green swirls. Through the north window, the sky before moonrise turned his catkin-burgeoning quartet of aspens, the neighbor's two-car garage, and the adobe-littered foothills the blue-green color of the bay at Abu Dhabi.

Maxine's chest heaved while she let him undo the three green buttons of her tailored jacket. She lifted her right leg when he crab-walked to the scimitar footboard. He gripped the heel of her left boot and tugged it free, then the other.

"Thank you, Mr. Pellington. I'm so embarrassed."

"Don't be. This old man wouldn't mind resting a moment himself. I've spent the whole day talking with volunteer gardeners and a young friend whose life also isn't working. Psyching up for war gives everyone the willy-wobbles. Perhaps I will take a break, if you don't mind."

She shook her head; the ribbon holding her hair sagged to her neck. Unbuckling the straps of his overalls, he moved between the driftwood dresser and the other side of the bed, where he hauled off his boots.

"You think maybe no one's life is working?" she murmured, gazing in the gloom at the herringbone pattern of the latilla ceiling.

"Don't know." He eased himself close to her. "I'd shut the door against the millers, but the stove is our main warmth."

"It's so peaceful. Even the wind humming in the other room seems right—Christ, what's that thing?"

"A pack rat," he chuckled, spying the ringed, pink-white tail swishing between two latillas. "Animals have always taken to me. Pay it no mind." He reached up and smacked his palms twice. The tail curled from sight and within seconds the scrabbling between batts of fiberglass scattered under the roof boards stopped.

As Maxine crossed her wrists on her belly, Dirk eased a red-flanneled arm above her leg and let his hand drop to her knee.

She rolled to face him, sniffing as she fingered one of his grizzled cheeks.

"You like sardines."

"I love 'em."

"Don't say anything about this, will you? Especially to Mr. Kirkpatrick. I could lie here for days. Though in a couple of hours my husband would call Jennifer and she'd call my cell. Though I wouldn't hear it."

Lifting his hip, Dirk rose to his elbow and touched one of her violet eyelids with his lips. His Songbird squeaked. He pulled at the tiny stem, yanked the device out of his ear, and flicked it into his overalls' breast pocket. He bent to her eyelid again, feeling her fingertips smooth the denim suppressing his erection.

"I wish I could get one of those," she whispered. "You have a lovely one, Mr. Pellington."

"Yes. See what's out the window, Mrs. Morgan."

She propped herself on both elbows to view the moon emerging at the right of the neighbor's garage, where the foothills formed a V, transforming distant cottonwoods and piñons and homes to lemon yellow. In the glow closer by, a mule deer munched catkins off the aspens, tail tipped white as its ears.

"It's so magical." Maxine said, sitting to help him undress her, letting him peel off her jacket, herself freeing the oyster-shell buttons of her blouse. She fluffed her hair while he reached behind to unhook her pink-rosebud-rimmed brassiere. Standing, she undid her wool pants and pushed them down, perching on the edge of the mattress while he tugged them off. She peeled rosebud-trimmed panties from her thighs and kicked the cotton into his hands. He tossed them onto a low bookcase, overalls bunched around his thick waist.

The bursting moon turned her flesh to custard, throwing crescent-shaped shadows from the footboard's scimitars onto the oval rugs.

He was unbuttoning the upper portion of his long johns when she beckoned him with all four fingers of her right hand. He hauled his overalls over his callused feet and left them on the floor. Bent by the red flannel, his erection hurt until she freed the remaining buttons and it sprang into the air.

"You're uncircumcised!"

"I was midwifed; no money to flay me. And you have an appendix scar. And a little mole on your nose." He took her cheeks in his palms.

"It curves like the shadows from those scimitars," she mused, gripping his erection. "Look, Abishag's crept in."

Maxine leaned forward to cradle the shaft between her breasts, then pressed them together and rocked from side to side. "I've never had an orgasm—I don't like touching myself, though I suppose I might if I owned one of these. I've never sucked an uncircumcised penis."

"Want to experiment?"

"We hardly know each other," she murmured, easing herself supine. Recovering his shaft, thumb and forefinger circling the folds of foreskin, she gazed at the ceiling, her curls forming a black halo. "I want you to tie my wrists and ankles to the ends of your bed. I want you to bite my fingers and my strawberries and my earlobes until I cry out—don't touch that erection yet. Will you do it, Mr. Pellington?

"I want to see what a man feels like dominating. And I want you to lick me. Perhaps you can bring on what I've never had."

His breath came in puffs as his palm massaged the white curls on his chest. "There's extra clothesline in the kitchen."

Stumbling over Abishag, who lay beside his desk, he hurried into the living room. The wind thrummed between the south windows' frames and sills as he flung open the plywood door under the sink and grabbed the nylon loops lying next to the box of baking soda.

She lay spread-eagled in the moon-brightened room. He took the knife he'd once used to slash the throat of his guard in Najaf from his desk drawer, its handle orange poppies tooled in blue leather. Flopped over her ribs, her huge-nippled breasts rose and fell as she shifted her tongue across her lower lip.

She wanted him to hurt her? He cut four lengths of line, dropped the rest to a rug, and began to square-knot her to the scimitars as blood further engorged his penis.

Watching her squirm, violet lids closed, he began massaging the sopping black nest protecting her vulva. Extending his arm, he sidled toward her head and bent to nip an earlobe, his lungs filling with her scent. She groaned and he bit harder, moving his right fingers from her vulva to a nipple, pinching until she cried out, "The left one!"

Back and forth he wrenched the dark, puckered bud until, thrusting her cheek to the spread, she croaked, "Both now."

Instead he sidestepped to the headboard and leaned across her near wrist to grip with his fingers the shorter two bones of her ring finger. The diamond surrounded by emerald baguettes ate into the pad of his thumb as he took the second bone between his lower teeth and the roof of his mouth and snapped his chin down.

Like the shell of a pecan, the joint cracked.

"Ahhhhhhh," she screamed, thrusting her buttocks off the mattress and straining to twist her shoulder so she could see what he had done.

Abishag unlimbered herself and, striped tail swishing, strolled out toward the stove.

Dirk scurried to the mattress's midsection and knelt. Filling his lungs, grasping the writhing Maxine by her rib cage and pelvis, he extended his tongue to probe.

"Ahhh, ahhh, oh god, what did you do?" she moaned, settling her buttocks and thrusting them again toward the latillas. He lugged her pelvis as close to him as the nylon cords allowed and pushed his face into her nest. Though he could not find her clitoris, he lapped her folds, up and down, back and forth, grateful her outflow smelled fresh. From her ribs he removed his left hand to free his forefinger.

Her writhing slowed, her groans quieted. Licking, he pumped his finger in and out. Drops beaded on his forehead and the dewlap between his jaw and collarbone. His heart felt like a dumbbell thudding against the floor as saltwater dripped from his nose.

"Mr. Pellington, I can't, my finger hurts too much. It's begun to pound, oh, god, what did you do, break it?"

Glancing at the moon passing like a bubble beyond the window's splintery frame, he pushed down on the edge of the mattress and stood.

Puffing, he strode to the headboard and leaned toward her wrist. Her shoulders twitched, flipping her breasts to the left as he pinched the platinum wedding band to examine the knuckle. It had swollen. In the lamp stand's creamy light he couldn't tell if the joint was reddening. "No blood," he said.

"Should I go to the hospital?"

"Probably. We'll splint it with a couple of scraps of oak to get you home and through the night."

"Oh, damn it. You must be aching—have you a condom? I have a spare. For variety my husband rents us motel rooms," she lied. "Is studded okay?"

"I've got my own smooth."

Packs a condom for her husband? Bullshit, he thought, listening to the now-constant complaints the wind sent into the living room. "Want me to untie you?"

"My left wrist aches."

Her hand was pulsing and had turned hot. So had her wrist. Loosening the knot, he pivoted, tramped barefoot into the bathroom, and hauled open the cabinet door.

"Mr. Pellington?"

"Shout."

"No, we've got a snooper."

"What?"

"Tiptoe out."

With his teeth he ripped the top strip from the foil, fisted the condom's wet latex, and tossed the torn packet into a tin wastebasket.

Peering around the jamb, he saw the voyeur working her jaw sideways, ear tips glowing in the moonlight like wicks, pointing her glistening nose at the windowpane. As Dirk stepped onto one of the braided rugs, the white tail flicked and, heaving her shoulders, the doe bounded through sowthistle toward the split rail.

Maxine popped her finger from her mouth. "She's never seen the likes of me, I'll bet."

"Harden me up, Mrs. Morgan." Dirk straddled her waist and shoved his penis toward her throat.

She stretched her lips over the tops of her teeth and began munching it.

"Never mind," he growled. He sat on his heels, buttocks squashing her belly.

"I'm sorry, I've never done uncircumcised."

He started to pump himself, tightening sweat-damp lids while she sucked at her swollen finger.

"Ready," he panted.

He unrolled the latex over his erection and, straight-arming the mattress, scooted back to her thighs. Kneeling, he bent forward.

Her ring finger flew free as he rammed her, in and in again. "Unh," he grunted with each descent. A half-dozen strokes later, crying out, he collapsed his lungs. He sank down, barrel chest pressing hers.

They lay gasping until, "You," she breathed.

In the silence he felt her ribs expand. Then, "Cut me loose and splint this thing before my husband wonders where I am."

GINGERROOT TEA?

Morning air. In the yellow housecoat she had buttoned to her thighs, Lila jumped from the sofa and flung open one of the French doors to the splintered scrap of deck still overhanging the greenbelt.

A rapid *clang clang* brought her sleep-deprived eyes to Manny and Joyce's chimney. Soaring far above her glass-topped table and deck umbrella, still tangled in the arroyo, its spark arrester glinted beneath scattering and reassembling clouds. On top of the arrester, a yellow-shafted flicker, spotted feathers tossing, attempted to drill a hole in the aluminum bonnet. The noise resembled cans bouncing behind a car of just-marrieds.

Fuck and shit. Lila could feel the damp from the after-midnight sprinkle chill her slippers' rope soles. Her loose, unwashed hair swirled as she wheeled.

She hauled the outside door shut and strode to the wall phone in the kitchen, from the housecoat's pocket grabbing the wrinkled sheet of Victor's estimates, his number typed at the bottom.

"Bueno?" answered a cracked voice she assumed was Victor's mother's. He'd promised her that Mom usually slept until nine.

"Is Victor there?"

"Perdón?"

"Victor, Victor. Son."

"Él ésta trabajando. Regresa a comer. Quién habla?"

Lila clacked the phone against its cradle, bit the end of her little finger, and dialed.

"Bueno?"

She slammed the receiver back and dialed a third time—as he had instructed her to do on the off chance his mother answered.

"This is Victor. Leave a message and your number and I'll call you back soon."

"This is Lila Kirkpatrick. Don't come in an hour thinking you and I are going to do what I agreed to do. It's no longer the Lord's plan. My husband is home sick with a hangover, so don't expect to lay tile. Expect to rebuild the deck. Bring deck tools, not tile tools, you comprehendo?"

She thrust the receiver into its cradle and thumped back to the sofa, snatching the TV's remote and punching the button to On. As Fox News crackled into focus, a toothbrush-mustached newscaster, dressed in a blazer and striped red-white-and-blue tie, barked, "Uday Hussein is the second of three reasons this country has decided to invade. He's confined to a wheelchair except when he's raping women or men. Defectors say he has masterminded monstrous methods of torture to ready him for sexual pleasure."

A watercolor rendition showed a man faceup, suspended at the waist by a chain—back arched, legs bent at the hips and knees, palms and skull touching what looked like a concrete floor. Someone in a white robe and white hood slit at the eyes seemed to be winching him into the air by a hook.

"Show the missiles!" Lila cried, averting her eyes.

"We'll be putting an end to all this within twenty-four hours," the newscaster declared as if in response.

"Five hundred Tomahawks, each with a computer in its nose, and three thousand smart bombs, like the Joint Direct Attack Munition and the Paveway Three, each with a computer in its rear, will allow us to shred the Husseinian spiderweb of evil while minimizing collateral damage."

Lila spread her legs, unbuttoned her housecoat to her ankles, and peeled the yellow flaps aside, her heels pressed to the carpet. I've got to get hot, she fumed, clenching her jaw. But kneading her vulva sparked nothing.

Her eyes watered with the strain as the newscaster continued. "You cannot compare our current effort to the bombing tactics of previous wars, explains Secretary of Defense Donald Rumsfeld. "The humanity that's going into this current effort makes any such similarity to scenes like the following unfortunate."

The set's forty-eight-inch screen—stationed between two windows whose shades Lila had lowered when she'd tramped down the night before to sleep on the sofa—filled with body parts of children littering a town square: ripped-open bellies; the blood-matted curls of a severed head lolling against the tire of a Mercedes in flames; three corpses with one arm each; a leg whose foot wore an ankle-high basketball shoe lettered *Keds*.

Lila's mouth spasmed. She stabbed the remote's button to Off. Long ago hadn't Jonathan been training to rain death on foreigners like these? She doubled up, wrapping her breasts in her arms.

When her breathing slowed, she locked her teeth, and staggered toward the stairs.

A band of yellow tape reading *No Admittance* sealed off the master bath. To her right, Ron lay snoring under the ivory-colored blanket, the side of his huge head crushing a bent forearm. His jowls disappeared past the sweat-darkened collar of the blue *Go Lobos!* T-shirt he slept in.

He sounded to her like the hogs slurping garbage on her father's farm. She hobbled across the wall-to-wall carpeting. She hoisted a badger by one ear from the koalas and pandas and lion cubs massed on the wicker hope chest at the foot of the bed.

"Wake up!" she yelled, as the furnace clicked on and warm air began to stream through the grate under his bedside table. Though he'd slept twelve hours except for lumbering downstairs to pee, his breath still stank of tequila. She stared at the stubble that darkened his cheeks and chin, the fat upper lip vibrating with each exhalation, and whirled to yank the drapery cord.

Cloud-speckled sunlight whitened the room. The navy-blue pleats of the drapes' cotton duck furled against the far end of the window. Beyond the Kirpatricks' lower tar-and-gravel roof, next door the flicker continued trying to stab through the aluminum of Manny and Joyce's spark-arrester bonnet.

Back Lila turned to her husband. "Wake up, I said." Swinging the badger by its ear, she whopped the side of Ron's head.

He grunted. She angled her arm behind her shoulder to strike again but he tossed to her side of the bed.

"Wha?" He clutched his forehead, luminous with sweat, and raised himself on his right elbow. "Go way." He sank back, facing the plaster ceiling, palm glued to his eyes.

The seam of the badger's ear had split. Grabbing it, she thrust her fists to her hips. "We trained Jonathan to be a killer of children, you and me. All those times he watched you and I fighting because of that piglet's dick of yours plowing Veronica. Now it's plowing Maxine Whore. A heart attack is the Lord's plan for you, no doctor can save you, and I hope he doesn't."

"Stop, will ya?" He clapped both palms to his brow. "I'm seein' the sawbones Monday."

"Good luck!"

Flinging the badger against the leg of his table, she ran to the dresser and tugged at the bottom drawer so hard it flew onto the carpet. She snatched her sex tools and ran back to the bed.

"Who makes me use these? You make me use these and I can't even get wet anymore."

Jerking his head aside, Ron puffed his cheeks and planted his fists on the mattress to lever backward, knocking the headboard against the wall. "You accuse me of adultery, Lile?" He thrust a sausage forefinger at her as perspiration gleamed in the folds of his neck. "Now's the third time I'm tellin' you: after lunch yesterday we drove to the Canyon Road Bar, where I fell asleep on her. So she drove me home in my car.

"And lucky she did. I saw Victor with his shirt hangin' out, I saw your panda on the sofa. Were you and him startin' or just finishin' up? And how come he was hidin' in the guest bath when I come home early Saturday? I suppose on the Plaza Monday night you set yourself up with neighbor Barnes. Where are you plannin' to bring that one off? Rear seat of the Escalade, now you've got keys?"

"Manny Barnes is a faggot."

"Oh, yeah?"

"He turned squirrelly after the singing—wouldn't let me even buy him an ice cream."

"You're wrinkled and saggin', babe. That disappearin' nipple hangs near your navel. Faggot? One thing sure. He or his galfriend let air outta my tire and I'm gonna pay 'em back good."

"You also going to pay back Maxine Streetwalker for bashing the Escalade's headlight on our mailbox? You're going to be busy, Big Shit."

Staring at her, Ron ran his palms down his T-shirt, splotched dark with sweat. "I think we oughta think about splittin' up, Lile, I surely do. Like you suggested last week. You go on back to Cowtown. Mug a milk."

She watched him slide off the headboard. Rolling away from her scowl, he grabbed the sheet and blanket and tugged them to his hairline.

Her eyes misted as she watched his shoulder rise and fall. Below the fingers that gripped the blanket's edge, he began to snore again.

Shuffling to the doorway, she stepped onto the landing. She twisted, stretched for the knob, and slammed the door with a sound like a blast from her father's shotgun.

———

Lila wrenched the yellow Mustang off Washington Avenue onto the dirt lot of Morgan Realty. Beside an associate's Buick Rendezvous and Jennifer's little banged-up Neon, Lila spied Maxine's golden Land Rover.

Out she stepped, still in her slippers and yellow housecoat, now buttoned to her knees. She had not stopped to cover her hips in a bikini or stuff her vein-webbed breasts into a bra. Through leaf buds of Chinese elms bordering the lot's northeast edge shone the eleven o'clock sun before clouds shut it out. Her loose hair streamed off her neck.

Shivering, she paused to stomp dirt into two gopher holes before marching across to the Land Rover. Snatching her key chain from her pocket, she clenched the car key's rounded end and scratched *Slut* through the door's gold-metallic lacquer next to the bobcat decal, then ran toward the building's arched entrance.

"Ma'am?" called the bespectacled Jennifer, swinging from her receptionist's perch and clacking in gold boots and brown jumper down the hall after her.

Lila's soles slapped the gray-swirled tiles as one of Maxine's associates, a thin, ponytailed man in his seventies, peered from his cubicle and then darted back in.

"Ma'am? Hello?"

At the doorway to Maxine's corner office, Lila goggled at Victor, who was reaching up from the top step of an aluminum ladder. Blue handkerchief drooping from the rear of his stained gabardines, he stood wedged between Maxine's cherrywood desk and the window, which opened on cottonwoods across the street. Next month, when their buds became leaves, they would shade French & French Fine Properties's two-story annex.

Victor peeled strips of plaster from the water-damaged ceiling and tossed them into the white pail on his ladder's fold-out shelf. Two fluorescent fixtures yellowed his skin.

Maxine sat hunched to Lila's right at the oval glass table, the back of a red sweatshirt proclaiming *USA All The Way*, her topknot of black curls wrapped in a red-white-and-blue ribbon. Facing her and Lila, Dirk held the sweatered Pixie on his thighs. He'd taken the same red leather chair studded with brass that Ron had sunk into three years before, when he and Lila signed the contract to buy their town house. Head and chin wooled in white, Dirk wore a green tie, a dark suit coat whose sleeves were too short, and a dress shirt whose frayed cuffs were too long.

An odor of turpentine made Lila's nostrils twitch as she cried at Victor, "You're supposed to be fixing our deck!"

Black ringlets jiggling at the back of his neck, Victor swung the beige bill of his *Proud To Be American* cap down and across. "Mrs. Morgan butters my bread, puta."

Anger stormed Lila's belly as she watched the tips of Victor's handlebar mustache flutter under his cheekbones. Her breath came in spurts as Maxine scraped her chair back, stood, and wheeled. Her necklace of bone and coral sounded like the struck wooden bars of a tiny xylophone.

"Who do you think you are?" Maxine shouted, larynx bobbing. She cocked her left hand above her topknot and threw it toward Lila, palm up. Cradled in padded aluminum, exchanged for last night's oak splint early this morning at St. Vincent Hospital's emergency room, the ringless finger gleamed.

"Don't give me the finger, bimbo. You're screwing my husband. I give you the finger times two."

Shaking, Lila thrust both fists at Maxine, middle fingers stiff as masts. She brought the heels of her hands against her breasts before thrusting them forward—retrieved and propelled them as though a spring had replaced her heart.

"Jennifer! Get this crazy person out of here!"

The electronic bell in the cathedral tolled the first of eleven clangs as closer by, a siren began to wail.

Maxine clamped her palms to her ears.

In the knit that matched his mistress's patriotic ribbon, the black-faced Pixie bounded from Dirk's lap and, yipping, scampered under the desk.

"Ladies. Still yourselves." Pushing away his chair, Dirk rose. He extended his arms as though they hefted the Ten Commandments, revealing two inches of threadbare white cuffs.

The siren's bleat crescendoed; Victor gripped the sides of the ladder's top.

As a white car lettered *Police* in red capitals flashed past, its lights winking, a creak sounded where the accordion drapes stood mashed at the window's edge. Rumbling, they began to spread past the desk toward Victor, turning the view a cement gray.

"Goddamned Giordy with his servo-curtains that don't work right and his goddamned remote—watch out, Victor, it's in my drawer," Maxine called out.

As she rushed to her desk, her chair fell over. The headmost, steel-stiffened fold of drapes knocked Victor's hip as he clambered down. "Mierda!" he yelped, throwing one leg toward the saguaro cactus, its spines festooned with Maxine's awards.

The square toe of Victor's trailing alligator-skin boot caught between the ladder's strut and bottom rung. He collapsed to the tiles, black-rimmed glasses skittering toward the cactus. The ladder toppled onto him, pail thudding against his shoulder as it spewed its load of plaster strips across his blue-checked shirt.

Distance muted the siren's screech; the cathedral bell tolled for an eleventh time and stopped.

"It's an air raid out there," Dirk guffawed. He looked at Maxine, who had retrieved the Bakelite remote control from the desk's top drawer, hesitating whether to furl the drapes or leave the view grayed.

"Who'll fix Mom's lunch?" Victor moaned, legs doubled up. "My sonofabitch right wrist's burning."

"We'll fix it together," Maxine snapped. She glanced back at Lila. "Jennifer, get this person out."

Tonguing the corner of her mouth, the receptionist lay faux-nailed fingertips on Lila's shoulder.

"Ouch!" she cried as Lila's elbow punched her ribs.

"I'm leaving myself," Dirk declared, striding around the oval table in white socks and scuffed black shoes. "You'll have that contract knocked out for tomorrow at Mama Cheetah's? Say noon?"

"Make it one o'clock." Maxine jammed the handheld to her right ear and bare palm to her left as Lila shrieked, "Nympho bimbo!"

With a rumble, the drapes began to pleat themselves toward the window's far end.

Clamping her upper arms, Dirk frog-marched Lila along the hall's tiles behind the retreating Jennifer. Lila stopped struggling as he soothed, "Whoever you are, you're a good-looking woman. Especially in yellow against that beautiful skin."

"IF THE PLUMBER DOESN'T SHOW UP SOON, THERE'LL BE frogs croaking in here."

In soft-soled boots, azure cotton skirt hemmed at the calves, and black velveteen blouse—nothing that Baby wove—Alexis squished across bath towels soaking up water from the office kitchen's broken pipe, bearing a glass and four clear-glass mugs into the conference room.

Outside the black-barred window that looked out onto Palace Avenue, a mid-afternoon gust rocked the blossomless stalks of hollyhocks that Chuck had planted to remember his mother. Alexis handed coffee to him and to Bret, who folded his half-lens glasses into the pocket of his petroglyph shirt, sleeves rolled to his elbows. She placed warm water with ice in front of Manny and Red Zinger tea in front of Joyce.

"New comb?" she asked about the yellow-and-brown tortoiseshell inlaid with horned toads that pierced one side of Joyce's hair.

"From Manny. This, too." Joyce pinched the hem of her new wool sweater strewn with asters.

"I'm not seeing a ring." Alexis lowered herself next to her friend. She sipped black coffee from the remaining glass mug.

In a corduroy shirt whose tan matched Joyce's skirt, Manny turned to peer above Joyce's head. "We look for that tomorrow night, after I rough out some marketing ideas for Bret." Eyes watering from the Bret's lime cologne, Manny slapped his chest and swallowed to suppress a belch.

"Mr. Wilkes? Supposing that plumber doesn't come when he said, are you by chance handy? Before we drown?"

"I'm iffy." Bret ran a freckled hand across his brushed-back hair and thinned his lips into a smile. "It's not why I promised to stay over."

"Stu Fisher's awfully good," Joyce said. "He fixed our hot tub. Why not call him?"

"There's an idea," Alexis shot back. "He invited me to go hear the Desert Rocks play the Paramount Friday night. Baby's furious, of course. Too bad—all she does is sit around mind-fucking on Fox News's hype of the coming blitz."

"Mind-fucking?" said Chuck, scratching the black beginnings of his beard.

"Sorry, boss." She pulled a brown sheaf of hair from behind her ear and twirled it.

"Stu called you?" Joyce whispered. She reached under the table to stroke the blonde hairs lengthening along her shin, re-entering the vision from lunch at the Cookhouse of Alexis's breasts squashing her own.

"Hey, you two, it's tax season; we don't have much time. But when Bret phoned me about the dinner last night, I thought all of us ought to meet. Joyce, welcome to New Mexicans Thrive."

"It's what our neocon neighbor—we think it was Ron—did to our garage doors while we were dining with Bret that made me decide to say yes. Plus saying 'Let's go ahead' to Manny this morning." She felt her brow heat as Bret and Chuck grinned.

"So you're putting your town house on the market and looking for something cheaper near the Community College? I gather this time you won't use Maxine Morgan."

"No way," Joyce blurted, clapping a palm to her cheek.

"Jake! Can you believe the dear woman called my cell phone at dawn? I was doing my Canadian Mountie aerobics. I guess Giordy told her to get me back as a client or he's closing her business down."

Chuck squeezed Bret's shoulder. "I'll be able to suggest another realtor—for Manny and Joyce, too—in a couple of weeks. Alexis is phoning references. So, Manny, you're turning your investments over to Murch?"

"On your tip. If you're still planning to stop advising."

"Tax work only. We'll have our hands full growing the state's small businesses." He gulped his coffee. "Last night Helen and I fought again—I spent the evening with your tax workbook, Manny. Let's assume you'll net at least a hundred and fifty thousand after buying down. Bret thinks he can keep you and Joyce busy, and New Mexicans Thrive can pay you a little something to begin with. Even if you have that baby you told Bret about, perhaps in a year you can stop trekking to Silicon Valley."

Manny reached for Joyce's hand. "I love you, Boodie."

She returned his grip but said nothing.

Manny's torso swayed as helium seemed to push behind his eyes. Glancing at Alexis, he drained his mug, intestines gurgling.

"Today and tomorrow Bret hopes to line up which data-mining and consumer software firms to approach once we incorporate. But a caveat to us all—you know, Alexis found on the Bloomberg this morning that, versus the euro, the dollar has fallen to its lowest level in three years, oil prices have passed thirty dollars a barrel, and has anyone seen estimates of how many hundred billions we'll need to reconstruct Iraq? I haven't.

"Perhaps our defense industries will fatten enough to float the Dow over ten thousand. Certainly Bret's encryption firm should prosper. But New Mexicans Thrive could take longer to profit our clients and those around this table than any of us imagine. Even me."

Alexis pushed her chair back. "I better go find some dry towels."

The few black hairs on Manny's chest waved in the hot tub's water as he punched the jets' button to Off. No breeze jostled the junipers and bark-beetle-browned piñons mottling the slope down to the greenbelt and arroyo.

"Here it comes, Boodie."

Just south of Mount Baldy, the nearly full moon peeped over the foothills, cantaloupe-orange as its hulk eased toward clouds scattered like flat-bellied sheep. Sparkling in the light, Baldy's thin crust of snow turned lemony.

"Manny! Two of them! I thought they were loners."

Steam feathered Joyce's shoulders, wetting her cheeks and hair. The orange-and-black monarch-butterfly earrings that Manny had brought from Pacific Grove in January to celebrate their three years together shook as she pointed her chin at the sunken cement birdbath halfway down the hill.

The larger raccoon was washing something—a mouse?—its hairless forefeet resembling human hands. Facing it, the other lapped a drink; drops flashed off its pink tongue. The ringed tails and reddish-brown fur seemed encrusted with moon-generated crystals.

"I want you close to me," Joyce whispered.

He left his fiberglass bench and sloshed across the tub, settling his hip against hers and arcing his arm over her narrow shoulders. "Better?"

She nodded, nuzzling his ribs, watching the animals waddle into the shadow under a clump of rabbitbrush.

"Mucho strangeness, bud. Just think—tonight this beautiful moon will be highlighting bombs that blast Iraqi mothers and children. And here I am agreeing again to marry you, have your baby, sell this place, work with you and Allie for a man I've called a fool. It's all so strange."

Emptying his lungs, watching the fart bubbles break the water's surface, Manny shut his eyes, relishing the heat that softened his flesh. "If we go ahead with May plans, I guess we won't be celebrating among Baby's sheep and lilacs. We could say 'I do' on Dirk's beds of chard. Alexis and Stu dating? So much for my jealousy. I still need to apologize to him."

Lowering his right arm to cup her hip, he tilted his head to kiss the side of her neck. Her stray blonde hairs tickled his lips. "You won't back out? Even if the war crimps our income?"

"Not if you do what you've promised, starting with those peace stickers UPS delivered a few hours ago."

"My doctor says he'll see me about all this gas I'm having the day after I return from the Valley. I'll have him recommend a psychiatrist."

"You're a lot easier to live with when you're in therapy, bud. For starters, you don't flirt with women." Water dribbled from the strands in her armpit as she drew her hand from the water to smooth his damp hair. "I'm glad your cut is scabbing over. And thanks for sawing off the broken plum branch so I can't see it. What about those stickers, Manny?"

"Okay if I plaster a couple first on Ron's front door?"

"Knock it off."

"I'll dump them tomorrow into one of the oil drums ringing the ballpark." He bit the corner of his lip. "You want to try to make a baby tonight?"

She stiffened, then relaxed against him. "I took my temperature again after you proposed at breakfast."

"Again?"

"I take it every month, hoping things will change between us. Tonight's a good time."

She straightened, twisting her shoulders. But when he brought his chin down to meet her lips, a gasket in the expansion tank that Stu had forgotten to replace burst. A harsh grinding commenced under the redwood decking. Manny leaped out and, dripping, knelt to unhook the cover of the electrical box screwed to the stucco. He thumbed the safety switch down and the gnashing stopped. Shaking, he grabbed his red plaid robe from its hook and sashed himself into it. "Maybe I should warn Alexis not to ask Stu to work on Chuck's cold-water pipe, you think?"

"You don't call Allie, I do." Joyce scrambled from the tub and wrapped her brown terrycloth around her, shuffling into leather thongs.

Rolling the foam cover off the railing Stu had rebuilt on Monday, Manny capped the tub's steam. "No rubber for me, no spearmint for you— we're starting our family tonight, Boodie."

"We're going to try."

He patted the rough cotton covering her buttocks as she moved through the converted guest room off the deck. His iMac G4 and the HP printer they shared sat at right angles to the leather-rimmed table that had been his father's, littered with engineering reports and stacked wire baskets. Above Joyce's own G4 on the room's other side hung a black-and-white photo of the poet, Elizabeth Bishop. Across her down-turned lips Joyce had taped the green-wired stem of a silk poppy.

"Massage first?" Manny asked, stopping barefoot on the carpet in the gloom of their bedroom and squeezing his testicles. The climb had left him breathless. A full erection rose through the opening in his robe.

"No massage; you'll need to make me wet, though."

"A pleasure." Padding across the carpet to the TV, he snapped on one of two night-lights, then remembered the moon. From the sliding glass door nearest the bed's head he pushed back the drapes and returned to flick off the night-light. From the lowest shelf, under Joyce's books on nutrition, he plucked a CD, *Music for Zen Meditation*.

She lay on her back in the moonlight, smelling of apricot-scented lotion. The sounds of a koto and a clarinet filled the room. The half-dozen, pink hothouse roses that Manny had presented to her this morning sat in a ceramic milk jar on her bedside table. Kneeling on the mattress, Manny peeled the electric blanket and sheet past her calves, stared at the golden hairs covering her vulva, and—gripping one wrist behind him—bent to kiss her.

Fingers spread on each side of her pelvis, he lowered his face toward her sweetness. He circled his tongue around her inner warmth, relishing the hint of salt until she whispered, lifting her hips and letting them fall,

"Okay, bud."

Her fingers slid up his shaft. "Manny? My gynecologist says I'm most likely to conceive if you take me from behind."

"Better let go of me or I'll come," he gasped. Using his fists, easing backward until he felt his shins slide free of the blanket, he stood.

Rolling to her side, she rose to her knees and scooted back to meet him. "Fuck me well, Manny Barnes." Raising her buttocks, she dropped her head between her forearms, butterfly earrings trembling.

Moistening the tip of his penis with spit, he bent his knees and guided his erection into her, sighing as it disappeared. "I can't hold, Boodie; we'll do it slower tomorrow night and the next, too, okay?"

He cocked his buttocks to unsheathe most of his shaft, then plunged it in, withdrew and pushed again; each time, she moaned and her torso quaked. From his groin the ache spread into his belly. "Ahhhh," he murmured, and by the fifth thrust he was spurting semen. He fell forward and wrapped her breasts in his arms.

Between midnight and one o'clock, clouds dampened the draught-parched hills with a misty rain.

Five hours later, the city's two dailies announced America's invasion. All over town, hands flung papers from the windows of trucks and battered sedans. Rolled in polyethelene, they thudded onto driveways. *US Strikes Baghdad*, proclaimed *The New Mexican*. *We Will Accept No Outcome But Victory*, boasted the more conservative *Courier*.

In the twilight, Manny awoke to scrabbling. In the nightgown she'd donned, Joyce lay curled up facing him, softly snoring. He realized that the two picture hooks above their bed still hung bare of her antiwar poems.

His mouth tasted as if he'd been gargling buttermilk spiked with vinegar. Forget Stu and his steel-wool barrier against varmints—the scratch, scratch between the batts of insulation in the drywalled ceiling sounded as if the pack rat or squirrel or raccoon was piling up gravel. He pursed his lips and swallowed.

Anxiety knit his chest as pain beat at his eyeballs. Had he truly again asked Joyce to marry him? He heard his ulcerous father phoning from Los Angeles before slitting his wrists under the shower, praising Manny's smarts for remaining a bachelor five years after his mother and her analyst—become her lover—had fled to Port Townsend.

Last night, had he not used a rubber? Had the country launched Shock and Awe against Iraq while he and Joyce slept? Was he truly heading for Silicon Valley on Sunday with two thirds of the reports on his table still unsummarized?

Joyce's soft snores and the beast's scrabbling persuaded him to rise. Stretching, he squeezed into his moccasins, bent to retrieve his robe from the rug, and moved across to the window overlooking Plaza Hill's rutted main road.

Through the glass he heard an engine straining up the incline. A Jeep Wrangler, headlights blazing, one hubcap gone, chugged into view. From the ceiling-lit back seat a woman, gray hair braided tight around her forehead, hurled a *Courier* toward the Kirkpatricks' drive. The Jeep disappeared past the piñon-strewn embankment, tailpipe spewing white.

Reaching to ease shut the bedroom door, Manny clambered downstairs, gripping the redwood-stained banister as blood pounded his temples. Before he unlocked the front door, he let gas into his robe. His thigh muscles seemed like jelly.

Past the clematis webbing the porch's trellis, he opened the gate under the adobe archway, sashed his robe tighter, and hurried over the drizzle-dampened stones, his moccasins' leather soles sounding like waves abandoning a beach. The chill air still stank of the Jeep's exhaust. A yellow light snapped on in Mrs. Miller's town house across the road. Rounding the embankment, he stooped to steal the Kirkpatricks' paper, and spun to hurry back.

He clenched his jaw, seeing once more Joyce's and his garage doors scrawled in capital letters a foot and a half high, *Peace Wimp #1* and *Peace Wimp #2*. Black paint dribbled down the wood-grained rolled steel.

Closing the front door, he stretched out his tongue to protest its sour taste, strode to the refrigerator, and drank a tumbler of grapefruit juice. He unwrapped the newspaper on the dinette table, flicked on the acrylic light panel overhead, and sank to the cushion.

"'Americans are scum,' Iraqi boy shouts at Al-Jazeera reporter as his mother behind him screams, 'Where is their humanity?'

"Iraqis claim cruise missile wipes out hospital by mistake," Manny read further on.

"Today at 5:34 Iraqi time, in the haze of a Baghdad dawn, lethal lights descended on a city of four million, 8,000 miles from Santa Fe. President Bush authorized the unexpectedly early attack to destroy Saddam, his two sons, and an unknown number of ministers whom the CIA reports were hiding in a bunker at Dora Farms under one of the ruler's forty-eight palaces.

"Within two days, 3,000 smart bombs and 800 Tomahawk missiles are expected to soften Republican Guard resistance. Three hundred thousand coalition forces, including 40,000 Brits, 2,000 Australians, and 200 Poles, await striking orders."

Manny swallowed. His chin hit his sunken chest. Below Baca Field a siren started up—police? paramedics? firefighters?—as the electronic bell in the cathedral near the Plaza tolled six a.m. In the rocking chair lay a hundred brand-new peace stickers. Had he truly promised Joyce to toss all $125 worth into an oil drum?

"DROWNING WITH SHAME; SOPPING," LILA BREATHED INTO the receiver.

First she had pulled down all the living room's shades. Now, one eyelid twitching, she slouched in Ron's corduroy armchair imprinted with cowboy hats staring at his Indian chief, who, in the mid-morning dusk, seemed a corpse propped against the plaster fronting Ron's office. Her yellow housecoat hung in folds at each hip.

"I want to apologize to you and she for how I acted yesterday. I will of course pay for repainting the door of her automobile. And I want Morgan Realty to handle this town house again—Mr. Kirkpatrick and I will be returning soon to Fort Worth, our hearts' true desire. Do you have her schedule? When can I come in?"

"Let's see," chirped Jennifer on the other end of the line. "She's just on her way for an eleven o'clock at Ruckbee's—we may already have a buyer for the home of the elderly gentleman who walked you out yesterday. She and Mr. Valdez will be with Mr. Valdez's mother for a while and then she's lunching with the elderly gentleman at one. How about three o'clock?"

Squinting at the broken yellow feather in the wooden chief's war bonnet, Lila flapped the rope sole of one slipper. "That's Ruckbee's Real Estate at Grant and Paseo?"

"I think it's the only Ruckbee's in town."

"Good enough. Three, then."

"You don't mean there, you mean here, right?" Jennifer asked.

"I'm capable of understanding perfectly. Morgan Realty. Three o'clock. Thank you."

She pushed the Talk button off.

Did I do Your will to let Big Shit drive the Mustang to work, so the headlight Nympho Bimbo smashed won't embarrass him with the banker person he's buying lunch for, Lord? I believe I did so.

Blood flooded her forehead and neck. She swiped a gray hair off the twitching eyelid, elbowed herself upright, and—gripping the sweat-slick, ivory-hued receiver—minced her way toward its cradle in the kitchen.

She yanked a pair of toothed, red-handled shears from a drawer and, re-crossing the living room, flung them into the guest bathroom. As she dashed upstairs, their clank on the tiled counter ricocheted in her mind.

Tuesday afternoon, driven home drunk by the Nympho Bimbo, once again Ron had derailed her attempt at adultery, catching Victor with his shirt out and her with her panda downstairs. At least Victor earlier had managed to chisel free most of the tiles — the mastic's stink of butterscotch pudding assaulted her as she ducked under the *No Admittance* safety tape stretched across the master bath's doorway.

Snapping on the halogen ceiling light, she sidestepped into the walk-in closet. Though this was Thursday, there was still a scent of the lupine-meadow spray with which she freshened her clothes Sunday mornings. She marched to the closet's rear.

From a quilted hanger hung a black-velvet jacket brocaded with pink and fuchsia blossoms and cuffs the same hues; a short-sleeved fuchsia velveteen pullover; and a black-velvet skirt brocaded with pink and azure diamonds. Around the hanger's hook drooped a silver-concha belt and three strings of turquoise stones. Ron, who kept most of his clothes in the guest closet downstairs, had bought her the outfit two years ago to celebrate their thirtieth anniversary. She pinched up a pair of black flats from the blue carpet.

The sound of the furnace clicking off rose from the grate nestled between two remaining tiles as, bearing her load across the subfloor's swirls of rancid mastic, Lila breasted the safety tape. The end of the tape that her upper arm ripped off the jamb fluttered to the floor behind her.

Bikini and bra added to the heap in her arms, she dumped everything into the guest bathroom's tub and, plopping the necklaces on top, flicked into brilliance four bulbs that beetled above the mirror. Jackrabbits of sky blue and Russian-olive green — ears twice as long as nature intended — scampered around the mirror's barnwood frame, a present to herself three months ago when she first suspected Ron of balling Nympho Bimbo and, in retaliation, determined to find someone besides him to ball her.

But there seemed no one left to spray on perfume for. Leaving the red-willow wastebasket out of reach beside the toilet, she grabbed the scissors, clutched some of the hair covering her left shoulder, and snipped, released, and snipped again until the saw-toothed blades had severed it to within an inch of her scalp. She flung the strands across the counter's ice-blue tiles.

Dark beneath from lack of sleep, her eyes moistened as she clinched another sheaf. Recalling Helen Ridley confiding her own anguish after Chuck had persuaded her to get her tubes tied—and Helen's subsequent resolve to spike her own hair—Lila cut free a second handful and flung it aside.

"No longer a trophy wife," she told her reflection, gold gleaming in the two molars she'd cracked following Jonathan's death. "No longer Lila Kirkpatrick, no longer Lila Hollis wearing the pinafore Daddy bought, that Big Shit reached into to squeeze my seventh-grade tits. I'm a guest in a home I hate; unwelcome.

"This bunch I whack off for Jonathan, this one for whoever I am, this for Mama tootling her oboe, this for the ripped-open bellies of those children on TV, this for the severed foot of that boy wearing the basketball shoe. Daddy, are you sad for us?"

Smearing her tears with her wrist, she goggled at the gray eyes staring back beneath the clumps of hair. She gazed at the basin and counter strewn with hair and snatched strands off her housecoat where it covered her breasts. She let them float to the floor.

The slate clock beside the mirror read eleven.

"You better move it," she scowled to her double. She hauled a zippered, scarlet-beaded bag marked *Estée Lauder* from a low drawer. It lay beside Ron's electric razor, which she'd brought here after the tiles upstairs started springing free and the bathroom became unusable.

Out of a tube labeled So Ingenious she squeezed foundation to massage into her nose, chin, forehead, and over the capillaries webbing her cheeks. She covered it with Pink Cloud blush and sponged on powder. She applied Midnight Plum liner; she penciled her eyebrows black. Moondance lightened, then darkened her lids.

Pinching away clots of Maximum Lash, she outlined her lips in vermilion, glossing the rest with Mambo Madness. Tubes, sponges, compacts, pencils, and brushes she left nesting in the tangles of hair that swirled across the sink tiles.

Kicking off her slippers, she shrugged out of her housecoat and let it rumple around her ankles. She bent for her black bikini and black lace bra.

Though her tummy hurt, in five minutes she looked resplendent from the eyebrows down. Turquoise stones looped across the fuchsia sweater. Her woven concha belt's square buckle gleamed. Through the slit in the top of a blue-and-orange pottery box she yanked a tissue to dry her eyes.

Scuttling stockingless to the hall closet, she changed the last line of a song her mother had crooned forty years ago to keep the twelve-year-old stuck to the piano bench:

> Papa Haydn's dead and gone
> though his memory lingers on.
> When his mood was one of bliss,
> he wore joyful clothes like this.

Wrapped in her padded, knee-length coat, her black handbag with the silver catch slung over a shoulder, she hurried toward the laundry room and, in the garage beyond, the white Escalade. Escalade rhymes with Kool-Aid, she recalled Ron joking.

While Maxine and Victor dealt with the agent inside Ruckbee's two-story adobe, the wind thrashed the stand of aspen outside, flinging catkins onto designer boulders and the front walkway's bricks. But by the time she'd jammed her orange-billed *Range Rover* cap over her black curls and was leading the limping Victor out the back door and down the ramp toward her SUV, the wind had disappeared. The curved brown pods on the New Mexican locusts that lined the back edge of Ruckbee's parking lot hung motionless.

"So Ronald's crazy wife wants to apologize at three? I wonder if I should have agreed to that."

"Why not, amiga? Jennifer told you she wants to put their place up for sale."

"She's hallucinating. Spring starts tomorrow? It's too goddamned cold for spring."

Ring finger stiff and aching in its aluminum splint, she wrapped buckskin-clad arms around the top of the navy pantsuit she'd worn to Dirk's. Her knee-high black boots clicked across the gravel. "How's that wrist I wrapped?"

"Throbbing. You better believe I'm seeing no doctor. You recall when I broke my nose? All that probing kept me sneezing for a year."

Maxine stopped and took his elbow. "You need a new jacket, amigo. This sleeve's in shreds."

From the quivering tips of his mustache she raised her violet-smeared eyes to his olive ones. "My sister called this morning. Slipped again—she's in rehab north of Vegas. Started weeping on the phone; same old thing. Wants to know if the Sandinistas are still holding your brother hostage."

Victor yanked the bill of his *Proud To Be American* cap over the flaring black hairs of his brows. "Tell Kate that he's dead, she's been a widow for seventeen years. Keep telling her that—my brother's not coming back. She has his dog tags. She's got the photos showing him dangling from an I-beam of that warehouse in Managua. We have all seen the machete shoved through his gut. She must not continue to believe that Armando survived."

Maxine released the beat-up leather covering his elbow. "I'm glad the Ruckbee's agent agreed to let you make Dirk's place ready for her buyer, assuming Ronald can qualify him and your wrist heals soon."

"Three or four more nights soaking in hot water should do it."

"It'll mean another check to send Kate."

"Two checks if the Kirkpatricks sell."

"That's her pipe dream," Maxine said. "In any case, Ronald can be trouble."

"More than his wife? I think not, amiga."

"A lot more if Giordy wises up to him and me. He'll be over a little after eight. At least I know you won't talk."

We'll see, Victor thought, lifting his brows at his Anglo boss. "And cut my income stream?" he laughed aloud. "I wonder how much I'll need to lose from your husband tonight. It's the third Thursday of the month? Five-card stud—Mom and I are hosting."

"Let's go see how she is."

"And make it fast. I forgot to pee."

A gust rustled the junipers that separated the parking lot from Grant Avenue. Victor fingered a box of unfiltered Camels from his jacket as they approached the Range Rover. Across its door, under the bobcat decal, Maxine had masked Lila's key-scratched *Slut* with strips of electrical tape.

Inside, as she turned the ignition on, Victor said, "Let's make us a deal. I buy a new jacket when you stop wearing that smell of old paint cans. Gives me asthma, mi amiga."

"Balanchy's latest, amigo."

Frowning, Victor tore a match from the book he'd grabbed from the Great Books Cookhouse on Tuesday, scratched it into flame, and lit up.

Sunk in the perforated Shale leather of the front seat, Lila clutched the steering wheel's arc of Zabrano hardwood. As heat whispered from four overhead grilles, she listened to war news, windows shut against the sporadic wind.

Lila had parked half a block north of Ruckbee's, beside a law office's pink-stuccoed building. The Escalade's 345-horsepower V8 engine rumbled like a truck's. Her eyes locked on the realty office's *Exit Only*, lettered against blue on the shoulder-high adobe wall fronting Paseo de Peralta. Every few seconds she removed a veined hand to scratch among the black-and-white tufts on her scalp.

From nine speakers—on the dash, on each door, and on the doors behind her—rushed New York commentator Bruce Barrett's words:

"Some learned about the bombing under the stuttering lights of Times Square; many learned the news from their televisions at home or in bars. Some faced it with tears, others with contempt.

"Last night at nine-thirty Eastern Standard Time, cruise missiles from the Red Sea and Persian Gulf joined Stealth fighters to eliminate Saddam, Uday, and Qusay early, hoping to end the war by surprise. Unsuccessfully, officials believe now."

That's because you and your counselors, Bushie, didn't hear the Lord right. Lila stabbed a black button to turn the radio off. You fucked up. But I'm not going to fuck up, am I, Lord? She rattled the strands of turquoise hiding the wrinkles in her neck.

Through the tinted windshield, past the jittery branches of Chinese elms on either side of Paseo, she spied the wraparound brush bar protecting the grille of a Range Rover that halted at the parking lot's exit.

Her heart knotted. She appraised her makeup in the rearview mirror. Maximum Lash had begun to run from the outer corner of her left eye but no time now to tissue it away. Jerking the leather-wrapped gearshift on the steering column from Park to Drive, she inched forward.

Neither the nearer elms nor the thorned black locust towering from the law building's dead grass blocked her view. Look at those curls sprouting from the driver's orange cap, and thank you, Lord, for placing that piss-all-the-time, pee-tee-es-dee, walking-hard-on wannabe Victor Valdez beside her.

Two warmongers with one stone, Lila exulted, feeling perspiration cool the steering wheel's leather and spring hot between her thighs. She hauled the seat harness across her fuchsia pullover and clicked its buckle into its slot.

Her upper arms tensed. She looked left to the signal at Old Taos Highway turning yellow and murmured again, "Thank you, Lord." Under an archipelago of dark-bellied clouds a white bus whose side read *All Aboard America/New Mexico Park & Ride* clattered past, spewing smoke from twin pipes. Pickups, a mail truck, a green garbage truck, a gray hearse with the Stars and Stripes flapping from its antenna, a yellow Beetle, and an Isizu Trooper SUV whooshed by, leaving the north lane of Paseo de Peralta empty.

Maxine's Range Rover eased right into traffic to head east, where Victor and his mother lived in a rundown adobe on hillside land the family had owned for 300 years. Culture epicures from Texas, New York, Florida, and California surrounded them in faux-adobe mansions.

As Lila jammed the pedal to the carpet, thrilling to the big engine's thrum, a battered purple pickup stopped near the Montoya Federal Building, which harbored the main post office, half a block from where Maxine was accelerating. The truck blocked her from any sight of Lila. In the back of the truck paced a German shepherd.

The dog bumped the tailgate to bark at a pair of golden-brown Lhasa apsos leading a woman north along Grant's concrete sidewalk. The woman wore a black fur cap and an ankle-length, turquoise-buckled coat whose hem flapped behind her.

The Lhasa started yapping at an old man dressed in shreds—a scrap of gunnysack wrapped his ears—who wobbled toward them south off Paseo. He pedaled a bicycle humped with a box atop a sleeping bag strapped to the rusty rear rack. Tied to its handlebars by a rope, a black-and-white mongrel with black floppy ears padded beside him. It began to bark back.

A block behind Maxine another signal had turned red, and now no traffic roared in either direction along potholed Paseo de Peralta, as Lila and Maxine sped at right angles toward each other.

Fifty yards in front of the Range Rover, the purple pickup started up from the stop sign to swerve left. But the German shepherd, riled by the barks of the three other dogs, leaped from the truck's bed to join the fracas.

The driver of the pickup managed to swing clear of Maxine, who still had not noticed Lila. Rather than strike the galloping shepherd, Maxine wrenched the Range Rover around the corner, heading south past Grant Street's weed-fringed apartments instead of continuing east.

Bouncing toward her target at thirty-five miles an hour, Lila had jerked her gaze right to scream at the purple truck's retreating bumper. The knob on the trailer hitch seemed to rise like Victor's erection. *Kick Saddam's Ass* read the bumper sticker.

As she piloted the Escalade through the stop sign, Lila trained her gaze forward again, gasping to see Maxine swerve out of reach. Instead, from where she had meant to demolish the Range Rover, the shepherd leaped toward the snarling tangle of Llasa apsos, mongrel, man, and bicycle that had fallen to the sidewalk. Under a nearby cottonwood, the woman in the black, ankle-length coat flailed her arms.

To Lila, it seemed that Big Shit had hacked through her thorax and was twisting her lungs with pliers. "Unh," she wheezed, wresting the Escalade left, not to strew pieces of shepherd across the asphalt.

She clenched her eyes and jammed her black flat onto the brake pedal. Like a speared hippo, the SUV hurtled past the safety triangle bristling with privet, jumped the curb, snapped off a fluted lamp pole, sent an iron bench flying, and slammed into a waist-high planter girded in concrete.

Lila jerked forward as her seat harness snapped tight, vising her brocaded tummy and right breast. Her foot drove the accelerator to the carpet, urging the injured engine to rip from its mounts and grind through the planter. To a stink of burnt matches and a cloud of talcum, the air bags blasted like pistols and burst free from above the glove compartment and the steering wheel's hub at 200 miles an hour. The left-hand bag whopped Lila's ingrown nipple as if Ron had roundhoused it with the heel of his hand. Her lips smudged orange gloss onto the air bag's gray nylon before it and its twin deflated—after the glass on the passenger side had been smashed into a mass of stars.

Hearing the crash and seeing the Escalade's accordioned front end, the woman in black ran toward the post office, her two Tibetan dogs chasing behind, their leash ends whipping. The homeless man stood thrusting his bicycle at the German shepherd's snout while the flop-eared mongrel cowered on the concrete between the cardboard box and sleeping bag.

"Hunh, hunh, hunh," Lila grunted, forcing breath past the seat harness's grip. She stopped trying to claw the lap belt from her spasming tummy— though she managed to drag her shoe sideways off the accelerator, ending the engine's desperation and stopping the spinning tires from burning themselves up. She opened one eye, then dared to open the other, and started to blink.

Through her saltwater scrim she discerned a goateed, hatted figure on horseback. His plaque read *The Founding of Santa Fe/Don Pedro de Peralta*. Beside him she glimpsed his full-bearded companion, bronze walking stick jammed among the planter's clumps of buffalo grass. Don Pedro's horse gazed down through Lila's windshield as the conquistador himself stretched an arm over the Escalade's puckered hood, mouth wide in seeming amazement. Gusts whipped the limbs of ponderosa, locust, and cottonwoods scattered across the lawn that separated Lila and Don Pedro from the Federal Building.

Both signals had turned green again, and traffic rushed east and west along the Paseo. Sirens wailed from the ambulance and fire engine charging down Old Taos Highway toward the stricken SUV. "Jonathan, your mother's coming," Lila whispered. "I don't think there's much left to do—oh, Mama, help Helen with the music festival, will you?"

She did not say this at once. She had to stop to force air into her lungs.

"JUST HAVE A SEAT. AN AIDE WILL COME OUT FOR YOU."

An hour after Lila's smashup, Ron replaced the receiver of the wall phone in St. Vincent Hospital's emergency waiting room. On the other side of the bulletproof glass, the registration nurse began picking something from the corner of her eye with the nail of her little finger.

Stuffing into his jacket the get-well card he'd bought Lila in the gift shop, Ron took up a white spray can lettered *Antimicrobial Foam Hand Rinse* and thumbed the button. He rubbed the spume into his hand; a gob caught between his flesh and the white gold of his wedding ring.

Ron bunched his face at the odor of spoiled beef that permeated the room. Under the window, patched with a square of knotty plywood, a man in rags threw back his head and sneezed. Next to him, an Hispanic teenaged girl leaned against the shoulder of an older, bucktoothed woman. Through an unbroken pane, Ron glimpsed an aide in lime-colored scrubs tossing sunflower seeds toward a flock of pigeons, then lumbered toward a wiry Native American who sat gazing at the TV blaring above the drinking fountain beside the registration nurse's bay.

A silver barrette inlaid with lapis lazuli crimped the man's black hair against his neck. Incised lightning bolts garnished a silver bracelet circling each wrist. His face was pocked—acne? Smallpox? Held by adhesive tape wrapped at an angle around his forehead, a bloody patch of gauze covered one ear.

Ron lowered himself to the padded chair farthest from the man's dressing and pressed his palms to the knees of his corduroys. He clacked his boots a couple of times on the checkerboard of red and green vinyl tiles and looked up at the TV.

The newscaster's hair swooped like a theater curtain over an eye as she declared:

"Punishing sandstorms rake the war zone along a sixty-mile front. Though troops seized a port and strategic oil fields near Basra, the mass surrenders that followed the Iraqi military collapse in Kuwait in nineteen ninety-one have not yet occurred.

" 'This is a sad day for the United Nations,'" asserted Secretary-General

Kofi Annan. "Millions of people around the world are deeply alarmed. But many US commanders expect that the capture of Basra will generate images of Iraqis welcoming us, boosting support for the war here and across the globe."

"You bet your ass!" Ron cried, thrusting his right fist skyward. He winced and lowered the thumb to suck its cracked end. As he did, he lifted a hip to haul out the gold pocket watch that Los Alamos Mortgage had presented him last year. He flipped its cover open and glanced at the man beside him. "You a vet?"

The man squinted at him, then resumed staring at the screen.

"What's with the ear?" Ron began to fiddle with the *Onward Christian Soldiers* badge pinned to his jacket.

The man shifted on his cushion. "Guy jabbed a pen into it two years ago. It bleeds sometimes."

"Judas Christ!"

"Jabbed a pen into it and then he sliced it off."

Ron jerked his eyes toward the teenager, who was now vomiting into the bucktoothed woman's lap. One of the woman's hands reached to clasp the girl's head as the other pulled tissues from a white cardboard box sitting on the drum-like table.

"You puttin' me on?" Ron looked back at the Native American. "What pueblo?"

"No pueblo, man. Jalalabad." He smoothed the right side of his hair.

"Juh-what-a-bad?"

"UNESCO sent me there to share silversmithing know-how with the Afghans before Bush bombed Kabul after nine-eleven. Four Taliban hustled me by jeep into Tora Bora cave country near the Pakistan border. I persuaded my attacker that him and me were brown-skinned brothers. When he untied me, I kicked him cold and cut off his balls. Strung them around his neck on a goat tendon."

All this he delivered in monotone.

Pain seized Ron's heart as he stared at the cratered face. "How'd you get away?"

The steel door to the emergency room squeaked open. Shaved to the scalp, an aide in aqua scrubs called, "Mr. Naranjo?"

Naranjo rose and looked down at Ron. "Hot-wired the jeep. The other three guys were drunk on arrack."

Gawking, Ron pocketed his watch. Before driving to Maxine's tonight for the hammock treat she'd promised—no, Lile, you're not going to take that from me—he had to arrange a loan for the buyer of Dirk's place that Max said the Ruckbee's agent had found. Damn you, Lila, I can't believe what the cops told me on the phone. How much is this going to cost us?

"Mr. Kirkpatrick?"

Ron leaped up and followed the scalped aide's cigarette smell. The aide shoved his coded acrylic badge into the slot and pushed the door open.

Nurses and more aides stood in a central nursing station shaped like a corral, making and taking phone calls, typing diagnoses into processors, dispensing gauze and drugs to doctors in scrubs or white lab coats, who strode into and out of the surrounding bays. Moans and curses blew through the bays' white-cotton curtains. Aides pushed gurneys and wheelchairs along two perimeter aisles. A tousle-haired man in a green-and-black robe, parked in a wheelchair near a fire extinguisher, kept lifting his head like a coyote baying, but no sound came from his mouth.

Ron started at the stink of rubbing alcohol that cut the room's odor of blood.

"In the rear, where the guard's sitting, Room nineteen," the scalped aide said, veering into a different bay and drawing the curtain shut behind him.

"I'm the husband," Ron barked at the muttonchopped guard in cobalt jacket and pants. A pager hung clipped to his shirt pocket.

Without replying, the guard fitted a key into the door and pulled. Ron noticed the canister of pepper spray and the telescoped, black baton dangling from his belt.

Lila sat on the edge of the bed in an off-white gown tied at the back. Forest-green socks soled with rubber grips hugged her feet. He gasped at the purple that mottled the left side of her neck, the black-and-white tufts that had replaced her shoulder-length hair. As if her cheeks were maps, capillaries swirled between clots of powder; mascara dribbled from the corner of one gray eye. Straight-arming the mattress's edge, she stared at the doorway, jaw drooping. A second guard sat in the corner, chewing gum.

Room 19 held five people, including Ron. A woman in a lab coat, beige slacks, blue tennis shoes, and cropped blonde hair tapering toward her neck turned to him. She removed black-framed glasses as the muttonchopped guard rose and left, locking the rest of them in.

"I'm Dr. Harris."

"Ronald Kirkpatrick."

She shook his hand; hers was cold. "Apparently your wife suffered no internal injuries, but we're placing her in the Adult Psychiatric Unit for observation—she kept banging her head against that wall until we gave her a shot. A crisis counselor will be here shortly."

"Hello, Big Shit." Lila's voice had become as husky as Maxine's.

"This is for you, babe." Out of his jacket's side pocket Ron wiggled the envelope on which he'd scrawled *To My Sweetheart*. She took it, but soon it fluttered to the floor of speckled beige.

"Mr. Kirkpatrick, will you come with me? We'll be back in a moment, Mrs. Kirkpatrick. Watch her," she instructed the gum-chewing guard. She took a key from her pocket.

Lila gazed at them.

"That's my wife? What the hell's wrong with her?" Swiping his forehead with the heel of his hand, Ron leaned against the outside wall, next to the guard who'd left the room.

"They'll find out in the Adult Unit. She told me she tried to kill someone; is Nympho Bimbo a nickname you know? She said she cut her hair to stop the slaughter—what slaughter she wouldn't say—and to reunite with her mother and son. Does any of this ring any bells?"

"She's been talking crazy for a couple of days."

"The crisis counselor may want to ask you more questions later."

"So I should show up when again?"

"Visiting hours in the unit are six to seven. Call Behavioral Health Services around three—you'll need a four-digit pass code. Let's go get her clothes."

I like those ankles, Ron thought, following her. She locked the door behind him.

Lila's words streamed out in an undertone. "I'm going to teach Jonathan to play the oboe as soon as I can get rid of more of this." She closed a tuft of hair in her fist. "Will you bring my shears and tools?"

"Tools, Lile?"

Grinning, her two gold fillings gleaming, she smoothed her palm down the breast with the ingrown nipple, across her lap, and along her inner thigh, pressing the gown against her flesh. "You know."

"Oh, those," said Ron, flushing. "But you said they don't work anymore."

"They'll work here. The Lord wants me here. Here I'm not a visitor."

Frowning at Dr. Harris, Ron hunched his shoulders.

A click sounded; the door pushed open. Unprotected by scrubs or lab coat, a tiny woman in a red sweater, around which embroidered mice chased each other's tails, pushed a wheelchair. A T-shaped, chrome-plated hanger rose behind it. Her brown hair was French-rolled to the left side of her head.

Nice butt, too, Ron thought as Dr. Harris bent for Lila's thirtieth-wedding-anniversary outfit, her strands of turquoise, and her black flats, which lay jumbled on the seat of the second chair. She handed the pile to Ron, saying, "This is Felicity, one of our crisis counselors."

"I want those, Ronald."

Dr. Harris and Felicity moved toward Lila as Ron, clutching her bundle to his chest, stooped to pick the envelope off the floor.

"My makeup." Her bare, outstretched arms fell against her gown; the other two women helped her stand and into the wheelchair. "Meeting Mama, Jonathan."

"We'll take good care of her," Dr. Harris said.

"Where's the car she cracked up?" He raised his hand to nurse the split end of his thumb.

"You'll need to check with the police. The ER registration nurse can give you the phone number. We'll need you to fill out a form first—your wife's health insurance, age, social security, other basics. She wasn't able to help. Felicity will take the data. I'm sorry, I need to go."

The muttonchopped guard wheeled Lila out of the bay and toward the perimeter aisle, the gum-chewing guard strolling alongside. The heavy heels of her shoes smacking the floor, Felicity said, "You and I go this way, Mr. Kirkpatrick."

"How long will it be?"

"Not long."

He hauled his watch from his corduroys.

AT FIRST, BOTH HAD KEPT THEIR TEMPERS. BUT WHEN MANNY shouted that he planned to let air from the rear tire of every parked vehicle he saw sporting a neocon sticker, Joyce yelled, "Alpha male! You don't care about us. I may be pregnant. Fix your own dinner, and slam the door to the garage when you leave."

Her father's laminated-wood clock read 7:30 when she heard the door smash closed, shaking the floor above it. She sat on the bed, propped by a pillow. The wooden tray bridging her thighs held an empty cup of chamomile tea and scraps from two tofu enchiladas.

Lifting the tray, she folded its legs and pushed it past her feet. In a blue sweatshirt that covered her nightgown, she swung out from the electric blanket and bent to tug mukluks over her brown socks.

As she stood, the doorbell rang. Had he forgotten his stickers? Why not come back through the garage? Leaving the stand lamp blazing beside the tattered armchair, she wrapped herself in her brown terry-cloth robe and ran to the window. A UPS panel truck was grinding back over the gravel, its headlights yellowing the canes of a blossomless rose that traced the entrance gate's archway.

Had the driver delivered the green-tea lotion and lipoic acid she'd ordered last week from Bronson's? To keep her skin supple for whomever she planned to father her next child? she sneered. Would she shave her armpits and calves smooth for him?

She kicked the straw wastebasket holding Manny's bouquet of roses, which she'd snapped in two. "Why are you doing this? Why did you lie to me last night?" she cried out.

Maybe I'm barren, she thought, shoving a wisp of hair off her forehead with her palm. She grabbed the cup and plate, the wadded napkin and silverware, and, flicking on the light above the stairs, padded down.

She set the kitchen's ceiling fluorescents glowing. Tears misted her eyes as she breathed the scent of split-pea soup from the can Manny had left on the sink. Had he persuaded Stu or Allie or Dirk—or all three, think big—to help him tonight? How much bail would she need to post when the police called? His name must already be on record following the peace march Sunday.

Snatching the soup can, she placed it on one of the floor tiles, cocked her right leg, and kicked it past the dining table. It clanked against the black face of Manny's CD player, spattering green and orange clots across it.

Ron Kirkpatrick got my side of the garage right, she thought. Wimp is what I am, waffling with a jerk I say I love, whose stomach gurgles and who probably knocked me up. It's over, bud.

She padded to the front door and unlocked it. Wind rattled the clematis leaves as she grabbed the brown package labeled *Bronson's Labs* off the bench.

Striding into her and Manny's office, she clicked on the ceiling light and her gooseneck lamp. Warm air whispered through the grate under her desk. Outside, past the hot tub and the railing Stu had repaired, gusts flapped the tips of junipers, turning into strobes the lights of the Coyote Apartments down the slope.

She stared at the poem Manny had found in the arroyo and taped above his computer:

> *Dubya, why don't yuh*
> *scoot back tuh Texas, yuh*
> *got the beginner's curse. Crawl on*
> *home tuh Crawford, yuh*
> *cost more than yuh're worth*

At lunch they'd watched a replay of Bush's 9:30 pm announcement that he'd launched strikes against Baghdad—which had aired about the time she'd urged Manny to go into her from behind, she remembered. She winced. They'd watched Bush shake his fist and smirk, "Feel good." Seconds later, Manny had pushed out of his chair to make his own announcement.

"I couldn't toss those bumper stickers, Joyce. I've got to do what I promised myself to do."

She moved to the five-legged chair she'd wound half a foot higher than his. Planting her mukluks on the red cushion beneath her desk, she stabbed the button on her iMac G4. It glowed lime green; the processor whirred, clicked once. Waiting for the screen to turn blue, her eyes swept the silk poppy taped across Elizabeth Bishop's downcast lips.

Joyce's list of files and other icons filled the screen. She aimed the arrow at Mail and tapped her mouse. As Microsoft's Outlook Express blossomed into view, she jumped as the wind shook the window behind her. Christ, Manny, where are you?

At least Elizabeth Bishop kept a woman lover loyal, to wriggle against at night in Brazil. Gentle, as Allie would be. Will you come to Palo Alto with me, Allie, help me raise a baby? But what about your date tomorrow night with Stu?

Her palms grew damp. She wiped them on her nightgown, pointed the cursor to New, swelled her lungs and typed in *JoyHunt@hotmail.com*. She hit the tab key for Subject, typed in *coming home*. She hit Tab again, typed, "Mother, I'd probably weep or start screaming if I phoned. I'm moving back there. May I come live with you? I could help with the gout."

On Washington near the Plaza along the east wall of the Palace of the Governors, Manny eased his Prius hybrid backward to park between a pair of red motor scooters and a Yukon XL SUV. The waving branches of two Chinese elms gleamed in the yellow glow of a high-pressure sodium lamp.

He switched off the ignition, gazing at the crew in orange vests and white polypropylene safety hats gathered around a hole in Palace Avenue. Two of the men held lanterns while three others hoisted out dirt with shovels. Another jiggled on the perforated seat of a backhoe, its engine grumbling.

Always something wrong in Santa Fe and I love it here, Manny brooded. Down the lapels of his sheepskin he fitted cord loops around their pegs, turned up the coat's collar, and tugged black mittens from its pockets. Jamming his knit cap over his ears and yanking the key, he pushed the door handle down. He waited for the red-lettered squad car to roll past and opened the door.

This was the night we'd planned to buy an engagement ring, he agonized. Mostly what's wrong here is me. What do I do well, anyway? Marketing documents and making trouble. Yes, I've stayed true to Joyce, so what? My libido's gone limp.

He slammed the front door, then yanked open the rear one to haul out a black Sierra Club polyester pack from which fanned a hundred bumper stickers. As he hoisted it to his shoulders, he felt the yellow-and-black safety tape rip from the elbow of his coat. He slapped the loose end back on.

He beep-locked the car and waited for a swarthy man in an ankle-length overcoat, briefcase under his arm, to stride past. Then he started toward the Plaza, planning to practice his stealth technique before reaching the three big parking lots on Otero and Nusbaum that he'd scouted this afternoon before delivering marketing suggestions to Bret in Chuck's office a block away.

Gasping, he jerked his head down and to the side and clutched his belly. Acid fountained up, burning his throat. Though the pain that raced across his belly forced him to crouch, it soon subsided.

He stopped to blink away the tears and catch his breath. In the glow of the sodium lamps arching overhead, he thought he saw Lila's yellow Mustang whip around the corner. The car darted to the curb fronting Bonnie's Caring Bouquets. But instead of Lila, Ron jumped out in his straw hat, red polyester fleece jacket, and neon-blue boots.

Manny ran across the cracked asphalt, backpack bouncing, straps biting his collarbone. "Hey!" he shouted, dodging a family heading toward the Hotel Plaza Real—wife hatted in black felt and silver stars, husband chewing a toothpick under a Stetson, boy capped in red knit, the girl wearing a white turban.

Ron wheeled in front of the florist's glass door, which sported a decal of hollyhocks. His turtle eyes widened; furrows carved his forehead.

"Hello, Manny, my man. Who you rendezvousin' with here this time?"

"You're the one defaced our garage doors, right?" The aroma steaming past the edges of vinyl curtains that surrounded two groups of tourists dining outside the Burrito Company Café next door roiled his stomach.

"You're the one deflated my tire, right?"

"Neocon asshole." He leveled his eyes on Ron's. They matched the turquoise in Ron's wedding ring, with which the big man scratched his neck.

"Son of a peccary, screw that head back on. We need to march in tandem. Bush is savin' our butts. Lemme see a smile, friend."

"Scare off." Manny pushed his face closer. "I'm no friend of yours."

"You should be, sucker. But no more chances gettin' your paws on my wife. You'll excuse me, I've a few posies to buy."

Ron had already turned toward the florist's when Manny grabbed the red cuff puckering at his wrist. "I'm not chasing your wife."

"Not any longer you aren't. She's in the hospital. You'll let loose if you don't want that cut on your cheek opened up again."

"Hospital?" Manny dropped his mittened hand.

"Smashed up the new Escalade good. No broken bones but somethin' snapped in her mind. What're those tail feathers stickin' out behind you?"

Manny threw his fist to his lips as pain slashed sideways through his gut and disappeared. "Bumper stickers," he managed. "I'm attending an antiwar get-together."

"Kinda late for that, ain't it?" Ron guffawed. "I've got to race back to St. Victims. You take care, hear?"

Shaking, Manny stared as Ron lunged at the glass door, pushing into a cornucopia of lilac and alstroemeria, hyacincths and jonquils and gladiolas. This was where Manny had bought Joyce the pink roses the day before; now as then, an outpouring of romance acted like fingers grabbing his heart.

His hiking boots crunched the elm leaves strewn along the bricks as he hurried toward the corner, wincing at the thud of the jumping jack with which a polypropylene-helmeted worker compacted earth. Exhaust from the lowriders cruising north off Old Santa Fe Trail made him cough.

His shadow lengthened as he strode from under the mercury-vapor lamp that whitened the Frank Howell Gallery's bronze warrior. Beside Sena Plaza shops fronting Palace, a man in basketball shoes was throwing his shoulder against the rear end of a Grand Cherokee. Its red lights glowered; a woman in scarlet muffler and matching knit cap sat hunched inside, steering.

Across the street, along Cathedral Park's iron-picket railing, waited the practice target Manny sought—a silver Lincoln Town Car with a Sunshine State plate, illegally parked. Along the bumper stretched a neocon slogan in red, white, and blue.

Three men huddled in blankets on the park's dead grass twenty yards away, their backs against the cathedral's sandstone wall. As one of them aimed a flashlight at a long-haired dog panting on its side, Manny darted across the asphalt. Reaching to crimp the end of a sticker and jerk it from his pack, he knelt behind the Lincoln's bumper. He ripped away the sticker's protective strip and over *These Colors Don't Run* slapped *Somewhere in Texas There's a Village Missing an Idiot.*

He belched and glanced up. The men were ignoring Manny as they passed the dog—dead? wounded?—its matted hair plastered against its belly, from one set of arms to another. Two black-haired teenagers who shuffled past ignored him as well, the bottoms of the boy's pantlegs mopping the bricks, the girl's head bobbing on his shoulder.

Unsnapping the flap from his sheepskin's top pocket, Manny snatched a ballpoint and crouched. The asphalt iced his knees as he screwed off the rear tire's cap and jammed his pen point down to the valve stem. He averted his face from the hiss of stale air. The Lincoln's right haunch touched the pavement.

So don't watch, Manny exulted, rising. Read in the morning all about the hamstrung gas-guzzlers, ogle them on network TV, a hundred trucks and SUVs pleading for peace.

His head seemed to fill with helium. Weaving, he slanted across to where Otero Street ended at Palace and leaned against a lamppost, sucking air. Tightening his sphincter, he laughed at the soles of a pair of black dress shoes that clacked in the wind like castanets, looped over a branch of a big-tooth maple.

Pushing from the post, he spied Chuck and Bret through the grille protecting the adobe-office window facing Otero. They bent over the mogul's table, Bret in the blue shirt displaying daisies that he'd worn for dinner with Manny and Joyce at La Concha Tuesday night. Manny watched Chuck reach around the table's corner to squeeze Bret's shoulder.

He shivered as he recalled Chuck's gloved fingers touching his cheek during the peace march. How comforting they felt! Was Chuck truly gay, as Alexis had told Joyce at the Cookhouse he might be? Or was he simply exploring ways to show affection? Whatever, Manny envied Chuck. In comparison, his own back-and-forth dance with Joyce made him sick.

Otero lay empty of tourists and traffic, but vehicles filled the parking lot between *The New Mexican*'s headquarters and Robert's Cutting Edge barbershop. A row of aspens stood sentry at the back. Manny hurried across.

Against an aspen's trunk slouched a woman gurgling, asleep or drunk, chin pressing the lapel of a splotched leather coat. Her gray hair cascaded down to a banjo resting on her green skirt, her scabbed hands draped over the instrument's curve. He lifted the hem of his sheepskin, tugged out his wallet, pinched a $10 bill, and tucked it under the splintered banjo's four strings.

Now he began. To the right of a pickup's plate, over a short sticker that read *Give War a Chance*, he slapped *There Is No Way to Peace/Peace Is the Way*, letting its free end flap in the wind. With his uncapped pen he deflated one of the truck's tires.

To a Chevy's bumper he affixed *To Keep the Peace/We Kill Those/Who Kill Others;* on a Pontiac Grand Prix's bumper he smoothed *Heil Bush;* where the owner had affixed *Thank God for America* to the left back door of a green GMC van, Manny pasted *Sure You Can Trust Our Government/Just Ask an Indian.* The van's right rear sank with a hiss as he jabbed his pen point against the valve stem.

Under scattered Chinese elms, up and down the rows of vehicles, Manny marched, tormented by pain become a rhythm that clamped and released his insides.

He hurried onto Nusbaum, moving into the unguarded corner lot abutting the Hotel Plaza Real. In the twenty minutes it took to add stickers to fifty SUVs, panel trucks, and pickups—deflating the tires of fifteen— no pedestrians and only a *New Mexican* van used the narrow, shadowed street. Breathing faster, biting a corner of his lip each time the intestinal agony struck, he hobbled off the curb toward the Owings-Dewey Gallery, where a dozen bronze ravens clung to marble plinths. One pressed a green-enameled apple in its beak.

He'd meant to empty his pack in the main library's lot that bordered Owings-Dewey. But now, complicating the spasms, his colon seemed eager to relieve his distended belly—he'd not been able to move his bowels since early yesterday morning.

The throb of the backhoe's engine farther on jangled his nerves as he again neared Washington. The men in orange vests had bunched near the

Make Love Not War sticker on his Prius. They stood watching the backhoe spade into the pile of dirt and dump it in the hole.

Gulping back acid and kicking aside a brown bottle of Bud Light, he tried to hurry to the corner, tilting forward as if battling wind. Half of the stickers remaining in his pack slid over his left shoulder. Smacking the sidewalk, they spread out, but he couldn't stop to retrieve them.

He also doubted he could drive. Better to hobble into the Plaza Real, call Joyce. Jolting down the dirt road from their town house took only three minutes. Of course she would come.

When he reached the corner, his thigh muscles stopped lifting his knees. From their three-story arcade across Washington, the lighted windows of Underpinnings Fine Lingerie, Smith-Barney Investments, Merry-Go-Round Children's Clothing, and Niman Fine Art smiled at him. Overhead, a gust rattled the brown pods of a thorned black locust.

Two men arm-in-arm—one in a Russian cap like Chuck's and a black-and-white checked coat, the other wrapped in an orange muffler whose fringed ends bobbed near his belt—stepped off the curb.

"Help," Manny bleated, his right palm pressing his belly, which was drumhead tight.

They turned their faces away, toward the arcade, as visions of ejaculating inside Joyce last night and of handing over his boarding pass for his upcoming flight to Silicon Valley filled his mind.

He managed to stumble to the concrete slab angled between the library's children's wing and a patch of dead grass before crying out. Crumpling onto his side as the rest of his bumper stickers shot from the pack, he jerked his knees to his elbows, hoping to lessen the ordeal, which felt as if someone were wringing his guts dry.

Gagging, he writhed; split peas and bits of carrot flooded out. He pursed his lips at the sour reek. Eyes clenched, he rocked back onto his pack, then shifted his head to cool his cheek against the icy concrete.

"Now those ain't the dry heaves, is they, bro? You know what? You smell worse than I do." With the whiskey voice came chattering, as from a rattled squirrel.

Spewing the next wave of vomit, moaning as its acid seared his throat, Manny peeked at the apparition standing near him. A woolly monkey squatted on the man's shoulder, attached by a rope to another rope holding up paint-spattered khakis. Unshaved, two lower teeth gone, brown hair falling to the collar of an army jacket splotched in green, the man grinned and stepped closer onto the bricked sidewalk. Eyes glistening like black marbles, the monkey proffered a Styrofoam cup toward Manny and covered its nose, pivoting its face to the side.

"Gotta guess you're in no shape to contribute to Beryl's and my well-being. I seen drunks and I married a drunk; been one myself. But I never seen the insides of one come out like yours."

"Call nine-one-one," Manny gasped, elbows ramming into his thighs as another cramp struck.

"What zat?"

"Go into the library. Call an ambulance."

The family he'd seen heading toward the Hotel Plaza Real after he spotted Ron detoured into the middle of Washington to avoid Manny and the beggar. The toothpick-chewing father grabbed his son's forearm to keep him from breaking away for a closer look at the monkey. Its chattering turned to shrieks as it raked the black hairs on its head.

"You say ambulance," the man repeated.

"Yes," Manny croaked before abandoning himself to spasms that twisted his torso in what felt like an epileptic fit.

BLESS THEE, SPICY TOMATO.

At the marble kitchen sink of the Morgans' Sierra del Sol faux-adobe hacienda, nine miles up Hyde Park Road, Maxine shook tomato mix into the bottom of a blue tumbler and filled the rest with vodka, forgoing the lime wedge and ice.

She rolled the first mouthful around inside her cheeks, swallowed, and gazed past patches of snow at the lights quivering like fallen stars on the three mesas of Los Alamos, thirty-five miles northwest across US 285. Scattered ponderosas and clusters of transplanted aspens, each group ringed by granite boulders, thrust into the eight o'clock sky.

Tonight, for Ron, she wore the outfit Giordy loved her to fellate him in, the strapless red slippers with inch-high heels and the spaghetti-strapped red satin that reached her ankles, appliquéd with purple peonies over her nipples.

She covered all this in a robe. Blue stars adorned its red wool; strands of white yarn held her black curls in a topknot. She wore the same perfume as she had at the Great Books Cookhouse, Saint Grêve's Beaver — the animal's ground-up sex glands mixed with lavender.

But though she felt curious about the toys Ron had phoned to tell her he was bringing, she wished she could open the front door to Dirk and unsash her robe for him. She yearned to squeeze that uncircumcized shaft again, feel it slide into her mouth, her cunt, her anus, her armpits, between her breasts. So what that he seemed only a few years younger than her seventy-two-year-old husband? She even missed the squeak of Dirk's hearing aid. And with him she hadn't wanted to drink.

She took another swig from her tumbler.

The sudden rumbling of the garage door sent the splint on her ring finger clanking against the bottle of Stolichnaya. The pain felt as if Dirk had shoved a sliver of bamboo under her nail. Giordy home from his poker game? He'd left only an hour ago; he never returned before eleven. Victor made sure of that.

Grimacing, she shook her left hand to calm the smart. She clacked across the hallway's slate tiles and over the black, red, and white kilim, a ten-year anniversary gift from Giordy last April. She approached the massive, brass-studded front door, in which Victor had carved an image of St. Francis feeding sparrows.

Standing on tiptoe, she pulled its wood flap open to peer through the iron grille. Not Giordy's Jaguar but Lila's yellow Mustang crawled across the gravel toward the garage, headlights blazing.

Maxine sprang across the prayer rug. She leaped over the damp splotch left by a ruptured radiant-heat tube, dashed past the door to the pantry and laundry, and flung open the door at the back of the garage, now bright as a car wash.

The top edge of its articulated steel door banged the aluminum stop bolted to the ceiling. A gust blew into the drywalled space; the sports section of yesterday's *New Mexican* floated off the stack awaiting trash day on Giordy's workbench.

"No, no!" Maxine shouted as Ron nosed the Mustang in beside her Range Rover. "Park where you always do, by the visitors sign."

He backed the car out. She punched the button that started the door grinding down toward the slab and retraced her steps to the foyer.

"Goddamn computerized, engine-sensing bullshit Giordy installed last week. I guess now the garage'll be opening for everyone," she said to Ron, having unlocked the front door and flung it wide.

"Son of a peccary, Max—hoo, do you look good. And smell. These are for you, kemo sabe." He handed her a dozen red roses and baby's breath wrapped in rice paper.

"Come in, it's cold."

"That splint's larger than I thought when you told me you'd sprained your finger liftin' boulders. Does it hurt?"

"It's manageable." She bolted the door behind him.

Out of the master bedroom Pixie started down the hall, nails clicking on the slate. Spying Ron, the black-faced Pekingese skidded to a halt between the rugs. His yips became barks; he whirled and ran back, high-ceiling halogens sparking the long hair that bounced up off his sides.

"Did you bring that treat?" Maxine asked. "If we're going to spend more time together, you and he need to come to terms."

"Too much on my mind—gimme a hug, sexy."

In red polyester jacket and a brimmed, green felt hat he'd exchanged at home for the straw one, he waited for her to set the flowers on a side table, then locked her in his arms.

She kept her eyes closed until his grip relaxed. "You're fat, you know that? Did you get back to the hospital?"

"She refused to see me, so I left her toothbrush and yellow housecoat and mouthwash with the desk nurse, who wouldn't even say Lila had been admitted. Psych-unit visitors need a four-digit pass code and the patient decides who gets it."

"She actually tried to broadside Victor and me?"

"So she told the sawbones. The cops say my Escalade is pretty much history."

"Don't you feel a bit guilty about all this, big boy?" She led him into the kitchen.

Ron staggered to a pigskin-backed chair next to the pewter-topped table on which sat a telephone and a pencil. "Comanche motherfucker," he wheezed as a viselike pain beneath his breastbone forced out a gasp.

Staring from smeared eyes, thumb and two fingers of her splinted hand gripping her hip, "There's no blood in your face," she blurted.

"Little dizzy. Gotta be the 'guilt' word—Lila and me been together thirty-two years. I'll be mug a milk in a minute." His jowls sagged as he blew out air.

Maxine downed half her Bloody Mary. From one of the glass-faced cabinets she fetched a cut-glass vase, unwrapped the roses, and stuck them in. She filled it halfway with water, then brought up the bag of kibble from under the sink, its brown paper crackling.

"That's better, " Ron managed, though the inner side of his left arm burned. "How about you? No guilt?"

"Giordy and I have an understanding," she lied.

"I never knew that."

"Your color's coming back."

"A double tequila martini would speed the healin', Max."

"No way. You get as crazy as your wife. Anyway, for what I've planned, you won't need a drink. Giordy says staying sober heightens the thrill."

"What's this war hammock you been tellin' me about?" Ron blinked his eyes to clear his head.

"In a minute—you secured a loan for Dirk?"

"It's all set."

"I couldn't get his signature today on the listing agreement, so we're lunching tomorrow at the Cookhouse. Victor and I found his mother on the floor of their bathroom with a broken hip."

Emptying his lungs, Ron peeled off his jacket. The freezer bag holding Lila's sex tools and tube of jelly weighed down one pocket. "You haven't asked about—"

"Victor's agreed to fix Dirk's place up to sell."

"The man should stick to carvin' santos."

"The man's brother was my sister's husband, Ronald."

"What?"

"Nicaraguan guerrillas strung his brother up in a warehouse and jammed a machete through his gut. Victor helps me send money to my sister in Vegas. So keep your mouth shut. We need to find him more work, now that his mother's in the hospital."

"How long to fix her hip?"

"Surgeon figures she'll be there seven days at least. She's got no health insurance."

Ron grabbed the edge of the pewter-topped table as the garage door rumbled again.

"Stay put," Maxine barked. She clacked past him and flung the inside door open. Three bulbs behind the engine-sensor's acrylic panel flooded the garage with light. But no headlamps aimed their way toward her parked Range Rover as the wind fluttered another section of *The New Mexican* on the workbench.

"Goddamn it." Wrapping her arms around her robe, she thrust her thumb at the black button implanted in the wall. The articulated steel again grumbled down.

"Totally fucked-up computer; nobody there," she told Ron back in the kitchen. "Maybe these gusts are doing it. Let's go hit the bed."

He picked up his jacket. "I need a drink, Max, I surely do."

"For you, no; for me, a touch-up."

She shook the red mix into her tumbler and topped it up with vodka.

"You sure Giordy won't come home early?"

"On the Thursdays you're here, has he ever broken away before close to midnight? You know I reimburse Victor for everything he loses to my husband."

The bag of kibble jiggled along her thigh as they entered the master bedroom. The blaze she'd started in the kiva fireplace beside the double window was snaking up a tripod of oak. White scale like that at the Cookhouse splotched the floor, alkali scabs left from occasional snowmelt trickling under bricks set on sand. Kitty-corner to the two queen-size beds pushed together, the windows looked uphill toward the aspens springing from their rings of boulders.

White muslin ruffled the windows' upper halves; on the left one's sill sat a storyteller from Cochiti pueblo, a ceramic matron in azure and red glazes, her eyes closed, her mouth an O, telling an eternal tale to three chubby girls on her lap, a boy on each shoulder, and a papoose clinging to her ceramic shawl.

"Son of a peccary," Ron blurted. "What the hell?" Maxine stepped forward to press her breasts to his back as he stood ogling the hammock.

Not a foot above the further bed hung a churro wool blanket like a canopy. Four brass hooks Ron had never noticed, screwed into the ceiling's pine vigas, held the knotted ends of four hemp ropes that looped through stacks of wooden pulleys to support the hammock's corners. A five-inch slit reinforced with rope opened in each long side of the blanket.

"I told Giordy the story," Maxine breathed against Ron's neck, "that it's a chief's hammock, loomed to guarantee him victory. I lied that San Ildefonso chieftains slept in it the night before doing battle. The two slits on the sides and the hole in the bottom were my brainstorms. Giordy arranged the pulleys and stops to make raising and lowering it easy. Sometimes I climb into it; mostly he does. C'mere."

She nudged Ron forward. "I commissioned a friend at San Ildefonso Pueblo to weave it. For a war hammock San Ildefonso seemed appropriate — it's the closest pueblo to Los Alamos. You see the themes in salmon and yellow against the scarlet? A scalping, the brave spearing his foe in the chest, the slow burning of a foe roped to a stake?

"But this one" — she prodded the wool nap with the tip of her splint — "is my favorite. That's honey the squaw's pouring on the head of the prisoner buried to his chin. Can you imagine what the badgers will do to him?"

Gulping from the tumbler, she thrust her splint through the round, two-inch hole reinforced with silk thread in the middle of the blanket. "What this is for I needn't go into, right?"

Little Prince strained against Ron's slacks. It sprang upright when he pulled the corduroy free. He extracted the freezer bag from his jacket and threw the jacket on the bedspread, woven in a spread-eagle-wing motif.

From the walk-in closet, flanked by two black-on-black ceramic urns, came a whine.

"Pixie likes to watch. See if you can coax him to eat." Maxine set the tumbler on a bedside table, its legs fashioned of interlaced mesquite branches, pinched out some kibble, and passed it to Ron. Glancing at the see-through bag he held, she said, "I hate to tell you, big boy, but dildos have never done it for me."

"This one vibrates. And Lila uses somethin' else, too."

"Hunh?"

"Gold-plated balls in a rubber she shoves into her snatch."

"Maybe," she smiled, feeling her vagina begin to prickle. "Pixie, you little pisspot, come out of there."

"Hey, Pix, call a truce?" Ron took off his felt hat. Massaging his arm, he moved to the hammockless bed and lowered himself to its edge.

A whimpering commenced but no eyes glowed.

Breasts swinging, Max swished across the bricks toward the closet. Soon she clacked out, pulling the red wooden wagon. Through his black mask, Pixie stared through the branches of the red-willow cage. The wagon's jiggling caused water drops to leap from the dish at one end.

"I've changed my mind, Ronald—me first. I came up with an idea at dinner watching the news with Giordy. You talk atrocities, see if it helps me come—go light the candles."

As Ron moved to the bookshelves hollowed in the wall, Pixie started yapping at him. Below a row of Mayan masks, he pinched a La Concha matchbook from a green dish and flamed the six wicks. Pixie grew silent as he flicked off the row of track lights running between two vigas.

Tossing her robe over Giordy's pillow under the hammock and shoving her body against her own pillow, Maxine bent to pop a John Coltrane CD into the player on her bedside table's shelf.

"Don't you want to lower the drapes?"

"We've got three electric-fenced acres up here and an electric gate, you know that. No bears, not even deer can get in. Tonight should be a nearly full moon. I want to watch it rise while I'm bringing you off." She smiled, remembering the moon highlighting the doe that had peered in Dirk's window on Tuesday. Hoisting her red-satin hem past the appendix scar, she spread her thighs and massaged the folds of flesh under the triangle of black curls. "Show me Lila's toys."

Out of the bag and onto Maxine's belly Ron dumped the cherry-colored condom holding the 24k-gold-plated ben wa balls, K-Y Jelly, and the knobbed polypropylene shaft with its rigid testicles. The devotional candles and crackling flames from the kiva fireplace sent shadows of the black urns and a palm in an orange pot shimmying across the plaster.

"You've never much liked touchin' yourself," he muttered.

"Tonight I'm feeling lucky." Slithering down her pillow, she marveled how quickly her juices had begun to mat her nest. "You stay dressed until I'm through." Pulling her left forefinger from her vagina, she stretched the spaghetti straps off her shoulders and pushed her breasts together. "Suck."

Ron knelt on the Navajo rug, arching his right arm over one of her wrists. Zigzagging from note to note like a chased cottontail, Coltrane's tenor sax energized Ron's lips. He drew one of Maxine's pocked strawberries into his mouth until she groaned, then released it and flicked his tongue around the rim of the other. The lavender-and-alcohol Beaver that she'd rubbed between her breasts made him giddy. Once his cheek rammed the tip of her splint and he jerked away. Laughing, she shoved her breasts closer.

"Good work, big boy. I'll double that prick's length before we're through. Put those ben wa things in me, I'm drenched. Forget the jelly— you washed the condom?"

"I found a fresh one in her drawer."

Puffing, he thrust his fists to the mattress and pushed himself up. She spread her legs, pulling wide the lips of her vulva. The balls clunked as, inhaling the odor of latex, he twisted them into her vagina until only the condom's knotted end showed like an oversized, second navel.

"Yes; nice." Maxine wiggled her pelvis—the balls made her nerve ends spark. "Start talking atrocities—I'm in charge of Afghans at Guantánamo Bay. How do I find ways to get them to spill the beans? This damned gizmo, how do you turn it on? Never mind, I got it. Talk."

To the notes of Coltrane's sax, the vibrator added its buzz. It clicked against the aluminum bracing her ring finger until, by keeping her pinky straight, she managed to insert the knobbed curve. Maybe, maybe! Clutching the polypropylene testicles, denting the mattress with the back of her head, she closed her eyes from the rows of vigas in the off-white ceiling. "Talk," she murmured, as waves rolled through her vagina's swelling tissues.

Ron pulled at the beige corduroy pressing against his erection. "Commanche motherfucker, Max, I—." Then he remembered the bloody-eared Native American in the emergency room. "Here's one. You jab a pencil into an Afghan's ear and say you'll skewer the other if he doesn't come clean. He screams but he spits in your face, so you cut off his ear with a hacksaw."

"I didn't think you had it in you. It's working, keep talking." Thrashing from side to side, she felt her upper lip twitch.

"You take fingernail scissors to the sac holdin' a guy's balls and snip a quarter inch at a time. You slam a metal pipe into a guy's knee. You cut off his eyelids." He recalled a punishment his father used on his sister. "You get him barefoot and stomp on his toes with your boot heel."

It was a sensation she'd never had. Forcing her head up to see herself work, she longed for the whirlpool her insides had become to never stop spinning.

"With your penknife you slit a guy's armpit and crush a lighted cigarette in the wound."

"Ahhhh, jeez, goddamn—son of a bitch!" Maxine wailed. She threw her head back, using the vibrator like a jackhammer. Her topknot loosened and flailed the pillow. Could she climax again? She plunged the shaft between her folds, pressing her clit. "Yes, oh my god, *yes*."

Yanking the shaft free, she squeezed the ben wa balls with her thighs until they seemed one.

"Judas Christ, Max," Ron wheezed, grabbing and releasing his testicles. Searching for a chair, he backed toward the stuffed one by the door and sat down, his bulk flattening the white cushion. Sweat covered his forehead and armpits.

"Not even Dirk could give me that," she panted.

"Whaddaya mean, 'not even Dirk'?" He narrowed his eyes.

"Something happened a couple of nights ago I hadn't meant to tell you."

"Like with that Bret? Look at Pixie's tongue hangin' out."

"He loves all this. Not like with Bret." How she wished it were Dirk in the white armchair grinning at her through his whiskers, instead of Ron scowling, sucking his thumb.

"How many men you had beside me, anyhoo, Max?"

"I don't keep count." She drew the mucus-slick condom out, kissed it and the vibrator's testicles, and placed them on the spread next to the unopened tube of lubricant. Reaching behind her to prop the pillow against the headboard, she scooted backward, pulled the red satin up over her breasts, and lifted its straps to her shoulders.

"I've been with you more than anyone except Giordy, if it makes you feel better. But Dirk's unencumbered. Bret has a runaway girlfriend and you have a wacko wife."

"I'm thinkin' we're gonna split up."

"Don't count on you and me pairing—my life's too complicated now."

"A few minutes ago you said we're goin' to spend more time together. At the Cookhouse you said you'd leave Giordy if I can make the bucks."

"Did I?"

Both their bodies tightened at new rumbling from the garage. Ron yanked out his pocket watch. "Nine o'clock," he whispered.

"Run out the laundry-room door and punch the black button to your left. No way he's back."

"This is unnervin'."

"Once you're in the hammock, you'll forget about it."

A minute later the rumbling began again. It stopped as Ron reappeared through the bedroom door. "You were right."

"Take off your clothes, big boy."

He slid the turquoise clasp down the rawhide of his bolo tie and lifted it over his head. He removed his boots and socks, corduroys, and maroon shirt. Stepping from toast-colored shorts, he lumbered toward where she stood, his own breasts swaying. When he passed between the wagon and the beds' footboards, Pixie began to yip.

Holding it by its quill, Maxine waggled at him a golden-eagle feather. "What's that for?"

"Illegal treat, big boy. I'm the Beloved Adopted Daughter of Northern Pueblo Elders, remember? A potter gave me this for displaying her bowl on the cover of last year's Morgan Realty brochure. She and her boyfriend use one to get their juices flowing. Climb up, if you can manage—on your back first. Watch the pulleys. Ouch!"

Reaching for the tumbler, still a third full, she'd jabbed it by mistake with the tip of the splint and sent the glass shattering on the bricks. Vodka splashed toward the window; she kicked the sparkling shards against the wall.

Grunting, Ron clambered onto the mattress and grasped a rope to hoist himself into the hammock. To the trembling shadows from the candles and the sputtering oak splits, Coltrane slowed for the start of "A Love Supreme" as Ron lay hyperventilating, staring at the two brass hooks in the ceiling above the foot of the bed. The sagging blanket's wool tickled the hairs between his buttocks.

"Close your eyes, Ronald, and leave your arms against those rolls of flesh. I can't turn that fellow into Bret's donkey dong, but I bet you I can make him sit up and beg."

Satin-sheathed tummy pressing the hammock's edge, she raised the feather and drew its vanes over his left nipple.

"Son of a peccary!" He snapped his eyes open.

"You like?" She feathered the other nipple, making its black hairs wave, then slid the vanes down the mountain to where Little Prince lay curled.

Ron twitched; he rose on his elbows to watch, feeling sweat-damp skin bunch under his chin.

Back and forth she drew the brown feather, easing it between his thighs, tickling his pubic hairs, drawing curlicues on his testicles with its tip.

"Oh," he groaned and lay back. Glans purpling, his penis straightened and rose under the feather's ebb and flow. Maxine concentrated her wand on the nerve running down the shaft's left side.

His hands jerked from his sides to form a hut over his genitals. "I can't stand anymore, Max," he panted.

"Turn on your belly and shove Junior through the hole."

Under the hammock's canopy, she wriggled supine onto the spread and scooted toward the bed's foot so that her calves pressed the mattress and the heels of her slippers flopped against the footboard. Her mouth lay north of where she watched Ron's erection emerge, slanting toward her lips. His testicles followed.

Her lower back smarted from her wrinkled gown; she lifted her buttocks to smooth the fabric under them.

"Have I told you why I love swallowing cum? It makes me feel empowered. I hate playing sex servant to the bunch of you—and I love it. Look, here comes the moon."

Through the window, the rim of the still-almost-full orb shown bright over the ponderosa-choked hillside, where trails wound toward the ski lift 2,000 feet above.

"I can't shift position to look, Max. I'm dyin' up here, take me in your mouth. I'm beggin'."

"The hammock sags more with you but you're shorter than Giordy— I'll grab a pillow." She arced her unsplinted hand toward the headboard, gripped the open end of the cotton pillowcase, and scrunched the pillow under her head. Grasping the rope-wound slits on each side of the hammock, she tugged until Ron's erection disappeared between her lips. At his "Oh!" she swung the hammock's end until his glans dangled above her chin, rocked him back into her mouth, stretched her lips over the top of her teeth and munched the shaft, then rocked him out.

"Yes?" she asked, violet-smeared lids half closed.

"Yeahhh."

Neither she nor he startled at the rumbling of the garage door. Half of the moon now glowed over the horizon.

In and out she pulled him, running her tongue along the nerve, nipping, increasing her pace until she felt the great belly that stretched the blanket shudder. She rocked him in and out as fast as she was able, until he wailed. The spurt of semen hit the fleshy uvula dangling from the roof of her mouth. She guided him in until her lips pushed the wrinkles of his testicles. Gulping the hot, acidic semen, she drew Little Prince free, sweat massing in the corners of her eyes.

"Judas Christ and Paul the Apostle," he sighed above her.

Closing her eyes, she pushed her breasts together and circled her thumbs over the satin-clad nipples, revisiting the night before last with Dirk, feeling again the exquisite ecstasy of pain when he'd cracked the joint of her ring finger.

A flash reddened her lids, hurling specks and threads across them. Ron cried out. Snapping her eyes open, in the moonlight she saw Victor grinning through the window, *Proud To Be American* cap shoved back on his hair, the tips of his handlebar mustache wiggling. Right wrist taped, left temple bandaged, he raised his Nikon; the second flash blinded her.

Yapping, Pixie twisted in his cage as though a wasp had stung him, his hind paw flinging water from the donut-shaped dish. Maxine's forehead pushed into Ron's belly as she jerked upright.

A third flash lit the dark.

"These will cost you big-time, amiga," he shouted through the double-paned window. "We'll talk tomorrow."

To Coltrane's moan she scrambled from under the hammock and stood peering at Ron, who was now silent. Forehead and jowls clammy with perspiration, his visible cheek gone ashen, he lay with his chin dimpling the war blanket. His right hand gripped one of the ropes; his left, knotted into a fist, stretched past the hammock's foot. The one gray-pupiled eye she could see, though wide open, seemed sightless.

"Ronald!" She watched the rise and fall of the hairs emerging from the fat that cushioned his shoulder blades. With the heel of her hand she pushed his hip. "Goddamn it, Victor—why?"

His truck engine roared. How she wished her husband had never given the man the code to their electric gate. Was Giordy still at Victor's mother's, playing poker?

"Shut up, Pixie!" Barefoot, she grabbed her robe from Giordy's pillow, and leaped over a mouse that had careered out of the closet and was scampering toward her bed.

"Ah, jeez!" Her heel came down on a sliver of glass. She hobbled to the white phone on her bedside table and with a forefinger stabbed out *911*.

BED REST _____

RON JERKED OUT OF A MORNING DOZE TO THE SOUND OF water roaring down the toilet near him. Whoever had flushed began talking about the war when she reached the window side of the white curtain dividing the two-bed room.

Was that rubbing alcohol or formaldehyde he sniffed? He wished himself one of the war's dead, and intended to pickle himself with tequila martinis as soon as he reached home. Following his angioplasty of the night before, the nurse who told him not to bend his leg said he could expect to be discharged late this afternoon. But who would drive him home? Maxine? Though the stent holding the artery open near his heart caused no pain, the left side of his groin throbbed where the dressing pressed in.

Someone knocked on the doorjamb. "Mr. Kirkpatrick?"

It was the muttonchopped guard who'd wheeled Lila from the emergency room the day before. "You up for a visitor?"

Flat on his back under the polyester blanket, Ron had been staring at the loose acoustical tile dangling from the ceiling. Warm air rattled the fins of the grate between it and a stainless-steel sprinkler head. Swallowing to erase the taste of roadkill furring his tongue, he stared down his belly at the guard. "She wants to see me?

"So she claims."

"Hold on." He wormed his fingers through the side rail to retrieve the remote control, pulled it by its cord onto the mattress, and stabbed a button. The bed's head ground upright. He yanked his pillow behind the bow securing his gown. "Bring her in."

"Okay," the guard called out the doorway.

A pair of forest-green socks with rubber-sole grips wheeled into view as an aide, his long blond hair tucked into a net, pushed Lila to the padded armchair under the wall-mounted TV. He turned her to face Ron and sat, his chapped lips smiling. The guard clumped back into the hallway.

"Hello, babe."

"Hello, Big Shit." She pulled the flaps of the yellow housecoat he'd brought to the psychiatric unit yesterday across the gown draping her breasts.

He stared at the tufts springing from her scalp—unbelievable. Her jaw slack, two gold fillings glowed in the fluorescent light from the fixture above him.

"Felicity needs to know when we're returning to Fort Worth."

"Felicity?" Clenching his eyes and swallowing again, he flattened his palm against his breasts.

"My friend who turns my bed down."

"The little gal with mice runnin' around her sweater?"

"Why not?"

"I don't believe Cowtown's in the cards right now, Lile; we got lotsa thinkin' to do. My ticker stopped last night."

"You're sitting up, anyways. I can't find our son, Ronnie. Is he waiting in Fort Worth, you think?"

"Could be."

"You didn't bring my sex tools last night."

At this the aide flexed his lower lip back over his teeth, patted his hairnet, and stood. "The doc in the unit said stay just a few minutes. We'll go get us some lunch."

As he turned Lila toward the door, Maxine—dressed under her trench coat in a lilac pantsuit too sheer for mid-March—burst in. Seeing Lila, she clapped a palm to her lips. Her left hand clutched the half-empty bottle of wintergreen cologne Ron had asked her to bring from the town house. Over her arm she carried his red, white, and blue-striped robe. Her perfume this late Saturday morning was Pure Tiffany—jasmine, tuberose, and magnolia, Giordy's favorite at $200 a half ounce.

She twisted to call into the hallway, "Giordy! Go buy some roses in the gift shop like the ones Ronald brought last night to thank us for our business. I'll meet you in twenty minutes in Victor's mother's room; a nurse will know where it is."

She turned back to face Lila. "Who's your hairdresser?" She leered, her voice hoarse. "I'm saddened you're under the weather."

"For you," she said to Ron, tossing the robe across his blanket and planting the square bottle in one of its folds.

"That robe's my husband's!" Lila half rose from her chair. "Nympho!"

"Easy, now," the aide said, pressing down on her shoulder, a gold ring on his pinky flashing. "Jerry, I could use some help."

Stroking an end of his graying mustache, the guard returned in black-soled shoes.

"Who's a nympho?" Maxine laughed, jabbing her splint at Lila's face.

"I want my husband back."

"He's all yours, sweet pea, I'm heading south."

"But you've soiled him."

"*I've* soiled him? He's an alcoholic." Leaning toward Lila, whose nose twitched like a caged rabbit's, Maxine cleared her throat. "I know all about it. My sister's an alcoholic. And what are you? White trash in the dumpster back of Albertsons."

Lila slumped down in her chair. "No, I'm sweet pea, I'm sweet pea," she mumbled, patting her left hand with her right as the aide wheeled her out.

"Let's take a breather, miss." The guard gripped Maxine's elbow and muscled her toward the hall.

"Headin' south?" Ron bleated.

"Selling out, big boy," Maxine called over her shoulder. "Dirk and I are buying a trailer near Socorro, though he doesn't know that quite yet."

"Then kiss the loan goodbye I set up for him. You comin' back this afternoon?"

"Maybe; someone needs to drive your wife's Mustang out of here."

"Comanche motherfucker." Ron slid down his pillow, snuffling to clear his nose.

"Can you lower the noise over there?" came the woman's voice from the other side of the white curtain.

"We're on our way," the aide said as he wheeled Lila out.

Joyce stepped from behind the curtain. Here since seven, she'd not washed her hair; a dull blonde sheaf dangled across one cheek.

"What the hell are you doin' here?" Ron groaned.

"'Comanche motherfucker?' I said to Manny. 'I bet that's our neighbor. We can't rid ourselves of him.' Thanks for keeping your mouth shut most of the morning. Manny collapsed last night—so what are you in for?"

"Peace wimps," Ron mumbled. "What a joke; we're all trashed." He closed his eyes and rolled to face the red biohazard bin that stood waist-high next to the bathroom wall. Three decaled pairs of scorpion-like pincers blackened its lid.

Joyce looked past the window's vertical blinds at the snow-patched Sangre de Cristos rising under puffball clouds. Closer by, two ravens ripped apart a green garbage bag on an apron of dirt that sloped to the stuccoed rehab building fifty yards away.

A nurse walked in. "Ready for lunch, Mr. Kirkpatrick?"

"Ready for a shot."

"Sorry, I can't. How about some broth?"

"You got any strawberry ice cream?"

"We sure do. Be right back. No need for this," she muttered, dragging the biohazard bin behind her.

Returning to Manny's side of the curtain, Joyce sank into the wooden armchair beneath the other TV. "I'll bet he had a heart attack, he's so obese. Who were the women, I wonder?"

Manny lay half upright, his thinning dark-brown hair matting his forehead. From the back of his left wrist, above his identification band, emerged a tube leading to a blue infusion pump and a bag of saline-dextrose solution clamped to a stainless-steel pole.

From one nostril emerged a clear tube, snaked through his throat last night in the emergency room. Through it a wall pump slurped speckled digestive juices from his stomach into a polypropylene bucket. Swallowing felt as if the ER nurse had jammed a wad of foil behind his Adam's apple. On the sheet beside him lay a see-through urinal shaped like a headless duck.

Two tablets of Tylenol had not eased the pounding in his temple. "Boodie, keep sharing what you read in today's *New Mexican*, will you? Did you see anything about the flat tires near the Plaza?"

"Nothing; no."

"Probably tomorrow."

"Maybe. I wish he'd show up."

"Who?"

"Christ, who do you think? I know waiting isn't any easier on you. I read that thousands of protesters plan to leave work today and shut down highways. Can you picture the backup on the Golden Gate Bridge? Yesterday, forty thousand protesters milled outside the US Embassy in Berlin. Tomorrow, United for Peace and Justice is holding an antiwar march in Manhattan.

"I wrote down for you what Bush told the press last night." From her brown leather purse she extracted a stenographer's notebook and flipped its cover. 'We appreciate the sacrifice of those I've had to send into harm's way to make the world as peaceful and the lives of our citizens as prosperous as possible.' Can you believe that?"

Staring at the clouds, Manny raised his left hand, hoping to massage the pain from his larynx. "I feel so beside the point."

"At least it's the first day of spring. Your car's probably ticketed by now, and who knows where the backpack is, but I washed your sheepskin and cords—they're waiting for you on the bed."

"If I come out of this, might you still want to marry me? You might be pregnant."

"The thing is, Manny, you betrayed me." Listening to the pump sucking out his juices, watching the tremble of the sheet draping his toes, Joyce felt compassion muffle her anger. His hazel eyes, yesterday full of light, now seemed caves. Stubble peppered his chin and cheeks. Above him, on the wall beside the basket holding a blood-pressure cuff, hung a Japanese print of waves bashing a cliff. "I might," she said.

"I bet you are."

"Are what?"

"Pregnant."

"I mean I might be open someday to getting married."

"I want to help raise our baby, Boodie."

"Don't pressure me."

"You could abort."

"Shut your mouth, bud!"

Raking her fingers through her tangled hair, she jumped up as Dr. Seward, grinning as he had earlier this morning, strode past the end of Ron's bed. The stoop-shouldered, six-foot-two surgeon, his face dotted with moles, drew a second white curtain around Manny. Hauling the wheeled IV stand and its infusion pump with her, Joyce came closer. Seward grabbed Manny's side rail—moles dotted the backs of his hands. As he bent, his stethoscope swung over Manny's chest.

"How are you feeling?" His aqua scrubs smelled of bleach.

"Scared. And starving."

Laughing, Seward straightened. "Good signs. We'll be looking at what's going on in there in about half an hour. Last night's barium swallow shows a blockage, but we can't tell what's causing it. They'll be coming for you any time now."

He leaned over Manny and gripped his right wrist. "The anesthesiologist will gift you with happy dreams, then we'll go to work figuring how best to get you back to eating and out of here."

Pushing up his surgical cap enlivened with red chiles, he turned and furled the curtain. Joyce stooped to lift her purse and followed him into the magenta-carpeted hallway opposite the nursing station.

"Dr. Seward?"

"Yup?"

He towered over her. She waited for a nurse in amaryllis-flowered jacket and sneakers, their heels steel coils, to wheel into the next room a wrinkle-cheeked woman breathing oxygen from a tank strapped to her chair.

"How serious is this?"

"Don't know. He may be home in a few days."

"But it might be more complicated."

"Think Iraq. The Bush people say we'll be mopping up over there in six weeks. Unless we have to fight the Republican Guard door-to-door; unless Turkey decides it needs to suppress the Kurds. A lot of 'unlesses.' I forget—you're Manny's wife?"

"Fiancée."

"So you'll be around." He jerked his gaze toward Surgical Admit at the hallway's end and back down to Joyce.

"I'm not certain."

"Just keep in mind that he's going to need help. Sorry, I have to go scrub."

"Sure."

A nurse humming "Amazing Grace" trudged past a polyethelene bag in an aluminum frame marked *Soiled Laundry*. A handle of her hemostat clicked against a ballpoint stashed in a pocket of what looked like a carpenter's apron.

The back of his scrub top fluttering, Seward strode down the hallway— toward Bret, Chuck, and Alexis, who had just rounded the corner from Central Registration, near the gift shop off the lobby.

Chuck and Bret were holding hands. Chuck wore his mohair, fawn-colored turtleneck and hip-hugging denims, Bret the knee-length, camel-hair coat of Monday, when he'd visited Joyce and Manny.

His partridge-feathered Stetson hid Bret's brick-red hair. Joyce frowned at the strength of his cologne as he released Chuck's hand. Love conquers all? she thought. Another lost cause. Wise up.

"Did we miss him?" Chuck's stubble had grown into long black sideburns and the short upside-down horseshoe of a beard.

"Not quite." She nodded toward Ron's and Manny's room.

"I'm staying till you want to go," Alexis said. "Chuck's letting me work Sunday to make up."

Bundled in the churro-wool sweater Baby had knitted for her in three tones of green, Alexis stepped around her boss and Bret and took Joyce in her arms.

Joyce started to shake.

"Giordy Morgan called Bret this morning," Chuck said, squeezing her left hand. "We're thinking he may want to invest in New Mexicans Thrive—we're taking him to La Concha for lunch after meeting up by the gift shop." He smiled as if he thought the news might cheer her.

Joyce shrugged, raising a sweatshirted wrist to swipe her eyes. Alexis released her as Bret followed Chuck into Room 2220.

A nurse bearing a tray holding half a pint of milk and a dish of pink ice cream followed. Behind her came a pregnant nurse pushing a blue, five-wheeled platform. Off its stainless-steel pole dangled an electric thermometer, a beak-like oxygen-saturation monitor, and a black blood-pressure cuff. They entered Room 2220.

Would these be Manny's last-ever diagnostics? Joyce wondered. "Christ, Allie, here comes old dumbo-eared Dirk."

"Dumbo-eared who?" Standing so close that their hips touched, Alexis blew out a pink bubble and sucked it in.

"Manny's oversexed pal. You have to shout when he forgets to screw in his hearing aid. Usually he stinks of sardines."

Dirk ambled down the hall in the flapping green tie, dark suit coat and pants, white socks, and black shoes he'd worn to Maxine's office Wednesday morning, though Joyce had seen him only in overalls and a red flannel shirt.

"Hiyuh, Joyce Hunt."

She sniffed the familiar scent of fish.

"Is he awake?" The dewlap between Dirk's jaw and collarbone wobbled.

"Two friends are in there already," she said as the nurse returned without the tray.

"I'll scoot in quick. I'm due to hook up with my realtor in the lobby — her handyman's mother's here with a broken hip."

"This is my best friend, Alexis Dahl. Dirk Pellington."

He narrowed his gray eyes. "Hiyuh, Joyce Hunt's best friend."

"Manny says you're thinking of leaving us?" Joyce asked.

"Hoping to head down to the Bosque del Apache to soak up some peace of mind."

"I've read watching the geese and cranes fly in and out of the marshes there during the winter months is a spiritual experience."

"Don't know. Do know they hurt no one doing their whatever."

As Dirk turned to go in, the nurse with the wheeled platform emerged from Ron and Manny's room, followed by Chuck and Bret. Chuck went to Joyce and hugged her, then took both of Alexis's hands. "Keep me informed, kiddo."

"I will," she said, securing strands of brown hair behind her silver-ringed ear.

Hand in hand, Chuck and Bret headed toward the lobby. They sidestepped two Hispanic aides—one burly, one thin—who brought a gurney on wheelbarrow-size rubber wheels around the corner from the operating room. The rattling of its side rails grew. In thick-soled tennis shoes, they paused beside Joyce and Alexis. The burly one glanced at the number of Ron's and Manny's room.

"They smell as fresh as you do, Allie," Joyce whispered.

Alexis wrapped her in sweatered arms as Joyce broke into tears again. What a hopeless mess, Alexis thought.

"Patient transport," one of the aides called, knocking. He waited for Dirk to pass before grasping the gurney's stainless-steel frame.

"Your man's showing a lot of courage," Dirk said to Joyce. "Do you have a cell phone?"

She shook her head.

"I'll pop in after lunch. Could that have been Ron Kirkpatrick slouched in the other bed?"

Joyce nodded. Still in her friend's arms, she watched Dirk retreat down the hallway. Alexis released her and the two women waited in silence for Manny to emerge.

The thin aide was whistling in starts and stops like an oriole. He tugged the gurney carrying Manny feet first past the daily weights board. The burly aide pushed the back end of the gurney with one hand and with the other guided Manny's wheeled IV stand.

"I got no sleep last night, Eloy—whoa." A side rail screeched against the jamb.

"Easy, bro," called the thin aide.

"Right on. Now we go."

"Couple a rhymesters," Eloy laughed to the two women, who had begun walking on either side of the gurney, near Manny's head.

"The tape on this tube stings my nose." Silent a moment, he brushed damp strands from his eyes. "Life partner, Boodie?" When she didn't answer, he turned to Alexis. "Will you tell Stu I apologize for what I said about Joyce and him?" He tried to swallow the phantom foil wadded in his throat.

"You mean at tonight's concert? I backed out, Manny; Baby begged me."

Joyce stared across Manny's chest. We're all crazy, she thought. She felt laughter rising—if she left Manny but stayed in Santa Fe and there was a baby, Baby and Allie could help her raise it; or Allie could if she left Baby; or Mother, if the gout hadn't crippled her. Or how about Stu? The surgeon and his unlesses, her own ifs, what a crackup. "Uh-oh, look who's leading the vacuum cleaner," she breathed to Alexis.

"Who is it?"

"Pancho Villa."

As if chased by the technician steering the tractor that sucked debris from the carpet, Victor limped toward them, the tips of his mustache bouncing, the bill of his beige *Proud To Be American* cap shadowing his cut forehead. From under the tattered sleeve of his leather jacket, two turns of the ACE bandage showed above his right thumb. His left hand grasped a manila envelope.

Not recognizing Joyce, he flattened himself against the wall to let her, Alexis, Manny, and the two aides pass. Slowing, the tractor rolled in the other direction, its grumbling softened to a drone.

"Where is Geraldine Valdez?" Victor asked the nurse in lime-green scrubs. She bent toward a computer screen in the triangular station.

"A patient?"

"My mother. She's in for hip surgery."

The nurse turned to another, who had a scarlet birthmark on her cheek. "Valdez? Room number?"

"Two-one-two-one."

"End of the hall and right."

From the counter where he'd laid it, Victor took the envelope holding eight-by-ten color photos from last night, quick-developed at The Image Maker this morning.

He entered Room 2121, shedding his cap by its bill. Near the window sat five people, three of them cross-legged on the vinyl flooring, gazing at a lighted TV. An Hispanic man with slicked-back white hair streaked in black hunched in a leather vest toward a sobbing, gray-haired woman who pressed, removed, and pressed a handkerchief to her eyes.

Victor heard an unseen newscaster announce, "To reduce the threat of terrorism as we push north toward Baghdad, Homeland Security is minimizing flights over Disney World."

"Enough of that, no?" The old gentleman rose and, stepping over one of the youngsters, jabbed the set into silence.

Victor peered around to make sure he was in the right room. There lay his mother, sleeping on her side, as at home. Gray wisps from her permanent escaped down the blanket she'd pulled up to her cheek. The flesh on her neck jiggled with each outflow of breath. Through one of the bed's snapped-up rails, an IV tube snaked up its pole to the saline-dextrose bag alongside the blue pump. A plate of cottage cheese and peaches lay untouched on a white, four-wheeled table.

Hanging his jacket on a chair's upholstered back, Victor stationed himself next to a red biohazard bin. He placed the manila envelope across his thighs, listening to murmurs from the group near the window and to tennis shoes squeaking along the hallway. She was pissed when I called but she'll show up, he reassured himself.

Which she soon did. He smelled the Pure Tiffany before seeing the black topknot dip past the doorjamb. Grabbing his envelope and rising, he hauled the ceiling-mounted white curtain around his mother's bed.

"What is all this, Victor?" Maxine faced him in her trench coat.

"Whisper, please. Mom's sleeping."

"Giordy will be here any minute with flowers, so make it quick."

"You see this?" He brandished the envelope. "The negatives are at home."

"No doubt."

Both started as his mother groaned.

"She has no health insurance."

"That you told me yesterday."

"I'm fed up with being your fetch-and-carry, amiga; I'm returning to carving full time. Your husband takes a look at these unless you pay for Mom's surgery and support us while I bring her back to health."

"Why don't you up the ante, make me also pay for Ron Kirkpatrick's convalescence? He's down the hall. Your flashbulbs gave him a heart attack."

"Giordy told us that Kirkpatrick collapsed, after you called his cell to pick you up outside the ER."

"He resurrected in time to help me get his clothes on before the paramedics showed. I followed in his wife's car after stowing the hammock. Giordy thinks he came over last night to consult about loans for Dirk Pellington and Bret Wilkes. You don't know Wilkes, but Giordy loves the man; he wants to invest with him in some harebrained venture of Chuck Ridley's—I guess you don't know Ridley, either. How'd you leave the card game early without alerting Giordy, by the way?"

"I told the guys I wanted to check on Mom before visiting hours were over. When I came back with the photos, I decided to try to win. Did okay until your phone call ended the evening."

"Ronald's going to have to take a cab home unless I drive him because god knows when his wacko wife can leave the psych ward. She lost her marbles when she cracked up his Escalade yesterday."

"Come Monday, I was supposed to replace their subfloor." Under the gridded fluorescents he gazed at Maxine's pale cheeks and violet-smeared eyes.

Her perfume started him coughing. He jammed a fist to his mouth, dipping his chin as Maxine flipped her splint at him.

"I wonder if I can sue you for attempted blackmail," she said. "You know what? Show those photos to whoever you want. I'm leaving real estate and following Dirk down to the Bosque del Apache. Though he won't know until our lunch that he's going to show me how not to act like a human being."

"Sure he is," Victor guffawed.

"Believe what you like. You want to drive Ron home?"

Victor did not return her grin.

"Tonight I tell Giordy what's been going on."

"And who supports Kate?"

"My sister needs to stay in AA—no more slips. Sober, she can find a job. You should watch her drive a cab."

"Victor?" came the cracked voice from the bed.

"Ah, Vieja, you're awake." He lifted the brown envelope. "You'll never leave Giordy's millions," he said to Maxine.

"No?" Her left thumb and forefinger unsnapped the woven-leather purse slung across her coat. Plunging her hand inside, she pulled out her wedding and engagement rings.

"I threw these into the purse figuring we might be negotiating. Last year I had them appraised. The diamond alone's worth twenty grand. You're tired of fetch-and-carry? Fetch these out and they're yours."

Pivoting, she yanked up the red, scorpion-pincered lid of the biohazard bin and thrust her fist toward the mass of soaked diapers, dressings, latex gloves, paper gowns, and towels. She twisted her lips at the sweet-sour stench of vomit, blood, and urine. Closing her fingers again, she yanked the fist out and pounded the bin's lid down, then shook the fist at Victor as if rattling dice from long-ago days in Giordy's Vegas casino. She straightened her fingers. "Gone!"

The soles of her black leather boots clicked against the beige vinyl as she marched past the bathroom and into the hallway.

In an off-white suit, white leather tie, and loafers, Giordy came swaggering toward her like a man twice his size, bearing a bouquet of red roses wrapped in tissue. The thickets of his white eyebrows were knitted in a frown under the wheat-colored fedora that hid his scalp's sheen. His wrinkled wedge of a face ended in almost no chin.

"What the hell," Maxine said through clenched teeth. She decided not to wait until dinner to share her plans. The nurse's station felt far safer than home.

Behind her, Victor limped to the doorway. "Rich white fucks," he hissed close to her ear. Grabbing his penis, he spun into the bathroom and slammed the door.

And so, finding no quick fixes for their fear-driven lives, they all pushed unhappily on as American-led forces continued to strike Iraq.

THREE MONTHS LATER

RON KIRKPATRICK SENT LILA TO HER FATHER ON THE RANCH outside Fort Worth; she died of grief at six in the morning while milking one of his Holsteins. Ron lost his job at Los Alamos Mortgage when caught bedding a couple of the secretaries. The shock led to a triple-bypass down at the Heart Hospital in Albuquerque.

Although the surgeon had to snip away fifteen inches of ileum, Manny Barnes recovered. Joyce Hunt stayed with him until a pregnancy test from Walgreens showed positive. By then Alexis Dahl had left Baby, who'd become both Christian Rapturist and full-blown neoconservative. Although workman Stu Fisher had already persuaded Alexis to accompany him to two rock concerts, her friendship with Joyce proved stronger. The two women left Santa Fe and rented an apartment in San Jose, just twelve miles from Stanford Medical Clinic and Joyce's mother.

Manny returned to cobbling together newsletters for Hewlett-Packard and Cisco Systems, though for a while he helped Chuck Ridley, Bret Wilkes, and investor Giordy Morgan jump-start their company, New Mexicans Thrive. After Alexis left for California, Chuck hired an Iranian exchange-student part-time. Manny fell for her long black hair and appetite for peace activism.

Chuck's wife Helen and the twins left to make the summer chalet outside Montpelier in Vermont their permanent home. Chuck and Bret experimented—mostly happily—with homosexuality until the Native American girl Hisi, to whom Bret sent money back in Silicon Valley, phoned him. She claimed that he'd impregnated her in February and that her uncle from Taos Pueblo was on his way gunning for him. That night Chuck flew to Burlington to plead with his wife to take him back. She refused. The last Manny heard from Chuck, he was recuperating in New Orleans; the last he heard from Bret, he was hiding out in Fargo, North Dakota at the Holiday Inn.

Dirk Pellington did buy a trailer and parked it near the Visitors' Center at the Bosque del Apache National Wildlife Refuge, 170 miles south of Santa Fe. Maxine Morgan agreed with Giordy in writing that he could keep the proceeds from her business if he'd pay her three thousand a month for two years. After selling Dirk's house, Maxine and her Pekingese, Pixie, followed Dirk to the Bosque. Within a month, a bald eagle had scooped Pixie up from the edge of a marsh. Maxine began drinking three, four, seven Bloody Marys a day. Soon she dispensed with the spiced tomato juice.

No problems loomed for Victor Valdez. He continued caring for his mother, made enough at poker games to support them both, and began to get commissions for carving images of Saint Francis feeding the sparrows. When New Mexicans Thrive went belly up, Giordy used freed funds to buy Victor the old adobe next to his mother's.

On May 2, six weeks after Operation Freedom began, President George W. Bush emerged in a green flight suit from an S-3B turbofan jet onto the deck of the USS Abraham Lincoln offshore San Diego. Under a banner that read, *Mission Accomplished*, he declared, "Major combat operations have ended. We can achieve military objectives without directing violence against civilians. Iraq is free." President Bush added that coalition forces would soon find Saddam Hussein, his two sons, and their weapons of mass destruction.